ᛒY THE ᛖDGE OF THE ᛋWORD

A MEDIAEVAL MYSTERY

BY THE EDGE
OF THE SWORD

A MEDIAEVAL MYSTERY

C.B. HANLEY

The
Mystery
Press

First published by The Mystery Press, 2021

The Mystery Press, an imprint of The History Press
97 St George's Place
Cheltenham, Gloucestershire, GL50 3QB
www.thehistorypress.co.uk

British Library Cataloguing in Publication Data.
A catalogue record for this book is available from the British Library.

ISBN 978 0 7509 9816 1

Typesetting and origination by Typo•glyphix, Burton-on-Trent, DE14 3HE
Printed in Great Britain

For M.L.
Who is older than he used to be

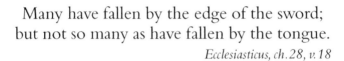

Many have fallen by the edge of the sword;
but not so many as have fallen by the tongue.

Ecclesiasticus, ch.28, v.18

Praise for C.B. Hanley's Mediaeval Mystery Series

'[*Cast the First Stone* is] brilliantly evocative of time and place, but with themes that are bang up to date. C.B. Hanley brings past and present together in an enthralling story.'

A.J. Mackenzie, author of the *Hardcastle & Chaytor* mysteries

'*The Bloody City* is a great read, full of intrigue and murder. Great for readers of Ellis Peters and Lindsey Davis. Hanley weaves a convincing, rich tapestry of life and death in the early 13th century, in all its grandeur and filth. I enjoyed this book immensely!'

Ben Kane, bestselling novelist of the *Forgotten Legion* trilogy

'Blatantly heroic and wonderfully readable.'

The Bloody City received a **STARRED** review in *Library Journal*

'The characters are real, the interactions and conversations natural, the tension inbuilt, and it all builds to a genuinely satisfying conclusion both fictionally and historically.'

Review for *The Bloody City* in www.crimereview.co.uk

Brandon Castle 1218

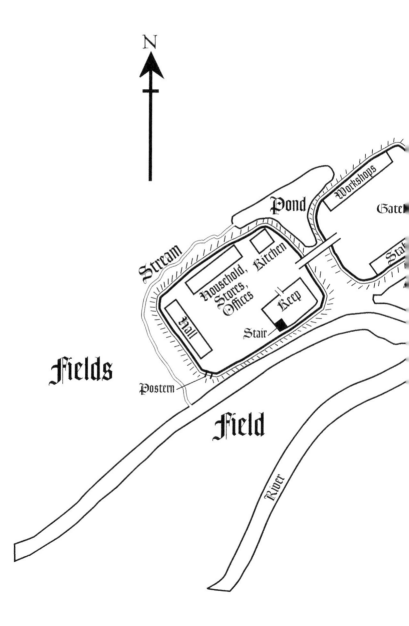

N

Pond

Workshops

Gate

Stream

Household, Kitchen Stores, Offices

Keep

Hall

Stair

Fields

Postern

Field

River

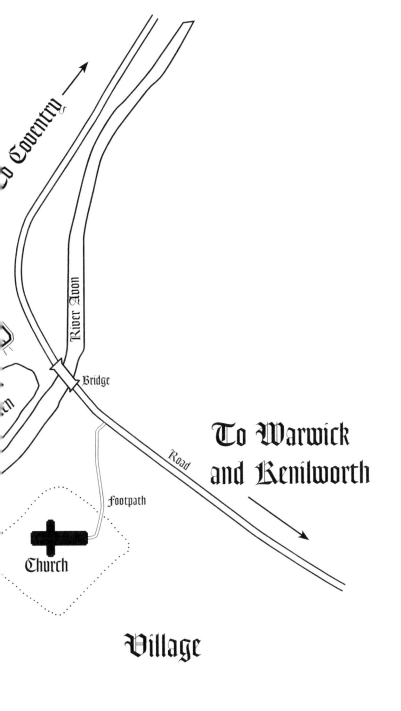

To Coventry

River Avon

Bridge

To Warwick
and Kenilworth

Road

Footpath

Church

Village

Prologue

Christmas Eve, 1218

The world was white and cold and endless.

The heavens and the earth were indistinguishable, frozen hills and valleys stretching out before him until they touched the ice-filled sky. The white blanket that was draped over the countryside might look soft, but the gentle, down-filled appearance was deceptive: the ground was as hard as iron, and the wind had knives in it.

The snow was above his knees as he struggled onwards, hoping he was still on the road. His horse had broken a leg some hours ago, but staying with the animal meant almost certain death; nobody would be out in this weather if they could help it, not at dusk on this holy day of the year – and nobody knew he was here, so there would be no search party. His mission was a secret; she had impressed that upon him before he set off and he had spoken to nobody of it on the way.

The road, if it was the road, now led into a wood. He was surrounded by trees and the swirling wind whipped up the powdery snow into his face, blinding and confusing him. Where was he? Had he turned around? Was he still going in the right direction?

One thought stayed fixed in his mind. Conisbrough. He had to get to Conisbrough because he had to deliver the message. He had to deliver it for her. It was this that kept him ploughing on, as well as the thought that there would be a fire when he got there, and warmth, and human company. *Keep holding on to that picture.*

But he was so cold. Every time he inhaled, he sucked more icy blades into his chest. His breath came in jagged gasps, like his thoughts.

He hadn't been able to feel his toes for some time, and now he stumbled as his feet became numb, disconnected from his body. He'd seen that tree before, hadn't he? Yes, he had – his own footprints were there.

It was hopeless. He had no idea where he was and he could see no smoke, no sign of any village or castle. The forest was silent, he was alone in the world, and it was getting dark. Perhaps it would be better to shelter here for a while, in the lee of this tree, out of the biting wind, maybe try to start a fire? He had flint and steel in his pouch as well as the all-important letter. He fumbled at his belt.

But now his hands wouldn't work either, and he let his legs give way. Some snow had piled up around the base of the tree, and the drift was soft and oddly welcoming; he allowed himself to sink into its embrace.

And now he was comfortable. He wasn't cold at all; why had he thought so? He was in a feather bed, covered in soft furs, warm and content as he fell into the sleep from which he would never wake.

Chapter One

Conisbrough, the Feast of St Stephen, 1218

Martin whooped as he urged his horse on to greater speed. To be out in the fresh, clean air and on the hunt was a glorious thing, and the energy grew within him as he outpaced the others. The hunting had been good these last few weeks, and he had been the one to slay the boar whose head had graced the earl's Christmas table. The thrill of the chase, the danger of the cornered wild animal, the bright, hot, spurting red blood against the snow – he was *alive*.

He knew he was going too fast, but he didn't care. He left the others behind, eager to be the first to reach the stag once the baying hounds had caught the scent again. What did he care if they couldn't keep up? What did he care, indeed, if he should be sent flying and then crashing to earth? If his neck should break? What did he care if his mount tripped—

It was concern for the horse that eventually caused him to pull up a little. Fauvel, the beautiful, powerful, *tall* dun courser that had been the earl's gift to him after the events of the previous year at Sandwich, was far too precious to be risked. Besides, they were now entering the woods, so the dangers of low-hanging branches were added to those of the uneven ground. Fauvel shied a little as the light dimmed, and Martin slowed to a walk as he ducked, knocking snow off the branches as he pushed them aside.

As he moved deeper into the dense thicket of trees, the clamour of the rest of the hunt party faded. He could still hear the hounds, but they were away over to his left and the only path in front of him snaked off to the right. He would have to take it for now, but it was no matter – he knew these woods well enough not to lose his way even in the snow. This path would lead down to the stream, where he could turn back to ride alongside it. He cursed himself as he realised that his speed had probably now put him behind the others, as they would have been able to follow the hounds' change of direction before they reached the trees.

He continued through the cold, white silence and was not far away from where he knew the stream to be when a splash of colour drew his attention. What was that, over there beneath that tree? He hadn't gone many paces further when he saw that it was a pair of booted legs sticking out from a snowdrift.

Martin dismounted, but with no particular haste – the man was clearly dead, and had probably been there at least a day judging by the sprinkling of snow on the hose and boots, and the greater amount on the upper body which must have fallen off the tree to cover him like a blanket. But which of the villagers would have been out in the forest on Christmas Day? No work was due, and they generally made sure they'd collected all the wood and supplies they might need beforehand so they could stay around the village, the church and their own warm hearths on the day itself.

As he hitched Fauvel's reins to a branch, Martin heard another rider approaching, feeling the warmth of man and beast steaming in the air before he could actually see them.

It was the earl himself. He pulled up as soon as he saw Martin. 'What's the matter? Come off, have you? Horse all right?'

'Yes, my lord, he's fine and all is well. I've lost the stag, but I've found something else.' He gestured towards the body.

The earl craned his neck to see. 'Not one of the hunt?' He continued before Martin could answer. 'No, been there too long. Well, we can't leave him here – start digging him out and I'll summon men to carry him back.' He had a horn hanging from his belt; he unhooked it and gave a long blast.

Martin knelt and began digging away the snow, half afraid of whom he might find under it. Thankfully he knew it wasn't Edwin, for he had seen him that very morning. He began to run through in his head which of the other villagers he had passed on his way out to the hunt. But when the face was uncovered, it was one he'd never seen before.

The relief made him sit back on his heels for a moment. 'A stranger, my lord.'

The earl had not dismounted, but he nudged his courser forward a couple of paces to look down. 'Well, that's something at least. Still, he deserves a Christian burial, whoever he is. We'll have him taken to the church and then the villagers can look at him to see if they recognise him. Some travelling kin, perhaps.' He seemed about to turn away, then added, 'When you get back, find Weaver and get him to have a look. I can't imagine it's anything other than an accident, but best to be sure in case the sheriff comes nosing.'

'Very good, my lord.' Martin finished uncovering the body and stood up, brushing the loose snow from his hands and knees as more of the hunting party arrived to help, and it wasn't long before he was mounted again, following a crudely fashioned litter on which the corpse had been placed. When they reached the village, he saw the men off in the direction of the church and made his way down the street to Edwin's cottage.

Edwin felt the joy spread through him in a blaze of warmth. 'You're sure?'

Alys nodded, her smile as wide as his own. 'Yes.'

He could hardly believe in such good fortune. Something would cloud it, surely. 'I mean, after last time …'

A momentary shadow passed over her face. 'I know. But this time it's been longer, and I can feel the quickening.' She took his hand and placed it on her stomach. He couldn't feel anything out of the ordinary, but he was happy to take her word for it. *A father.* He was going to be a father, and his beautiful wife a mother. They would be a whole family. Together. Could there be any greater bliss, any brighter sunshine, amid the darkness of the winter?

A loud knocking sounded at the door.

Edwin kissed Alys and then gently propelled her towards a stool by the fire. 'I'll answer it. Cecily, probably.'

But he knew that it wasn't his aunt, for she would never pound like that – the door had nearly fallen in. He opened it and was unsurprised to see Martin on the threshold. 'Come in, come in! Share some ale with us while you warm up by the fire.'

Martin shook his head. 'Can't, sorry.' He glanced over Edwin's shoulder. 'My apologies, mistress, but I'm here to take him away for a short while.' He looked back at Edwin. 'We've found a body.'

Edwin's heart sank into his stomach as the warmth inside dissipated. Could he not have one day, *one hour* of unalloyed happiness before something arrived to spoil it?

Alys had heard the words and was now next to him at the door. 'A body? Who …?'

Edwin could see that Martin wasn't particularly discomfited. 'Nobody. Or, that is, nobody we know. A stranger – we found him in the woods so he's probably just a traveller who got lost. But my lord wants Edwin to look over him just to see that there's been no foul play.' He hesitated. 'You know, in case the sheriff …'

Edwin winced and then realised he'd unthinkingly put his hand to his throat. 'Yes,' he said, drily, 'the last thing we need is him turning up.' He put his hand on Alys's arm. 'Nothing for you to worry about. Stay here in the warm and I'll be back soon.' He shared a look with her, a look about their secret, and he couldn't stop the smile spreading over his face despite the circumstances. 'And then we can keep talking.' He gave her another kiss and an embrace, aware of Martin shuffling behind him but for once unconcerned about it.

He wrapped his cloak about him before stepping out into the cold and following the tall, silent figure up the icy street. Today he refused to feel guilty about being happy. It was a year and a half since Martin had had his heart broken, and Edwin knew that he was jealous of

Edwin's happy marriage, though he tried not to show it. Not jealous of Alys herself, of course, for Martin's heart still lay with Mistress Joanna, who had lived for many years as a companion to the lord earl's sister before being sent away for a marriage not of her choosing. It was strange, perhaps, that Martin still pined over her when there were so many other girls who would willingly throw themselves at a tall, strong squire – but then again, Edwin himself could never have loved anyone but Alys once he'd met her, so maybe it wasn't so surprising after all.

They reached the church to find that Father Ignatius was already praying over the body, his blue hands clasped and steam rising from between his chattering teeth. Brother William, the earl's clerk, was also present, and he nodded to them as they approached.

Edwin forced himself to concentrate on the matter at hand. The face that looked up at him from the bier was both peaceful and unknown to him. He glanced enquiringly at the priest and the monk, and they shook their heads. A stranger, then. The clothes were nondescript – not rich, so he probably wasn't a nobleman, thank the Lord, but not those of a pauper either, nor a runaway serf. A townsman, a trader, a messenger? Ah, wait …

'Is that a strap across his chest? Under the cloak?'

With Brother William's help, he removed the cloak and turned the stiff body over. As he had thought, a leather bag had been concealed between the layers of clothing. He prised the strap over the head and passed it to the monk. 'He must have been on his way to deliver some letters to the lord earl – better take a look.'

While Brother William was opening the bag, Edwin examined the body as best he could. There was no wound, no sign of violence, and the frozen expression was content. He turned to Martin. 'He looks like he just fell asleep. As far as I can tell, he must have lost his way and died in the cold. Nothing to bother the sheriff about.'

Martin rumbled his assent.

Edwin draped the cloak over the body, covering everything except the face. 'I suppose he might be from one of my lord's other castles?'

'If he is, I've never seen him,' came Martin's reply. 'But I can have some of his messengers fetched, if you like, the ones who travel most widely, to see if any of them recognise him.'

'Yes. Yes, please do – if he can go to his grave with a name, so much the better.' Edwin turned to Brother William. 'Anything?'

The monk was puzzled. 'A few pennies, some bread, flint and steel, but only one letter.' He held it out. 'And it's not for the earl, it's for Martin.'

Martin was taken aback. 'Me?' He took it. 'It must be from my father, although he usually … Oh no, it's not. I don't know who it's from – I've never seen this seal before. How odd.'

He stood gazing at the letter for some moments before Edwin suggested that maybe he should open it.

'Yes, yes of course.' He broke the seal and moved to stand near a burning candle.

Edwin watched him as he laboriously made his way through the contents. Martin had learned to read and write when he was a boy, but he hadn't done much of it since and it was obvious he was struggling. Edwin longed to step forward and offer to read it for him, but he didn't want to embarrass his friend, and besides, what if it was personal? Some bad news about his family? So, he simply stood watching, his ears filled with the sound of the soothing prayers to which the others had returned, but his eye alert to every change of expression on Martin's face.

Whatever it was, it didn't seem like good news. Martin read, read again and ran his finger along some words, all the while becoming paler. It was probably just Edwin's imagination, or perhaps the candlelight, but it almost seemed as though the hand holding the letter began to shake.

At last Martin looked up. 'Edwin.' He stopped and cleared his throat. 'Edwin. Can you tell me if this word here says what I think it does? Just to be sure?' He was pointing at a word on its own at the bottom of the parchment – the name of the sender.

Edwin stepped to look over Martin's arm. The letter was short and written in a good black ink, but he did not read the contents. Instead, he focused in growing surprise on the name, for there could be no doubt: it said 'Joanna'.

'So then,' said Edwin to Alys a little later, 'I was going to ask him more about it, but he just snatched it back, said he had to get back to the castle, and left. I think he said he would try to come later if he could get away, but it depends on the lord earl, of course.'

It was getting dark, the short winter day almost over, and they were sitting by the fireside as Alys stirred the pot. Smoked pork in the pottage, in honour of the Christmas season; the house had smelled heavenly since yesterday after the long Advent fast, and there would be dried apples and oatcakes to follow, flavoured with a pinch of Edwin's favourite cinnamon. Truly, he was blessed.

There had been a time, just over a year ago, when he and Alys had been pressed to live up at the castle – a great step up in status – but they had declined. This was home.

It was also, by now, the centre of Alys's burgeoning business. A large and complicated loom stood in one corner, at which she spent many hours; when she wasn't weaving, she was either spinning or supervising the village girls whom she employed to produce the hundreds of yards of thread necessary. Her father had been a cloth merchant, and before she'd moved to Conisbrough to marry Edwin she'd run his shop in the great city of Lincoln. Her expertise was slowly being recognised by the inhabitants of all the villages around and she was often asked for advice.

There had been a time, last year, when the two of them felt that they had hardly a friend in the world, and certainly not in Conisbrough, but Alys had taken on the challenge. Despite what had happened she had been kind and generous to all, mending broken relationships, helping neighbours where she could and paying fair wages to her girls. The final barrier had been broken when she'd reduced a travelling salesman almost to tears by haggling down the price of his fabric on behalf of several village women, and now she received smiles and greetings wherever she went.

Edwin looked at his wife and his home and realised that he was happy.

This time the knock at the door didn't trouble Edwin, and on opening it he was greeted with the welcome sight of his mother as well as Martin. 'My lord wanted to play chess with Sir Geoffrey,' explained Martin, as he took off his cloak and hung it on a peg, 'and Adam and Hugh are perfectly capable of setting that up without me, so I left them to it.'

'And I decided that a walk and a chat would be better than a lone evening at my sewing,' added Mother as she kissed Edwin and bustled forward. 'Now, my dear, what have you there? Can I help you with anything?'

Edwin was about to follow when Martin put out an arm to keep him by the door. He stooped so he could hiss in Edwin's ear. 'I need to talk to you about my letter.' He hesitated, glancing over at Mother and Alys. 'It concerns you too, so shall we go outside somewhere? They'll overhear.'

'Me?' Edwin was surprised. What could Mistress Joanna possibly have to say about him? But it was no matter. 'They're my family. Whatever it is, they'll hear it soon enough anyway, so it may as well be now. Besides, I'm not going out in the cold when there's a good fire here.'

Martin looked uncertain for a moment, but then nodded. 'All right.'

They moved back towards the hearth. Martin was agitated, pacing up and down before he could be persuaded to sit, at which point he pulled out the letter and spread it on his knee. Then he seemed to change his mind and passed it to Edwin. 'You read it. Read it out loud so we can all hear. I still don't know what to think about it.'

Edwin held it up to the light. 'Martin,' he read. 'If it please God I hope this finds you in good health. I am in trouble, and I need your help. I cannot have it written here, but the man who carries this letter will explain all. Come to me at the castle of Brandon in the county of Warwickshire as soon as you get this, and bring Edwin with you if you can. I know this will be difficult to arrange, and I would not ask, but please – there is no one else I can turn to. My life and my immortal soul are at stake. Joanna.'

Edwin looked up at the shocked faces around him.

'The poor girl,' said Mother. 'She must be facing something dreadful to write such a desperate plea.'

'Yes, but facing what?' asked Edwin, his mind already working through the possibilities. 'Brandon castle, in Warwickshire. This must be where she went after her marriage, where her husb—' He looked at Martin's face and stopped. 'Anyway, the trouble can't be anything to do with him, or why ask you for help? No, it must be something more … personal.'

'But what?' asked Alys. She crossed herself. 'The poor messenger can't tell you.'

'And why you, Edwin?' added Mother.

Edwin thought for a moment. 'Something has happened. Something bad. And she wants to find out the truth of the matter, for there can be no other reason for her wanting me.'

'Agreed,' rumbled Martin. 'And she must need protection, or why come to me?' He looked at Edwin with a dark expression. 'Is someone threatening her? Because if they are, I'll …'

Edwin put out a hand. 'Calm down. There's nothing you – we – can do until we know more. But how shall we find out?'

'Well, that's obvious, isn't it?'

'Is it?'

'Of course. We'll go there, wherever it is – Warwickshire is south of here, we go through it when we go to Reigate or Lewes – and we find out. We sort out whatever is bothering her, and I'll deal with anyone threatening her.' Martin was on his feet again.

'But think, Martin. It's much more complicated than that. How will you explain this to the lord earl? How will you get a leave of absence? I don't know how far it is, but surely it would take a week or more to get there, and the same back, to say nothing of how long we might be there. And why would he let me go? I serve him – and so do you – so why would he be interested in helping Joanna?'

Martin started to make an angry retort, but Edwin cut him off abruptly. 'I'm only speaking the truth, hard as it may be for you to hear. And better you should consider it now, before you speak to my lord about it. Now sit down and let's think.'

'*Think*.' Martin's tone verged on contempt. 'We don't need to think, we need to act. I'll go to him and show him the letter and ask if I may go. Simple.'

'And if he says no?'

'I don't know. Maybe I'll go anyway.'

'Disobey him? And be expelled from his service? What good would that do?'

'None. But what choice is there?' Martin's agitation was ever more evident. 'Or maybe I could tell him that I've had a letter from my father and it's a family matter and I need to go.'

Edwin was incredulous. 'You would *lie* to the lord earl?' The fact that Martin would even think of saying such a thing out loud shocked him. His friend's feelings for Joanna obviously ran even deeper than he thought. 'It would never work. He would want to see the letter, to know some details. And besides, your father is the lord earl's liege man – he would write to him, not you, if he wanted to summon you.'

'Yes, but what else is there? Martin's voice was raised.

'Perhaps …'

It was Alys who had spoken, and Edwin looked at her sharply. 'Do you have an idea?'

Martin was also gazing at her in a kind of desperate hope, less surprised than many other men would have been at the interruption, for he knew that Alys was an unusual woman, and that Edwin valued her counsel.

'It's just … I don't know the lord earl as well as any of you, of course, but perhaps if you were to ask him – telling the truth – but try to find a way in which it would be in his *own* best interest to have you both go?'

Mother was nodding, and Edwin saw the wisdom of the suggestion. 'I thank the Lord every day that I married you,' he said, remembering also their earlier conversation and secretly blessing himself again. 'Martin?'

Martin rubbed his chin. 'That could work.' He held out his hand for the letter and Edwin passed it to him, watching as Martin ran his finger over Joanna's name. Then he looked up again. 'But if it doesn't, then I'm going to find a way to go anyway: I don't care what you or my lo— what anyone else thinks.'

There was an awkward silence, which Alys broke by asking if they would stay to eat.

This brought Martin to himself again. 'No – no thank you, mistress, I'll have to get back to serve at table. My lord will be finishing his chess game by now, or almost.' He managed a smile, pointing at Edwin's own rather rough-hewn board and pieces that sat on the table. 'Games against Sir Geoffrey last a while longer than those against you! He'll make you play blindfold soon, just to even things up.'

Mother was also declining, and Martin remembered his manners, fetching her cloak. 'My lady. Let me escort you back – it's almost full dark.'

They left, Martin taking a brand from the fire to light their way before he ducked under the door lintel.

Silence settled on the cottage. Edwin had more or less got used to his mother being referred to as 'Lady Anne' in the year and a half since her marriage to Sir Geoffrey, Conisbrough's castellan, but he was still sorry to see her go. Her apartment at the castle was much grander than the cottage, of course, but it was austere, and Edwin couldn't help thinking that she sometimes went back to it with reluctance. But perhaps 'home' meant something different to her these days.

Edwin sat at the table, idly pushing at a knight on the chess board while Alys ladled out their hot meal. As she blew on a spoonful of the pottage to cool it, she looked at him directly. 'So, it seems you'll be going away again.'

He nodded. 'If our plan – your plan – works. I'm sorry to do it to you, my love, especially now.'

She put one hand on his, 'It's all right. I've never met this girl – this lady, I should say – but I do know Martin a little by now, and that's the most emotion I've ever seen him show. It's clear that he loves her, so you should help.' She swallowed a mouthful before continuing. 'Although, if she's married, there's going to be no happy end to the tale, even if you can sort out whatever the problem is.'

'And that's what I'm worried about,' said Edwin. 'Do you remember the last line of the letter? "My life and my immortal soul are at stake." *My immortal soul.* I have a feeling that this is very much more serious than Martin might think it is.'

———

Edwin was due to attend on the earl the following morning. He'd had no further chance for a private talk with Martin, so all he could do was hope that Martin would make his request in as calm a manner as possible, and that he himself, if asked, could weigh in with an opinion on how the earl could benefit by letting them go.

Edwin had seen a mounted messenger passing through the village that morning, so it was no surprise, as he entered the council chamber and took up his position by the wall, to see the earl already in conversation with Sir Geoffrey and Brother William, several letters spread over the table and one in the monk's hand. Martin was over against the opposite wall and Edwin tried to catch his eye, but Martin was too busy with his own thoughts to notice. He was shifting his weight from foot to foot, his normal blank stillness replaced by a fidgeting that was making Adam and Hugh, the earl's junior squire and page, look at him in surprise and Sir Geoffrey with irritation.

'Ah, Weaver, good. I'm glad you sorted that business out with no trouble yesterday – natural death in the snow – for I have a new mission for you.'

This was not at all what Edwin had expected. For months now his service to the earl had been peaceful, and he had been hoping it would continue that way. But to be sent away now, just when he wanted to go somewhere else! This time he did meet Martin's eye, seeing the desperation there, but there was nothing to be done. 'Yes, my lord,' he said, as woodenly as he could.

'I have received a letter,' continued the earl, pointing at the parchment Brother William held and oblivious to the thoughts of his underlings, 'from de Lacy, a man who owes service to me.'

Edwin's attention was immediately engaged, for he'd had a thorough drilling from Sir Geoffrey over the last year on who was who among the earl's liege men, and who was related to whom.

'You remember the girl Joanna, de Lacy's cousin, who lived here for some while as my sister's companion? Yes, of course you do. Well, it's about her.'

'Yes, my lord?'

'Strange thing, really,' continued the earl, flicking his fingers at Hugh for a cup of the wine that was warming by the fire. 'De Lacy writes that he has received very troubling news that will reflect badly on him and his family, and he requests that I intervene to help resolve the situation.'

Martin really was twitching now, but Edwin tried to ignore it. 'And is there some way that I can help you in this, my lord?'

'Yes, I want you to get down there and find out the truth of the matter.'

He looked as though he considered this instruction final, but Edwin was still very much in the dark. 'If I may, my lord, where should I go? And is there any indication of what the trouble actually is?'

'Oh, didn't I say?' The earl took a sip from his goblet and gestured for Brother William to hand Edwin the letter. 'You need to go to Brandon in Warwickshire, where the girl now lives, and where she's being held before any charges are pressed.'

'Charges, my lord?'

'Yes, charges. And serious ones, too. It looks very much as though she's murdered her husband.'

Chapter Two

They had been on the road for days. There had been no new fall of snow since Christmas Day, but there was still plenty of it on the ground and, at first, they had made very slow progress indeed. Once they had reached the wider Great North Road, however, the going had been a little easier and they picked up some speed. Martin, indeed, would have pressed them on faster, but both Edwin and Turold, the senior of the four men who were accompanying them, persuaded him into caution so they would all arrive together and alive.

They had slept each night at an inn, for it was far too cold to camp in comfort. Turold was one of the lord earl's most trusted messengers, used to riding up and down the country, and he had been assigned to their party in order to guide them; he knew the way to Warwick and Kenilworth, and Brandon was only a few miles from each. He would also be able to ride back to Conisbrough with any urgent message if necessary. Edwin felt much safer having him along, worried that they would lose their way otherwise, and he was particularly grateful for Turold's knowledge of which inns served the best food and had the fewest fleas in their beds.

It was now just before dawn, and they were saddling up for what should be the last day of their journey; Turold reckoned they should just about reach their destination before dark as long as they met with no further delay on the road. Edwin stamped his feet and rubbed his hands to try to get a bit of life into them, watching as the steam from the breath of men and horses rose to join the smoke from the torches in the inn's yard.

He frowned as he saw Martin giving Lambert, the youngest of the party, a clip round the ear for not holding his stirrup properly and wondered if he should speak to him about it later. Lambert was a raw recruit to the garrison, admittedly, and clumsy with it, but he was trying hard, and Edwin could see that some of his ineptitude stemmed from nervousness: like many of the boys around Conisbrough, he held the earl's huge senior squire in awe. Martin's continual exasperation with him wasn't helping, and Lambert had started ducking every time Martin came near him, his clumsiness only increasing.

Martin's impatience, meanwhile, had grown with every hour they'd spent on the road, every mile they'd drawn closer to their destination. Edwin was going to have to come up with some strategy to keep him under control when they got there; no easy task, but if Martin's emotions boiled up too far it would jeopardise their mission.

Edwin's turn to mount came and he did so, swinging into the saddle with an ease that gave him continual joy after the difficulties he'd experienced when first learning. These days he could ride for a whole day and be no more than stiff or cold when it ended, rather than in agony.

The sun was just rising as they left the inn and made their way back to the road. The last few days had been so dull and overcast that it hardly felt like daytime at all, but Edwin thought, as he looked at the sky, that the sun might burn through the cloud and shine a little more brightly today. That would be nice; the endless grey had only emphasised Martin's agitation, which in turn had spread to the men. Edwin himself was relatively cheerful, despite the circumstances, and he decided to put into action the first part of a plan to keep Martin's mind off what they might encounter when they got to Brandon.

Some general chat about horses was always a good place to start. It was a subject in which Edwin had no interest at all, outside of being able to travel from one place to another faster than on foot, but Martin could wax lyrical about all things equine for hours. The ploy was a successful one, and it led on to much praise of Fauvel, Martin's own precious mount, which Edwin listened to with pleasure but not much attention. When the subject turned to Fauvel's having been a gift from the earl, however, Edwin felt a nudge was needed to steer the conversation away from any potential references to the great battle at Sandwich; he didn't want Martin's mind to turn to fighting. He attempted, therefore, to keep to the theme of gifts.

'Your father sends you presents from time to time, doesn't he?'

'Yes; he's very pleased that I'm getting on well in the lord earl's service.'

'But you don't see your family very often, do you?'

'No – my father wants me to stay with the earl as much as possible as it'll be good for my future. It doesn't bother me much, mind: I don't really like his wife, and she was glad to see the back of me so she could fill the place with her own brood.'

Martin was not normally one to engage in gossip or chit-chat, so this was new information to Edwin. 'His wife isn't your mother?'

'No – she died when I was born, God rest her soul, and he later married again. They have half a dozen children by now, but all much younger than me – the eldest would be about ten, I suppose.'

'But you're still your father's heir? You'll inherit his lands?'

Martin laughed, a welcome sound that Edwin hadn't heard for some while. 'It's only two manors – we're not proper nobility. The lord earl only took me into his service as my father did him some kind of favour years ago, which is why he's so keen for me to get on. I can further our family's interests, apparently, although why I'd want to do that for the sake of the little brats I don't know.'

'Well, an inheritance is something to look forward to, anyway,' said Edwin, aiming to keep the conversation light.

'Not for a long while, though,' was the reply. 'My father's only fifteen years older than me.'

'What?'

'Didn't I ever tell you? I suppose I didn't. It's simple enough – two men with neighbouring manors who wanted to unite them, and my grandfather keen to get his hands on the other as his friend only had one daughter, his heiress. So, they married their children off, my father just turned fifteen and my mother a year younger. They couldn't claim the marriage was valid until they'd lain together, so they did, and I was the result.'

'Wait – your mother was only fourteen when she bore you?'

'Yes.' Martin's voice assumed a less jaunty tone. 'And it killed her.' He paused. '*I* killed her.'

'It wasn't your fault.'

Martin sighed. 'No, not my "fault" exactly, but the fact remains that I was born and she died.'

The conversation had taken a direction that Edwin was keen to avoid, and needed to be turned, but he couldn't continue it; he was too busy contemplating the terror that Alys, too, might die in childbirth. It certainly wasn't uncommon – the churchyard in Conisbrough was full of women who'd perished during or after their labour. He tried to tell himself that Alys had some few advantages. She was seventeen rather than fourteen, a better age for childbearing albeit one that was relatively young by the standards of the village, where couples normally waited to marry until they were on a firmer financial footing. She was healthy and she ate well. And finally, Edwin wasn't quite sure how these things worked, but he himself was barely average height, so did that mean they'd have a small baby? That would make things safer.

The conversation had ceased completely. Edwin was now not in the mood for light-hearted chat, and Martin was always happy to ride in silence.

As they went on, Edwin became conscious of a new problem. The sun was indeed shining brightly today, but with the world still blanketed in snow the glare of the dazzling whiteness in all directions was hurting his eyes and giving him a headache. Flashes of light and spots were starting to appear. He pulled his hood further forward to try to shield his face as much as possible, but it was no good. By the time they stopped at midday to rest the horses his head was pounding and he was feeling nauseous.

As they resumed their journey, Edwin tried hard to concentrate on what he would be facing when they arrived. He had so little informa-tion to go on that it was almost impossible to know what they were walking into: all he knew from the earl was that Joanna was accused of murdering her husband – who had been called Sir Nicholas de Verdon – and all he could glean from her letter to Martin was that she wanted their help to exonerate herself. And no wonder: all murderers were executed, but for a woman to kill her lord and master was also petty treason, meaning that the penalty was to be burned at the stake, a particularly horrific and agonising end to face.

The main problem that Edwin could foresee at the moment – apart from the obvious one of finding out what had actually happened – was the conflicting motives he would have to deal with. Martin, of course, was already convinced that Joanna was innocent, and that they were on their way to prove that and rescue her. The lord earl, however, had taken Edwin to one side before he left and given him some different and rather troubling instructions. Edwin himself was trying to keep an open mind until he knew more: he liked Joanna, and in his heart he wanted to prove her innocent, but he could feel at the back of his mind – as Martin clearly could not – that there might be an explanation that none of them wanted. Women were often abused by their husbands: what if this turned out to be the case, and what if Joanna, driven beyond endurance, really had killed him? How in the Lord's name would he reconcile carrying out the earl's orders with Martin's probable actions?

Edwin shook his head, which was by now not so much pounding as being drilled and stabbed. The too-bright glare was still all around him, and the tell-tale splintering of the light had started. He needed it to stop. He couldn't afford for this to happen to him now; he had to stay vigilant so that their arrival at the castle went the way it needed to. *Think.* What were they to do? He couldn't remember. *Concentrate.* Yes.

They had agreed that they would not immediately announce that they had been sent by the lord earl to investigate; this would only make the culprit wary, and it might also antagonise the local sheriff. Instead, they would say that they were in Earl Warenne's service, which would guarantee them hospitality, and that Martin was in charge of a party conveying Edwin to take up a position as steward in one of his castles further south. Then, once they were inside and

Edwin could find out a little more about what was going on and make contact with the sheriff or his representative, they would take it from there. The earl had given Edwin so much free rein ('remember my orders, and do whatever you have to do, on my authority') that he could organise everything himself, which in one respect was comforting but in another was terrifying.

The splintering was getting worse, and the nausea was increasing. It was a real effort not to vomit. But the piercing light just wouldn't go away, stabbing constantly into his eyes and brain. He had to stave it off, had to keep going, for there was one other important thing. More than important: crucial. And it was that he had to control Martin. If they arrived and Martin started off belligerently – or, worse, if he showed any hint of knowing Joanna already – their plans would come crashing down. He, Edwin, had to stay awake, conscious and alert to manage the critical first moments of their arrival. He had to. He would.

The pain in his head got too much. Edwin's eyes closed and he slipped from the horse.

Martin swore as he saw Edwin hit the ground. He called the others to a halt, dismounted, threw his reins at Lambert and ran over. What was Edwin playing at? He hadn't fallen off a horse in ages.

He had a rough comment on the tip of his tongue, but Edwin wasn't picking himself up and dusting himself off; he was lying still in the snow.

Fear began to prickle along Martin's spine. 'Edwin?' He shook his friend. 'Edwin!'

'Is he breathing?' Turold was by now crouching next to them.

Martin bent his head. 'Yes.' Thank the Lord.

'Fainted? But why would he? He seemed fine this morning.'

Something stirred in the back of Martin's mind, cutting its way through the panic. 'He does get these pains in his head, sometimes, especially on bright days – I think they've made him pass out once or twice before.'

'Well, whatever it is, maybe we'd best get him up, before he gets too cold and wet. We can't do anything for him here.'

That seemed obvious to Martin now that Turold had pointed it out. Why hadn't he thought of it himself? *You're meant to be in command – start acting like it.* He slid his arms under Edwin's still form and lifted him easily. 'How far are we from Brandon?'

Turold looked about him at the flat, featureless landscape. 'If it's where I've been told, about six miles east and south of Coventry, then another hour, or not much more.' He pointed behind them. 'All that smoke over there is the city; we bypassed it instead of going through.'

Martin looked at the fading sun. 'We can still get there before dark, then. Here, you two hold him a moment.' Turold and Tom came to support Edwin while Martin turned. 'Lambert, bring Fauvel here, and be quick about it.' The boy obliged, his own jumpiness making the horse skittish.

'Oh, get out of my way.' Martin pushed Lambert away, eased the saddle as far back as he dared and then mounted. 'Pass him up and I'll hold him before me, so he doesn't fall.'

They tried, awkwardly, until another voice was heard. 'Stand aside, lads.' Willikin, the fourth member of the party, took Edwin from Turold and Tom, hefted him easily above his own shoulder height and settled him in front of the pommel, both legs dangling on one side of the horse and his head resting on Martin's chest. Martin reached both arms round his friend's limp body to hold the reins, making soothing noises to Fauvel. 'Easy, now. It's only an hour and then you can rest.'

He looked down and nodded. He was glad Sir Geoffrey had allocated Willikin to them in case there was any danger on the road. Like many another man, his real name was William, but the garrison, with their usual brand of humour, had decided to differentiate him from all the others by using a diminutive usually reserved for children. The 'joke' was that Willikin, although not tall, was the strongest man Martin had ever seen, capable of lifting two of his fellow soldiers above his head at the same time, one in each hand. He had once, for a wager, bent an iron bar with his bare hands, the veins in his bull-thick neck standing out as a young Martin had watched in amazement. Willikin wasn't the sharpest man in the garrison, to be sure, but who needed sharp when Edwin was around? Martin would certainly rather have the brawn if there was going to be trouble.

The others were by now back in their own saddles, with Tom preparing to lead Edwin's mount. 'All right,' said Martin, with more confidence than he felt. 'Lead the way, Turold – carefully now.'

As they set off, he concentrated on keeping Edwin in place, cradled against him, comforted at least to feel that he continued to breathe but otherwise worried sick. What, in the Lord's name, had happened to him? Would he wake up before they got there? And if not, what would Martin do? He tried to remember what it was they had agreed. Edwin was a steward, and he was taking him south. Yes, that was it. So, they could still go with that and just say he'd fallen from his horse. All the more reason why they should seek shelter and hospitality as the cold evening drew in.

As they continued, Fauvel grew used to the extra weight and steadied his gait, and Martin could turn his mind back to the subject that had overwhelmed him throughout the whole journey. *Joanna.* He could feel his heart beating faster even as he thought of her, as he framed her name on his lips and let it escape in a cloud into the cold air. What awful things must have happened to her since she went away from Conisbrough? How could he save her from all of them? And – he hardly dared think it – was there some way, any way at all, in which the present circumstances might mean that they could be together? Her husband was dead. However he had died, whoever had killed him, the fact was that he was dead and she was no longer bound in marriage. Martin wanted to spur onwards and gallop as fast as he could to reach her side. He wanted to fight any man who threatened her, who came between them.

As each step brought him closer to her, his thoughts grew more extreme. If her life was in danger – as it certainly would be if she were found guilty of murder – then nothing would stop him. It honestly didn't matter to him whether she had killed her husband or not: if he'd ill-treated her then death was no more than he deserved. He, Martin, would cut down anyone who stood in his way, the same way he had killed again and again on the ship last year, coming back to himself after the battle was over to find piles of bloodstained corpses at his feet. He felt the battle rage, long suppressed, beginning to roar once again.

His feelings were at such a pitch that he paid no attention to his surroundings until he heard Turold's voice. 'We're here.'

Martin looked up. The light of the day was almost gone. The road ahead of them ran over a bridge and he could see the smoke and light of a village beyond. Immediately to their right, commanding the road, was the gatehouse of a small castle, separated from them by a ditch. The gates were already closed, and a row of suspicious faces regarded them from the top of the wooden palisade.

Turold rode forward into what little light was cast by a brazier. He took a parchment from his scrip. 'We are of the household of the lord Earl Warenne, travelling on his business. I have letters here with his seal. We seek shelter for the night.'

Martin now expected that the gate would be opened, as would be the case at any of the earl's well-run residences, but there was only a murmuring between the men on guard. He gave them a few moments to allow for some kind of order to be given, but when none was forthcoming, he moved forward himself and spoke with some irritation. 'Open this gate.' Damn it, Joanna was inside there, and every moment's delay was painful.

His voice, both in accent and in tone, gave away immediately that he was a member of the nobility, and this did cause more movement and more of a buzz of conversation. But the gate still didn't open.

One man leaned over the palisade. 'What's the matter with him?' He pointed at Edwin.

Martin could feel his anger rising. 'I don't need to explain myself to—'

Turold interrupted him, speaking smoothly to those inside while making a 'calm down' gesture to Martin behind his back. 'He's steward to Earl Warenne; we are escorting him from Conisbrough to one of my lord's other castles. He's not ill, just injured: he fell from his horse.' He spoke with deliberation. 'Have no fear, there is no contagion.'

The gate still didn't open, but a man who seemed to be in charge now appeared. 'Who are you, to be seeking admittance?'

Turold tried to speak again, but Martin, really angry now, forestalled him. 'We're in the personal service of the lord Earl Warenne.' As best as he could while he was holding Edwin, he pushed back his cloak so the patch of checked blue and gold on his tunic could be seen. 'You are breaking all the laws of hospitality to be leaving us out here in the dark, not to mention offending the lord earl – the king's cousin – into the bargain. Now, either open this gate or fetch your mistress and she'll tell you to do so.'

'Earl Warenne needs to teach his men some manners,' came the reply, but the man did give an order to his subordinates. Within a few moments Martin heard the sound of the bar being lifted, and then one side of the double gate was slowly pulled back. As soon as the gap was wide enough, Martin rode through it.

The man who was in charge was making his way down the steps from the wall walk. Martin was so incensed that all he wanted was to grab him and shake him, but he was still holding Edwin on the horse and didn't want to drop him as he dismounted. So, he settled for remaining in the saddle and looking down. 'Who in God's name do you think you are, talking to my lord earl's men like that?'

'My name's Luke,' said the other, with not a hint of apology. 'Head of the garrison here, and my orders are to defend the castle – no easy task these days. You never know which lord is out for what he can get. You say you have letters?'

'I say again,' said Martin, through gritted teeth, 'that your hospitality is lax. We have an injured man here – see to his wants before you question further.'

Luke jerked his head at the others. 'Put him in the solar, and I'll see to these.'

Edwin was lifted down and slung, none too gently, over someone's shoulder. Martin watched them head off through the slushy courtyard and then another gate, which he assumed led to an inner ward and keep.

Now he was able, he dismounted. He was pleased to see that – as he had thought would be the case – he towered head and shoulders over Luke. He moved a pace closer, but the man didn't step back.

'Letters.' He held out a hand.

Martin motioned to Turold, who stepped forward and held out the parchment with the seal uppermost.

Luke glanced at it and grunted before handing it back. 'See to their horses,' he ordered.

Martin pointed at Lambert. 'Stay here and see they take good care. You others, come with me.' He turned to Luke. 'Show us the way.'

Luke didn't move. 'I'll take you in when you answer one question.'

'And what's that?'

'I've never seen you before, and you've never been here. So how did you know to ask for a mistress and not a master?'

Edwin stirred.

Where was he? There had been snow, and bright light, and confusion … but he wasn't lying in snow now, was he? His head was still screaming on the inside, but he could sense that he was lying down in a warm room. There was a fire nearby; he could smell it and feel the heat. And someone was pressing a blessedly cool cloth to his forehead.

A voice was saying something. A gentle, female voice.

'Alys?' But it wasn't Alys – the fragrance wasn't right.

He forced his eyes to open. No, not Alys. But wait, he did recognise …

'Mistress J—'

Quickly she put a hand over his mouth and a finger of the other to her own lips. When she was sure he understood and would say no more, she turned to someone behind her. 'He's waking up. Would you have the man in charge of their party fetched?'

'You're not the mistress here any more, to be giving me orders,' was all the reply Edwin heard. Another woman, though he couldn't see her at all.

'Yes, yes I am,' Joanna replied, with some asperity. 'And in any case, I'm not giving you an "order". I'm asking you, of your goodness, to send someone to fetch the head of this man's party.'

Edwin heard a sniff, and then footsteps, but they were coming towards him, not away. He met Joanna's eye and then let his head fall back, fluttering his eyelids and giving a groan.

'He's coming to.'

'Yes, that's what I said.' Joanna sounded as though her teeth were gritted.

'Wanted to see for myself, didn't I? After all, it's not like we can trust anything *you* say.'

The footsteps receded, and Edwin heard the sound of a door being closed.

He opened his eyes to find Joanna still by his side. It was about a year and a half since he had last seen her, but she seemed to have aged more than that. She had been a lithe, cheerful, humorous girl; now she was definitely a matron. It wasn't just the married woman's wimple that framed her face, but also the expression, the way she held herself and the authority with which she had spoken.

She spoke again now, her voice urgent. 'We don't have much time. What happened to you? Were you attacked on the road?'

Edwin struggled to sit up. 'No. But never mind that. Tell me in as few words as you can why you need us here.'

Her face crumpled. 'He's dead – my husband. And they all say that I did it.'

'And did you?'

'Of course not! How can you even—'

'All right. But I had to ask. How did he die? Who found him? And why should they think it was you?'

Tears came to her eyes. 'It was—'

But there were already footsteps sounding outside, and the door was opening again. Joanna's lips were already framing a word that began with 'M', but the same woman as before entered on her own. Older than Joanna, but difficult to see by how much. Her hair was under a wimple so Edwin couldn't tell if it was grey, but she had that slight thickening of the waist that middle-aged women had, and she didn't move like a young girl.

'Luke's still talking to them. He'll send that tall one up when he's finished.'

Joanna lost her patience. 'And who is Luke to be causing this delay, when I have asked specifically for the man to be sent here?'

'Luke was my brother's right-hand man – and still would be if you hadn't murdered him in cold blood.'

'I didn't—'

And he'll be as glad as I am to watch you burn for it.'

It was a vicious thing to say, and Edwin looked at the woman more closely. There was some kind of undercurrent, something in the tone she was using, that made him think that her words covered more than she was actually saying, but he didn't know what it was. He wished Alys were here; she would be able to tell him straight away. But no – Alys was much safer where she was, and could not go travelling about in her condition, to say nothing of the danger they appeared to be in already. Who was Luke? And was Martin being held some kind of captive? He wished his head would clear.

His stirring brought both women's attention to him, and Joanna was able to turn her back on the other while she held a cup to his lips. 'Your husband's sister?' murmured Edwin.

'Yes,' came the soft reply.

'Keep her talking if you can, so I can watch and listen.'

'There, is that more comfortable?' said Joanna, more loudly. 'Stay by the fire and keep warm, and I'll leave this wine next to you – we can't have any man of Earl Warenne's own household being left in discomfort.'

Propped in a semi-reclining position with his back against a heavy wooden kist, Edwin was able to survey the room and take a closer look at the other woman. Yes, definitely older, perhaps around thirty, and her expression was one of discontent in general and dislike in particular whenever she looked at Joanna. Of course, if she really did believe that Joanna had killed her brother then she had every reason to hate her, but was there perhaps even more to it than that?

Edwin's mind began to work, albeit slowly and unwillingly. A sister who was presumably either unmarried or widowed, more likely the latter given her age, or she wouldn't be here. Who had perhaps been the mistress of the castle until her brother had married, which of course gave his wife the precedence even though she was younger.

He watched them as they spoke, barbs concealed – or indeed in plain sight – in their every utterance, with Joanna trying to bring the conversation round in a direction that might interest Edwin.

'As I've said many times these past few weeks, Emma, I didn't kill Nicholas. I don't know who did, but no doubt this will come to light in due course.'

Emma merely snorted. 'Nothing will come to light because there is no other culprit. You never liked him.'

Joanna kept her voice level and threw half a glance at Edwin. 'No, I didn't, not particularly – why should I? But I knew my duty as his wife and I did it, as you well know. It's a long way from apathy to murder.'

Emma was just starting on a finger-stabbing reply when a new sound arose from somewhere behind Edwin. It was a kind of mewling cry that he recognised instantly, and he looked in wonder at Joanna. But of course, it was no wonder at all – she'd been married for a year and a half. Why hadn't he thought of it before?

'Speaking of duty,' said Emma, acidly, 'you'd better do yours. Or are you happy for my nephew to die as well as my brother?'

Edwin could see that Joanna was furious, but she said nothing. She cast him a glance as she hurried past; he turned his head just enough to see that she was passing through an inner door – a bedchamber, presumably – and then he heard her make the same sort of soothing noises that mothers of all ages and classes had made since the dawn of time.

She emerged, carrying a swaddled infant. Edwin was no expert – *not yet, anyway*, he thought to himself with a little glow – but he thought it was too big to be a newborn. Besides, if it was then Joanna would still be lying in rather than walking around. No, it was likely to be a few months old. And Emma had said 'nephew', so it must be a boy. Hmm. That gave events an interesting slant.

Joanna was now over by the room's other door, the one that must lead to a stairwell. 'Ada? Ada, are you there?' She turned in annoyance. 'Honestly, where is that girl?'

'Eating, probably,' replied Emma, who had made no move at all to help or to look at the baby. 'What else do wet-nurses do?'

Joanna clicked her tongue. 'But he's hungry!' Her voice softened. 'He's always hungry, aren't you, darling? Going to grow up big and strong?' She dandled the baby and her face lit up in a smile as she looked down at him, her face shining with the sort of love that could not possibly be fake. Edwin lost himself for a few moments as he imagined Alys gazing at their own child in a similar manner.

Then Joanna sat down, and her face became stony again as she looked at the hostile woman facing her. Edwin pulled himself together and forced himself to observe as closely as he could through the gradually receding thumping in his head.

＊

Martin was rapidly losing his temper. He'd been irritated even before they'd made their way into the inner ward, eager as he was to be taken straight to Joanna, but this oaf, whoever he thought he was, seemed to be delaying them on purpose, keeping them out in the cold. The only thing that was tempering Martin's ire was the fact that there were at least two dozen men around them – they weren't all armed garrison members, to be sure, but even servants and grooms would be prepared to defend their territory if necessary, and he had only Turold, Tom and Willikin. Oh, and Lambert had wandered over once the horses were safely stabled, but he wouldn't be much use either way. Even with Willikin on his side Martin didn't fancy odds of six to one, so he tried to keep himself in check.

He'd cursed himself several times over for letting slip the word 'mistress', for it demonstrated undeniably that he knew something – why would anyone assume a woman was in charge, in the normal course of things? The quick-witted Turold had made an excuse about them having heard something in the inn they'd stayed at last night, for what was more natural than that the innkeeper should have mentioned the big local news when they asked directions to Brandon? That had seemed to mollify the man slightly. But Martin didn't like his attitude, and he certainly didn't like being kept from Joanna.

Luke's next tactic had been to question them closely about Edwin. What was wrong with him? How had he fallen? Were there bandits abroad? Martin was half-tempted to tell him that there was a gang of outlaws in the vicinity and Luke should get out and chase after them, but he restrained himself. Lord, but he wished Edwin were standing next to him. He would know what to do, what to say. Martin felt a chill as he recalled having the unconscious Edwin before him while he rode. What if he never woke up? But he would, surely. He had to. Martin couldn't manage this without him.

It was when questions on their business, their reasons for travelling and specifically for coming here, started to be posed that Martin felt himself slipping from irritation to outright anger. 'That's enough,' he barked. 'You have no right to pry into our business, and if you don't take us to your m— to whoever rules here in place of your master, my lord earl will be told how members of his household were treated here. And I assure you that you won't like the result.'

His fingers were itching to curl themselves around the hilt of his sword, but he must hold back. He folded his arms and stared down. 'You will take us to the keep *now*.'

The man was obviously spoiling for a fight just as much as Martin was, but either Martin's physical size or the threat of a higher authority intimidated him, and he dropped his gaze.

Another man, less pugnacious, had his hand on Luke's arm and was murmuring in his ear. Martin caught a few words. 'We should show him up … situation … sheriff's man … powerful lord … any more trouble …'

He turned to Martin. 'Your pardon, sir. I'm Joscelin, Sir Nicholas's … that is to say, the estate steward. If you'll follow me, I'll take you to Lady Joanna in the solar. Your companion is already there – I saw him taken care of myself.'

He paused, but Martin was too overcome by hearing Joanna's name to reply.

Joscelin continued. 'Your men are welcome to join the evening meal in the hall.' He pointed to a long wooden building at the far end of the ward, to which other men were starting to drift. Willikin brightened visibly, and Lambert was almost in motion when Tom grabbed his collar. 'You wait until you're told,' he hissed.

Martin nodded to them. 'You all go. I'll send for you if I need you later.' He bent to speak in Turold's ear. 'Don't let them drink too much.'

As he watched them go Martin realised how hungry he was himself, but that could wait. He turned to Joscelin. 'The solar, you said?' His agitation rose, but he couldn't tell which of the mixture of churning emotions was causing it.

He followed the steward to the small stone keep and ducked under the lintel. Inside was a large room, a few tables lit by rushlights at which sat some indeterminate figures. There was a staircase in the far corner, and Martin could hardly keep himself from pushing Joscelin out the way and taking the steps three at a time. He was going to see her again, for the first time in more than eighteen months. Here. *Now*.

When they reached the upper floor Joscelin knocked on the door in front of him and two female voices cried out, 'Enter!' at the same time. Martin didn't know or care who the second one was, because he recognised the first. His heart was already beating quickly, and now it nearly jumped out of his throat. With the barest pretence at civility, he barged past Joscelin and into the warm, softly lit room.

She was there. She was standing in front of him.

His own Joanna. His lost love.

She was holding a baby.

Chapter Three

Edwin felt his stomach lurch as he watched Martin step into the room and stop dead. The expression on his face spoke volumes, and surely neither the man who had accompanied him in nor Emma could be under any illusion that he and Joanna knew each other. Edwin mentally threw away the plans he'd made on the road and hoped he could think quickly enough to come up with some new ones.

'Martin!' he called, as much to break the awkward silence as anything. He was aware that his voice sounded weak.

Martin shook his head as if to clear it, looked about him and noticed Edwin for the first time. He strode over. 'You're awake! Are you all right? Your head?'

The other man had followed. 'So glad to see you recovered. I had you brought up here as it was the most warm and comfortable room, and the ladies graciously agreed to tend to you.'

He wasn't well dressed – from his position on the floor Edwin could see that his tunic was patched and faded – but the keys hanging from his belt indicated that he held a position of responsibility. 'You have my thanks, Master …?'

'Joscelin, sir. The late Sir Nicholas's steward. As I gather you are too, although of course on a much larger scale. It's an honour to meet you.'

Edwin didn't think anyone had ever said that to him before, but he stopped himself from demurring. Martin might have given the game away to a certain extent, but best to keep the rest of the pretence going for a while until he could see what was what. Besides, such deference might come in useful later when he needed to deal with the steward or the other inhabitants of the castle.

The man seemed nervous, fussing around Edwin. 'Do you feel able to get up and sit on a chair? The rushes on the floor are fresh, of course, but perhaps you'd be more comfortable off them.' He fetched a stool, adjusted its position near the fire and threw on a couple more logs. 'There. Shall I—'

He didn't have time to finish before Edwin felt himself being hoisted up by Martin's strong arms and unceremoniously dumped on the seat. As this was happening, he managed to whisper, 'Remember – you're not supposed to know her.' That might at least keep Martin from making any further gaffes until Edwin could get to grips with what was going on.

'You've met Lady Joanna and Lady Emma, of course,' continued Joscelin. 'The late Sir Nicholas's widow and sister.'

'My ladies.' Edwin inclined his head, which made it throb again. 'I am truly grateful for your kind attention.'

'Travellers in need will always be sure of a welcome here,' said Joanna, forestalling Emma's attempt to get her words in first. 'It was something my husband cared about particularly, as I'm sure his son will.' She looked down at the baby again, joggling him in her arms as his mewling cries gradually rose in pitch.

Martin still hadn't said anything – which, given that he was supposed to be the one in charge of their party, was starting to look odd. Edwin could hardly kick him without everyone seeing, but he threw him a meaningful glance.

'Oh, yes – er, we were very sorry to hear of your loss, my lady,' he managed. 'We heard about it yesterday while we were on the road.'

His eyes were still wide and he seemed absolutely on the verge of stepping over to her; Edwin hoped he could control himself. 'And your loss as well, of course, my lady,' he interjected, quickly, at Emma.

'Yes, and all the greater, given the circumstances,' she replied, casting a look of daggers at Joanna.

There was another awkward silence, or at least there would have been if the baby had not now been shrieking at the top of its lungs. Edwin had no idea that a creature so small could make such a loud noise, but he supposed he'd better get used to it.

The room's outer door opened and a buxom young woman hurried in.

'There you are!' exclaimed Joanna. 'Where have you been?'

'So sorry, my lady. Here, shall I take him?' Joanna held out the infant and she took him, making clucking and cooing noises as she retreated to the bedchamber. After a few moments there came a blessed silence.

Edwin was amused to see everyone heaving a sigh of relief at the same time. Then Joscelin began to bustle about. 'Has nobody come to lay your cloth yet, ladies? The evening meal is already being served in the hall so yours should be on its way momentarily. I'll go and check.'

'Yes,' said Emma, 'and—'

'These gentlemen will be our guests, of course,' interrupted Joanna. 'And if Master Aubrey is back yet then of course he should take his meal here rather than in the hall.' She sounded so much in charge, such a voice of authority, that Martin seemed taken aback, but Edwin could see that it all masked a fragility, a tension – she was displaying more confidence than she really felt. He certainly recognised *that* feeling.

There was a table over to one side of the room, under the one window – shuttered now, of course – and various serving men started to enter with a cloth, dishes and cups. Those in the room remained silent while the activity was in progress. Each, as far as Edwin could see in the dim candlelight, was intent on one of the others: Joanna was looking at Martin as much as she dared, while both Martin and Emma had their eyes on her, albeit with very different expressions.

Just as the meal appeared to be ready Joscelin entered once more, along with two others. One was a boy of around fourteen, the tell-tale heraldic patch on his tunic indicating that he was, or had been, Sir Nicholas's squire. He aimed a bow carefully at the centre of the space between Joanna and Emma before slipping in silence to stand behind the chair at the head of the table.

The other new entrant was a finely dressed man who at first glance didn't look much older than the squire, although on considering him properly Edwin guessed him to be in his mid-twenties. He also bowed, with grace, before glancing enquiringly at Edwin and Martin.

'Master Aubrey,' said Joanna, 'These travellers are from the household of Earl Warenne; they sought shelter here as darkness fell, and one of them was injured after a fall from his horse. This is Edwin of Conisbrough, steward to the earl, and this is …' she remembered just in time that she wasn't supposed to know who Martin was, and paused to let him introduce himself.

'Sir Martin?' enquired Aubrey, looking the towering figure up and down with a certain amount of trepidation.

Martin broke into his first smile since their arrival. 'Soon, I hope, but it's just Martin for now.'

They were all moving towards the table. Edwin stood up, but it made his head spin and Martin had to support him. 'My apologies,' he said to Aubrey. 'I hit my head when I fell.'

This was an entirely plausible excuse, so no more was said. As he made his way slowly over, leaning on Martin's arm, Edwin was able to observe the others. Nobody moved to take the chair at the head of the table, the one that under normal circumstances would belong to the lord, but both Joanna and Emma headed for its opposite number. He wondered if they were genuinely going to jostle for it, but Aubrey, who was a pace ahead, drew it out with a murmured, 'My lady' that was definitely aimed at Joanna, and she sat down. He then took a space next to her, and Edwin felt Martin tense.

Clearly it was not going to be a comfortable meal, but Edwin consoled himself with the fine food; it was not quite of the sort served at the lord earl's top table, but certainly a cut above anything he would normally get served in the hall. It was a shame they'd arrived on a Friday, but the fish was delicately poached and a far cry from the rubbery eel stew often produced for the lower ranks at Conisbrough. Edwin savoured it while appreciating the chance to sit in silence and observe everyone else.

Most of the talk was carried on between Martin and Aubrey, who spoke of the roads, the weather and politics with occasional interjections from one of the ladies. Aubrey, it transpired, had been sent here by the sheriff of Warwickshire following Sir Nicholas's death, from which information Edwin was able to deduce several facts. Firstly, that there was something untoward about the business; if Sir Nicholas had merely died of a seizure or obvious illness then the presence of a sheriff's man wouldn't be necessary. Edwin had already heard the word 'murder' from several quarters, but it was good to have that confirmed. Secondly, the identity of the culprit was not obvious, or at least not confirmed: Sir Nicholas had died some three weeks ago now and, as yet, nobody had been convicted or even formally accused, or Aubrey wouldn't still be here. And thirdly, despite a lord being murdered in his county, the sheriff had not bothered to come himself, instead sending a man who was, judging by his age and demeanour, inexperienced.

Next Edwin looked at the squire, whom Joanna had called Milo. Like all squires he remained silent while serving, but Edwin could see that his hands were trembling as he poured the wine. There was no chance of being able to speak to him now, but he would have known his lord as well as anyone, so he shouldn't be overlooked as a source of information.

The conversation around him was faltering. Joanna, at her end of the table and with Aubrey on one side of her and Martin on the other, was starting to let slip some of the pressure she was under. Emma, opposite Edwin, had made no attempt to talk to him during the meal but was still trying to continue her power struggle with Joanna, a game she looked unlikely to win.

By the time the meal was over Edwin was exhausted again. He could feel himself swaying and leaned against Martin in an attempt not to fall off the stool.

This did, however, give Joanna an opening. 'You're not well enough to resume your journey tomorrow. Please accept our hospitality for as long as it takes you to recover.' She glanced at Martin. 'I know you will be in a hurry to reach your destination, but surely the lord Earl Warenne would prefer his steward to arrive late and in good health rather than too ill to work?'

There was no arguing with that, and even in his woolly headed state Edwin could appreciate both the smooth, plausible suggestion and the way she had casually dropped in the name of one of the realm's most powerful men.

Back when he had first come to know Joanna, the year before last, he had got the impression that she was clever, and he saw no reason to start doubting it now. How that would either help or hinder his own situation, however, he couldn't tell. What he really needed was to be able to speak to her alone – by which he meant without Martin, as well as everyone else – but how was that to be managed? If only his head would clear. And he didn't think it had helped that he had been served wine rather than the ale he was more accustomed to.

At last the meal was over. Nobody was inclined to stay at the table to chat.

Joscelin appeared again from somewhere and addressed Martin. 'Your men are welcome to sleep with the others in the hall. We have a couple of small guest chambers downstairs here in the keep, so I've had one prepared for you and your companion. I hope you don't mind sharing, as Master Aubrey is in the other.'

'Not at all,' said Martin, getting to his feet and casting a sudden shadow so huge that it made Milo shrink back as he was stacking dishes. Martin hesitated, clearly (to Edwin at least) wanting to stay and talk to Joanna but realising with reluctance that this was going to be impossible. Instead, he looked down at Edwin. 'Can you manage the stairs?'

Edwin wasn't sure, but he certainly didn't want to be carried out like a baby, so he stood up as carefully as he could. 'Yes, if we don't go too fast.'

'Good.'

Aubrey was also on his feet. 'I'll come down too.' He executed another courtly bow. 'My lady. Ladies, I mean. Thank you once again for your hospitality.'

Martin didn't attempt anything half so elegant, but he nodded and added his own thanks before ushering Edwin towards the door.

Once they were safely down the stairs, Edwin could see the space there for the first time; he had no recollection of being carried through it earlier. Sir Nicholas had probably used it as a room to conduct business and to receive tenants and guests who wanted to speak to him in more privacy than the hall would provide but who were not important enough to be invited up to the private space of the solar. A couple of doors over at the far end must be those to the guest rooms; they would be directly under the main bedchamber. The rest was the usual sort of thing: various tables and kists, the entrance to a garderobe, and a fire that somehow failed to take the chill off the cold stone of the walls.

Aubrey stoked it up. 'It's a little early to retire to bed,' he said. 'Would either of you like to join me in a drink, maybe a game of merels?'

Edwin was desperately thirsty, but he certainly didn't want any more wine. However, a jug of watery ale proved to be available so he happily sat down with that – the more liquid he got into himself now, the better his headache would be in the morning.

Aubrey drew out a leather pouch. Merels was a game for two, but Martin didn't seem to have any interest in either playing or watching. He couldn't sit still, restlessly pacing about before flinging himself down on a stool only to get up again moments later.

Eventually the room seemed too small to contain him. 'I'm going out,' he said, abruptly, grabbing his cloak and interrupting Edwin's train of thought as he planned some six moves ahead.

'Out?'

'Of here, I mean. I'll go and check on the men and the horses before we turn in.'

He left, and Edwin turned back to his contemplation of the board.

Martin yanked the door open with unnecessary force. A blast of freezing air hit him, and he gasped as he fastened his cloak and pulled it around him before stepping outside. Then he stood for a few moments, breathing in the cold air and feeling it reach deep into his chest.

He didn't know what to do with himself. He knew what he *wanted*, of course, which was to run back into the keep, up the stairs and into the solar, to spend the evening sitting with Joanna in front of the fire, asking her all about what had happened and then making plans for him to get her out of here and away.

That was impossible, of course. But he couldn't let go of the thought, of the picture of the two of them riding off together, and he decided he would keep it at the back of his mind as a last resort. He would give Edwin a chance first: he had found a way out of seemingly impossible situations before, and there was nobody Martin trusted more. But in the meantime, what was he to do? The thought of Joanna being there, in the same building, only just above his head but out of his reach, was a torment.

And the baby. Of course, he wasn't stupid, he knew she'd been married for a year and a half, but somehow, he had just never envisaged such a thing – or maybe he had, but he'd tried to block it out of his mind. If he could take her away, would she want to bring the child as well? Surely not, not if it was the relic of a husband she had disliked.

He was getting cold, standing still.

Martin looked about him; it would be as well to get his bearings. As he stood with his back to the keep door, he could see three buildings in the ward. The one directly ahead, with light and sound and smells spilling from the open door and unshuttered window, must be the kitchen; the long one over to his left, from where the noise of men emanated, would be the hall; the other, between them, was in darkness, but was probably household offices or stores or something. To his right was the footbridge that led over the ditch to the outer ward, now in darkness.

The hall would be the place to start. He had to tread carefully as he went; the slush from earlier was now frozen solid again and the ground was treacherous. It would certainly be difficult to fight or train on it.

The fug hit him as he reached the hall: smoke, warmth, ale, sweat. It was almost physical. As he ducked through the doorway and then straightened, silence fell among those nearest to him, and all eyes turned in his direction. He wondered if this sort of thing would ever cease, but of course it would always be much worse away from home. The men of the lord earl's household and garrisons were used to him and barely noticed, but strangers were a different matter. Still, as had been pointed out to him more than once, it was better than being marked out by being short or misshapen.

His eyes found the Conisbrough men straight away. Willikin was – inevitably – involved in some kind of arm-wrestling match, while Turold looked on, but they were both sober. Lambert was sitting a little apart, joining in a game of dice, but the steady, grey-haired Tom seemed to be keeping an eye on him. He met Martin's eye and nodded over the top of the cup of ale he'd probably been nursing all evening.

Turold slipped away from the table to Martin's side. 'Edwin?'

'He's awake, thank the Lord,' murmured Martin, 'though he still looks a bit wobbly. But it's given us an excuse to stay longer so it's no bad thing. Keep your eyes and ears open and let me know if you pick up anything that he might find interesting.'

'If anyone can find out what's going on, he can,' replied Turold in an equally low tone. 'And yes, we'll see what we can do.'

There was a sudden loud exclamation from the nearest table: Willikin had not merely won his arm-wrestling bout but had sent his opponent sprawling to the floor, and men were laughing at the discomposed victim.

'Don't let this get out of hand,' said Martin. 'It's all good-natured for now, but if he takes money for it, or accidentally breaks someone's head, there will be trouble.'

Turold nodded and made his way back to the table to lay a calming hand on Willikin's arm.

Thinking of trouble made Martin look around for Luke, but he couldn't see him anywhere in the hall. Perhaps he was out supervising the wall guards or checking that they weren't slacking – an unenviable duty on a night like this.

Satisfied that the men were both comfortable and under control, Martin decided to head to the stables; there was no way he wanted to go back to the keep just yet, not under the same roof as Joanna, not while he was still so wide awake. Thinking too much was never a good idea – not unless you were Edwin, anyway – and the way to avoid that was to keep busy and keep moving.

He slithered and slid his way across to the footbridge that joined the two wards, and then took great care stepping on to it; the last thing he needed was to end up in the fishpond on one side or the ditch on the other. Someone had helpfully thrown salt on the icy wood, so he was able to get some grip and to reach the other side in safety.

The outer ward was silent and mainly in darkness, the workshops shut up for the night and the stables quiet. The only light came from the brazier up on the wall walk of the gatehouse, around which several shadowy figures were gathered.

The cold here was raw, but at least it wasn't snowing again. Martin picked his way across to the stable, feeling for the latch on the door, sliding in through a narrow crack and then pulling it closed behind him. It wouldn't do for any of the horses to get chilled.

Inside it was completely dark, but of course he couldn't strike a light. He made his way down the row of stalls, calling Fauvel's name softly until he heard an answering whicker. Yes, there he was – unmistakeable by his height as Martin put his hand up to stroke the soft head.

He spoke to the horse for some while, not embarrassed while he was alone to address him as a companion – 'Have they treated you right? Given you your oats? Are you warm enough?' – rather than an animal. For he *was* a companion, and one with whom Martin would hopefully share the best years of his life.

It wasn't long before the talk slipped gradually from Fauvel's concerns to Martin's, and he found himself whispering out his love and hurt and frustration. It was odd that his proximity to the horse was making his eyes water, something that had never happened before.

He felt a sudden cold draught. The stable door was opening.

Martin had no reason to fear being seen there – after all, it was perfectly natural that he should check that strangers had stabled his horse properly – but a combination of suspicion and not wanting to talk to anyone made him unbolt the gate of the stall and slip inside. Fauvel didn't mind, of course, so no disquiet on his part would give away Martin's presence.

He couldn't see anything, but something about the movement told him that the new entrant was not a groom, who would have no reason to act furtively. And in fact, it wasn't one entrant; there must be at least two, because Martin could hear whispering as the stable door was pulled shut again. Oh, great – it would be just his luck to get stuck in here when someone was having a tryst. Stables anywhere were always a popular location, what with the warmth and the hay, though at this time of night the only women in a castle would normally be the lady and her attendants.

That thought made him pause, but Joanna was definitely not one of those who had entered – he would have known. And, come to think of it, he hadn't seen any other women since they'd arrived apart from Emma and the wet-nurse, but it was always possible that a laundry maid or groom's daughter might have hidden herself somewhere before the gates were shut for the night. He would wait until their attention was distracted and then make his way out.

After some few moments, however, he realised that he had been mistaken. The newcomers – yes, two of them – made no move towards any of the stalls, but stayed near the door, still talking.

Martin strained his ears, but the figures were not particularly close to him and there were half a dozen horses in between, all making occasional movements that masked the sound.

'… today,' he made out. 'Why?'

Words with 'S' in them often carried further, even when people were trying to speak quietly, and Martin was sure he heard both 'steward' and 'mistress'. That brought him to even more of a state of alert, for surely these men – or a man and a woman? he couldn't tell – were talking of their arrival.

He crouched to keep his head below the level of the stall partition but inched his way into a turn so that his ear was towards the conversation. He closed his eyes and concentrated on what he could hear.

'*Told* you …' came one voice, the words reaching Martin a little more clearly due to their emphasis.

Then there was more whispering that he couldn't make out, maybe because they were talking over the top of each other, before he caught three words very clearly indeed.

Kill them all.

'I don't think I've ever seen anyone that tall,' said Aubrey, conversationally, as Martin stalked out and shut the keep's door behind him.

'An inch over six and a half feet, last time we measured him,' said Edwin, taking one of his opponent's pieces off the board. 'But we think he's stopped growing now. I wouldn't mention it to him, though – he gets fed up with all the jokes.'

'Understood,' replied the other. 'And I certainly wouldn't want to antagonise him.'

Edwin's memory flew back a year and a half to the pile of bloodied corpses on the ship, and he decided to change the subject. 'So,' he said, in as casual a tone as he could muster, 'you work for the sheriff of Warwickshire? What sort of thing does that involve?'

Aubrey sighed. 'Mainly, dealing with all the things he wants to avoid.' He waved his arm. 'Such as this, for example. The murder of a lord would be sensitive at the best of times, but with his widow, whom everyone thinks is guilty, being connected to a great house, it's even more so. He sent me because I'm of good family – my father is a friend of his – and he told me to stay as long as it took to find someone else to blame. But it's just impossible.'

Edwin was immediately suspicious. Was this man a simpleton, to be laying his business so wide open to a complete stranger, or was this part of some plan on his part? Did he suspect Edwin's motives for being here?

'Why do you say it's impossible?' he asked, carefully.

Aubrey made a helpless gesture. 'Because it's so obvious that she must have killed him. Sometimes when I talk to her I can't believe it – she seems so *nice*, and of course from such a good family. And I'd like to find her innocent, if only for the good of my own career. But you never know with women, do you? They can be unpredictable.'

'I think that's my game,' said Edwin, taking another piece, which only left Aubrey with two men on the board.

Aubrey clicked his tongue. 'So it is. I should pay better attention.'

Edwin didn't think that more attention would have helped, for his opponent's strategy had hardly been better than that of the eight-year-old Hugh back at Conisbrough, but he didn't feel the need to say that out loud. 'Another game, then?' he asked, telling himself that he should spin this out for longer so they could continue their chat. 'We're not playing for money, so there's no harm either way.'

The fire was still going, and the candle between them looked like it would be good for some while yet, so Aubrey set up the pieces again.

Once the game was in progress, Edwin risked touching on the all-important subject. 'So, women, eh? Unpredictable, like you say. But perhaps he mistreated her.'

'Not that I hear,' said Aubrey, who was contemplating the board, having signally failed to spot the deliberate mistake Edwin had just made in order to make the game last longer. 'He didn't beat her or anything, or keep her locked up.'

'So why,' continued Edwin, cautiously, 'is everyone so sure that she killed him?'

'Oh, didn't I say?' Aubrey looked up from the board and his eyes met Edwin's in the candlelight. 'He was killed in his bed – here, upstairs in the chamber. His squire went in first thing one morning, just as usual: Sir Nicholas was lying there with his throat sliced wide open, blood everywhere. Nobody in the room except him and his wife, and she was leaning over him with the knife still in her hand.'

Chapter Four

Martin's hand fell to where his sword hilt would have been, but he wasn't wearing it. He'd left it in the keep, for it was the height of bad manners to walk around armed in someone else's home – an indication that you didn't trust them – and Edwin had been clear, before his unfortunate incident, that they should try hard not to arouse any suspicion.

Which was of no help now.

He wondered if he could take them both with only the knife at his belt, but reluctantly decided against it. He didn't know who they were; they might be anything from grooms to hardened members of the garrison, and whoever they were, they would be on more familiar terrain. Besides, Martin had no way of knowing whether there might be a third or even fourth man stationed outside the stable door. No, it was just too risky.

They didn't say much more, and it wasn't long before the stable door opened again and they were gone. Martin waited a long while just to be sure they weren't going to come back, and to give them time to get far enough away that they wouldn't see him emerge, and then he made his way out of the stall with a final pat for Fauvel, drawing his knife as he tiptoed to the stable door.

He opened it the merest crack. There was no outcry. He pushed it a tiny bit more, so he could cautiously poke his head round. The sound of conversation from the top of the palisade floated across to him, but the ward seemed otherwise deserted.

He decided to risk it, stepping outside and closing the door softly behind him. There was still no sound of alarm, so he assumed a confident manner and walked across the icy open space back to the footbridge.

All was well; Martin made it back to the keep unscathed. The kitchen was by now in darkness, and although some light still spilled around the edge of the door and shutters of the hall, it was much quieter. He entered the keep to find that the main space was empty save for the squire and a few dogs sleeping by the remains of the fire.

Both of the guest chambers had their doors open, probably to allow some of the residual heat to circulate. Martin put his head into one but was fairly sure that the slumbering figure in it was Aubrey, so he tried the other. Yes, that was Edwin.

Martin considered whether he should wake his friend to tell him of what had happened. In the end, he decided against it; Edwin had continued to look unwell even after he'd come round, and if he were to be on best form tomorrow, he would need his sleep. He would be little use in a fight, anyway, so the best thing to do was for Martin to stay awake and guard the door.

Martin went back out into the main room to examine the keep's door. There were sockets in which a bar could be fitted, but he couldn't immediately see the bar itself, and he didn't want to blunder around too much and wake the squire or the dogs, one of whom was sleepily beginning to growl. As an interim measure he picked up two stools and stacked them on top of each other just behind the door; that wouldn't stop it opening, if pushed hard enough, but the noise of them falling would alert him.

Then he went back to the guest chamber. He considered shutting that door but realised that trapping themselves inside wasn't a particularly good idea. Finding his sword, which was lying with their other baggage, Martin drew it. He poked Edwin until he rolled over to the far side of the bed, and then sat on the near edge, facing the door, with the sword across his knees.

It was a shame he couldn't warn the others in the hall, but he couldn't possibly leave Edwin unguarded, so they would just have to shift for themselves. If the lord earl or Sir Geoffrey were here, he knew what their orders would be.

He settled down to wait.

Edwin woke up. In the darkness of the windowless room, he had no way of telling what time it was, but he had a feeling that he had slept long and deeply, and that it must therefore be nearly dawn.

He had retired to the guest chamber not long after Aubrey's revelation. Their baggage had already been placed there; with a momentary alarm, Edwin looked through it all but was relieved to see that the bags of pennies, issued to them to pay their way on the road, were still all in place.

He was momentarily irritated at discovering he had left his cloak upstairs in the solar: it had been wrapped round him when he was carried up, but he now recalled taking it off in order to sit at the table for his evening meal, draping it over the kist he'd been leaning on, and then not picking it up when he left the room. It was fur-lined and would have made an excellent extra cover for sleeping, but the bed here did at least have plenty of blankets on it. He had removed only his boots and his belt before burrowing under them, but he must have ended up warm enough or he wouldn't have slept so well and have such a clear head now.

The news about Joanna, and how she had been found with her dead husband, was shocking. Just as everyone believed, it didn't seem to admit of a doubt – and yet Edwin's mind was already working. There were two principal lines of thought. The first was practical: could anyone else possibly have got into the chamber to kill Sir Nicholas? And how would they have done it without waking and alerting Joanna? The second was more nebulous, but was equally as important, if not more. *Why* would anyone want to kill Sir Nicholas?

If only he could find a way to speak to Joanna, things might be clearer. But that would be difficult. She was in a strange, in-between position: until she was found guilty of the crime, she was in theory still the mistress here, on behalf of her young son, until such time as his wardship was bought by another lord. But on the other hand, if she could not prove her innocence then she might be executed anyway – and there appeared to be few here who would support her. Nobody could possibly swear to her being elsewhere, for example, not if she had been found in the chamber with the body. At the very least she would be tainted, always under suspicion and the subject of gossip and ill-will.

The only thing that currently stood between her and the pyre was her social position and the consequent hesitation of the sheriff to find against her. But that would not last forever; the government that ruled in King Henry's name was keen to restore the mechanisms of justice after the chaos caused by the recent war. Joanna was thus stuck in both a legal and physical limbo: neither innocent nor guilty, neither mistress nor prisoner. She was confined to the solar, Aubrey had told Edwin, but was still – more or less – being treated there as though she were the castle's mistress.

Added to Edwin's difficulty was the fact that he had no official status at Brandon. He had been sent by the lord earl, yes, but not in any sort of proper legal capacity. That responsibility rested with Aubrey, who had already spent several weeks here without discovering anything and who did not, at least judging by his gaming skills, have much of a head for forward planning. Perhaps he had been given the job on the basis of his social position rather than any particular skill or expertise. Still, if Edwin could help him, nudge him in the right direction … yes, that might work. If he could find out the truth, but have it emerge via a man who worked for the local sheriff, that might save a lot of trouble.

Edwin had been staring through the darkness at the ceiling, but now he turned his head and belatedly became aware that Martin was already awake, sitting up on the edge of the bed.

He touched his friend's arm. 'Martin?'

Martin jumped almost out of his skin, leaping to his feet with his sword in his hand. After a flustered look about him he lowered it again. 'I must have been dozing.'

Edwin sat up, pleased to find that he could do so without his head spinning. 'What in the Lord's name are you doing?'

Martin stepped to the chamber door and looked out. 'It's all right, they're both still asleep.'

'Yes, but what …?'

Martin put his finger to his lips and returned to sit on the bed. 'I think we're in danger.'

Edwin listened while Martin told him of the previous night's events.

'And you're absolutely sure that's what he said?'

'Yes. And it might not have been a "he" – I *think* they were both men, but I didn't see them at all, and it's difficult to tell just from whispers.'

'But how could anyone possibly suspect us already?' A foreboding struck Edwin. 'Can you tell me what happened – exactly what happened – when we arrived yesterday? I don't remember any of it, from passing out in the saddle to waking up in the solar.'

Even in the almost-darkness Edwin could see Martin grimace. 'Oh.'

'Well, it was just that—'

A sound came from the outer room, and Martin leapt up again. It was Milo, the squire, who had risen and was now taking the shutters off the windows, allowing a grey light to enter.

Edwin shook his head. 'Martin, you need to stop being so jumpy.'

'But—'

'Yes, I know. But this isn't going to help. If someone here is aware that we're not what we seem, that's bad enough, but we can't let them know that we know.'

'What?'

Edwin sighed. 'If we want to keep up the pretence that we're just travellers,' he said, under his breath, 'you storming around with a sword in your hand isn't going to help, is it?'

'But—'

'Please, just … look, keep your eyes open, by all means, and maybe warn Turold as well, but otherwise try to remain calm. And unarmed,' he added, looking meaningfully at the sword.

There was another clatter from the outer room. Edwin looked out again to see a serving man pushing at the main door, which for some reason was blocked by a couple of stools that had fallen over behind it.

He went to help Milo move them. 'Sorry – we must have shuffled things around last night without realising.'

As soon as the door was open wide enough, the dogs streaked outside and the serving man entered, carrying a basket of logs. Edwin shivered in the freezing morning air, but at least it was fresh after he'd been shut up inside stone walls all night, and he took some deep breaths. The sky was grey, thank goodness – he didn't need a repeat of yesterday's bright, blinding reflection.

Martin appeared behind him. 'I'll go over to the hall and check on the men.'

'You don't think …'

'I don't know. And everything looks so normal, it seems hard to believe that I heard what I heard. But I'm sure I did.' He looked out at the peaceful inner ward, just starting to come to life with the day's activities. 'At least, I *think* I'm sure.'

Edwin watched him cross the ward, Martin's tension easing considerably when the Conisbrough men emerged from the hall just as he neared it. Everything seemed fine. So, had Martin really heard what he thought he heard? Something that appeared frightening in the middle of a dark winter's night often took on less sinister proportions in the cold light of day, so maybe that was it. On the other hand, there *was* a killer on the loose somewhere inside the castle, so Martin's caution was understandable.

Edwin's mind turned to how he might best put into action the plan he'd made. Would Aubrey become suspicious if Edwin kept tailing him, asking him questions, prompting him to action?

Aubrey emerged from the other guest chamber, yawning, and Edwin greeted him. 'Cold outside,' he began, by way of a conversation-starter, 'but it's not snowing.'

'Good.' Aubrey moved to the door. 'I was going to head into the village this morning.'

'Oh?' said Edwin, casually, as he led the way back to the now-lit fire and held his hands out to it. 'Something to do with your investigations?'

It was fortunate for him that Aubrey seemed to have no idea of discretion; once again, he showed no hesitation in telling Edwin all about it. 'Yes. Yesterday I went to speak with the priest – you must have arrived while I was out there – and he was telling me that Sir Nicholas had a woman in the village who'd been his concubine for a long time before he was married. Mabel, her name is. Father Clement didn't seem too pleased about the arrangement, so I just wondered if it would be worth talking to her.'

'And what will you ask her?'

Edwin immediately felt he'd been too direct, but Aubrey merely replied, with a deep sigh, that he didn't know. 'I didn't have anything particular in mind – just a thought that she might have known Sir Nicholas as well as anyone. I'm at such a dead end that I'll try anything.' He turned round so he could warm his back at the fire and gave Edwin a sideways glance. 'You must be quite a clever fellow if you're the steward on a large estate. What would you ask her if you were in my shoes?'

Edwin was again unsure whether to thank the Lord for his luck, or to be suspicious that Aubrey was playing some kind of game. Surely nobody who worked for a sheriff could possibly be this naïve?

'We-ell,' he said, slowly, likewise turning his back to the fire, 'maybe it would be useful to know exactly when she last saw Sir Nicholas? And was that out in the village or here in the castle? And how did he seem to her at that time?'

Aubrey was looking at him as though he were some kind of genius. 'That's splendid! How did you think of all that so fast?' And then, with the air of a hopeful puppy, 'I don't suppose you want to come with me?'

Edwin tried not to look too eager. 'Well, if you think I might be of any help … you know, if we're going to be here for a day or two anyway …'

'Excellent! I'll get my cloak.'

He was halfway back to his chamber when Edwin stopped him. 'Maybe leave it an hour.'

Aubrey was confused. 'Why?'

'Village women have a lot of work to do first thing in the morning. Well, they do most of the time, but especially first thing.'

This wrinkled Aubrey's brow even further. 'Women? Work?'

Edwin tried to smother the picture in his head of how Alys would react if she were in the room now. 'Yes. Lighting the fire, getting the day's food ready, soaking the barley, making bread dough, fetching water, sorting out everyone else in the house, maybe looking out for small children?'

Aubrey's face cleared. 'Oh, I see. That sort of thing. I thought you meant, you know, actual *work* work.'

'I would maybe avoid saying that to her when we get there, not if you want to stay on her good side.'

'Oh. Well, if you say so …'

'I do. Now, speaking of cloaks, I appear to have left mine upstairs yesterday, and I'll need it if I'm to go to the village with you. I'll go up to ask if I might have it back.'

It was, of course, a very useful excuse. He was still hoping to be able to speak with Joanna on her own, but since he'd been awake, he hadn't seen anyone come downstairs apart from the serving man with the logs, which must mean that Emma and the wet-nurse were both still up there with her.

He was correct; when he knocked, two voices simultaneously claimed the right to admit him.

Edwin entered, Joanna's face lighting up when she saw who it was.

He gave the tiniest shake of his head, hoping she would understand. 'I beg your pardon, ladies, but I left my cloak in here yesterday. I wonder if I might collect it?'

'Of course,' said Joanna, quickly, before Emma could open her mouth. She looked about her. 'Is this it?' She picked it up and brought it over to the door herself. 'We'll need to talk,' she said, under her breath, when she reached him, before adding, out loud, 'This is very finely sewn. Did your wife make it herself?'

'No,' he replied, for Emma's benefit. 'My wife is extremely talented, but this particular cloak was a gift from my lord earl.'

Joanna was momentarily taken aback, presumably having said the first thing that came into her head and with no idea that Edwin actually did have a wife. 'Really?' she mouthed.

He smiled and nodded, making sure that Emma couldn't see. 'Are you ever left alone?' he murmured.

'And such fine fur! … Tomorrow, when they're all at church. I'm not allowed to go.'

He nodded. 'Many thanks, my lady. May I wish you both a good day.'

He was almost out into the stairwell when Joanna spoke aloud once more. 'I hope you will rest today, Master Edwin, after yesterday's accident. And your companion will no doubt have men or tasks to attend to while it's light. But I would be delighted if you would both join us for the evening meal.' She cast a look at Emma that even Edwin couldn't misinterpret. 'We do get so *bored* of each other's company in here, don't we, with nobody to vary it.'

'Thank you, my lady, we'd be glad to accept.' Edwin left Joanna to her own personal hell and retreated down the stairs.

Later that morning, with Willikin trailing behind them at Martin's insistence, Edwin and Aubrey walked out of the castle gate. Aubrey, like any nobleman, had made for the stable, but Edwin had pointed out that it wasn't worth saddling up horses for such a short journey and there would be nowhere to put them in the village anyway. The road was fairly clear, or at least clear enough for passing on foot; Edwin wouldn't have liked to try driving a cart along it. The footpath that led from the road to the church also looked well-trodden as they passed it; Edwin wondered about the priest Aubrey said he'd spoken to, and if he might be a useful source of information.

The first few houses, if you could call them that, were less than a hundred yards past the church. They were little more than hovels; Mabel wouldn't live in one of them. Edwin turned off the main road to lead the way to the central part of the village where the more substantial cottages stood, watched by men as well as women and the inevitable gaggles of curious children; with all this snow on the ground there could not be much work in the surrounding fields, and besides, it was the last day of the Christmas feast.

Having enquired for Mabel, they were directed via several winding lanes to a respectable cottage. The place was in good repair, Edwin noted as they made their way up the path, and there was a good deal of smoke coming out the hole in the roof, which indicated a decent fire. He could hear the sound of children larking about inside and a woman's voice telling them to stay away from the flames.

All noise ceased as Aubrey knocked on the door. After a few moments it opened a crack and a woman peered out.

'Mistress Mabel?'

'Might be. Who wants to know?'

'I'm from the sheriff's office, and I need to talk to you about Sir Nicholas.'

The woman looked in two minds, but the word 'sheriff' evidently held enough weight to decide the matter. 'You'd better come in.'

It was beautifully warm inside, and Edwin was glad to be back in a proper wattle-and-daub building rather than one made of cold stone. His eyes didn't take long to adjust, for it wasn't much brighter outside than it was in here, and he was able to take a surreptitious look around as the woman called to the children – three boys – to keep quiet and fetch seats for the guests.

The cottage was much better appointed than he would have expected: furniture, crockery on a sideboard, smoked meat hanging from the rafters, what looked like plenty of dried food stocked in barrels and bags, and a proper box bed in the corner piled with furs as well as blankets. Money was certainly coming from somewhere.

Willikin took up a station by the wall, the boys staring at him in awe as he settled into the timeless stance of a man who could stand guard for hours without thinking while he awaited instructions.

Aubrey was by now seated and looking expectantly at Edwin. Edwin realised that Aubrey hadn't introduced him, and that the woman would probably assume he was another sheriff's official if he didn't disabuse her of the idea. 'My name is Edwin,' he said, carefully.

'Thank you for seeing us, Mistress.' He cleared his throat. 'Do you have a husband, or anyone else you'd like to join us?'

'I'm a widow,' she replied, firmly. 'My husband died seven years ago. And no, there's nobody else.'

Edwin's eyes strayed to the boys, the youngest two of whom were clearly no older than about five and three.

'Sir Nicholas's sons.' Mabel's tone continued to be firm, even aggressive. 'It's no secret, and I'm not ashamed of it, for all Father Clement calls me a whore.'

'Your priest? He called you that?' Edwin was incredulous, thinking of good, kind Father Ignatius back at Conisbrough.

Mabel snorted. 'Have you ever met Father Clement?' She continued before Edwin could reply. 'Anyway, what did you want to ask me about?'

Edwin exchanged a glance with Aubrey, who indicated that he should continue. 'We're just trying to find out as much as we can about Sir Nicholas's last few days.'

'Why?'

'Well, because we're trying to find out who killed him, of course.'

'What do you mean, "trying to find out"? We all know already who did it. The only question is why haven't you taken her away yet?'

She was getting agitated. Edwin tried to be as calming as possible. 'I know that many people have strong suspicions, but—'

'Strong suspicions?' She was incredulous. 'That woman was found bending over him with the bloodied knife still in her hand!' She added something else under her breath that Edwin didn't quite catch, but he was almost certain it was 'Bitch'.

'How did you know that?'

'Know what?'

'How did you know exactly how Sir Nicholas and his wife were found? Presumably you weren't there yourself?'

She was momentarily taken aback. 'Well, I …' she floundered, before recovering. 'It's common knowledge, isn't it? Can't remember exactly who I heard it from, but everyone knows about it.'

'Hmm,' said Edwin, deliberately. Now would be the time to press an advantage. 'So, when was the last time you saw Sir Nicholas yourself?'

'It was two nights before he died.'

'Here?'

'Yes, here – I could hardly keep going up there after he married, could I?'

Edwin was shocked. 'You mean – he kept up his liaison with you even *after* he was married? From the age of your boys, I'd assumed …' He looked over at the children, who were by now giggling, all holding on to one of Willikin's arms as he lifted them up and down with ease, their feet kicking in the air.

Mabel made another derisive noise. 'Are you a monk?'

'No, of course not, but …'

'Look.' She leaned forward. 'Sir Nicholas and I had an understanding for many years, since we were children, almost. I knew we could never be married, and that was fine, because I knew it was me he loved.' She emphasised the word, defiantly.

Edwin did not react.

His silence encouraged her to continue. 'I deliberately chose to marry a man much older than me, and that suited all of us. And when I was widowed, so much the better; Sir Nicholas would sometimes come here, and sometimes send for me to come to the castle. He acknowledged the boys as his and made sure I was all right for money.'

Edwin was trying hard not to judge.

'And then *she* arrived.'

Taken aback by the malevolence Mabel managed to fit into one short word, Edwin felt that he had to clarify. 'You mean, Lady Joanna?'

'*Lady*,' spat Mabel. 'Of course she is, with her fancy gowns and her uppity way of talking. But she didn't love him. Not like I did.'

'But that's not surprising, is it?' asked Edwin. 'I mean, the marriage will have been arranged for her – she didn't choose it.'

'She got to swan about in the castle, though, didn't she? With her furs and jewels. And it'll be *her* son that gets it all, not mine.'

'Ah.' Edwin wished again that he had Alys here with him to help with all the nuances, but he thought he was beginning to understand.

Mabel continued to seethe against Joanna until Edwin cut her off. 'So, to return to my earlier question – you last saw Sir Nicholas on the night he died?'

'Yes. I mean no! Two nights before, that's what I said.'

'And how did he seem?'

She immediately tensed. 'Who told y— I mean, what do you mean, "how did he seem"?'

Edwin made a vague gesture. 'Was he happy? Sad? Angry? Anything out of the ordinary?'

She hesitated, as if unsure. Then, 'No, nothing out of the ordinary,' followed by a more confident, 'No, he was just the same as usual. Definitely.'

'Very well.' Edwin thought he'd leave it there, for now. Another thought struck him. 'How will you manage for money now that Sir Nicholas is gone?'

A shadow came over her face. 'We'll manage,' was all she said, before rising. 'So, if that's all …?'

Edwin raised his eyebrows at Aubrey, to see if he wanted to ask anything else, but he seemed content to be ushered towards the door. Willikin followed, allowing the boys to pretend they were pushing him by force.

It was snowing again, but it was a very wet sleet that might even turn to rain later. Edwin pulled up his hood. There was no bright glare, but the sudden cold after the warmth of the cottage was already starting to make his head ache again, and he shivered. He took a moment to orient himself and they set off in the direction of the main road.

Several people emerged from one of the other large cottages as they passed, and Edwin recognised Joscelin, along with what were presumably his children: two girls who he guessed to be around fourteen and twelve and a younger boy. They were all as badly dressed as he was, and Edwin thought to himself that the late Sir Nicholas hadn't been particularly generous with his wages. Still, this wasn't exactly Conisbrough, and Sir Nicholas didn't have anything like the lord earl's resources, so allowances must be made.

He hailed Joscelin. 'We're just on our way back to the castle.'

'We may as well walk together, then,' said the steward. 'Have you had business in the village?'

'Aubrey wanted to talk to a woman called Mabel,' replied Edwin, before Aubrey could open his mouth. 'So I thought I'd come with him to test how my head was faring.'

'Well, I trust?'

'Fairly well, on such a short walk. But I'm afraid I wouldn't yet be sure of my ability to ride all day,' he added.

Immediately the steward was all concern. 'Well, I'm sure Lady Jo— … Em— … the ladies will extend their hospitality until you are fully recovered. Besides,' he looked at the grey sky and the fat, wet flakes falling from it, 'it's not a good time to be on the road.'

They tramped on for a few moments, reaching the edge of the village. 'And did you also have business here?' asked Edwin, for the sake of conversation.

'Just checking on my family,' came the reply. 'I wasn't able to get back last night, as there were accounts to settle as well as guests to see to. My wife worries – as do I about them, of course, in this weather – so I popped back to see they were all right.'

'I hope you found them well? Our steward at Conisbrough is unmarried, but his predecessor's wife lived in the village. So much more comfortable for a family than a room in the castle.'

'Oh, for sure,' said Joscelin. 'Although I suspect that Conisbrough is a much grander castle than ours.'

'That doesn't necessarily make it warmer,' replied Edwin, with feeling.

Joscelin laughed. 'And are you married? Will your wife be joining you when you take up your new position?'

Edwin realised he should have anticipated such a question. 'Yes, I have a wife,' he answered, ignoring the rest of the question and hoping to change the subject. 'No children yet, but we haven't been married long. Those were yours, I take it?'

He'd managed to pick a subject close to Joscelin's heart, and for the rest of the short walk Edwin was happy to listen to the steward's doting descriptions of his clever son and his two pretty, talented daughters. It was only once they passed through the gatehouse and Joscelin bid them farewell that Edwin had leisure to turn his mind to the fact that he was sure Mabel had lied to him.

———

Martin had not even reached the hall when Turold and the others emerged from it. Unharmed, unaware of any threat. Martin shook his head. Had he really heard those words during the darkness of the night? Or had he let his imagination and his suspicion run away with him? It all seemed so fantastical now in the light of day.

'We'll be staying for a while, as planned,' he said. 'So we'll have to find something to occupy ourselves with.' He knew that he was talking to himself as much as to them. He was here, so close to Joanna after all this time, so agonisingly close and yet unable to really do anything. If he didn't find something to keep his mind off the situation, he would go mad.

Martin had a feeling that Edwin was going to sit talking for much of the morning, and he couldn't stand the thought of being cooped up in there, not while she was in the same building. But was there any present danger …? He dispatched Willikin to watch over Edwin, with clear instructions to protect him from any physical danger but to stay out of his way otherwise. If Edwin was in the middle of doing something clever – which he no doubt was – then he wouldn't want to be interrupted. It was the sort of duty for which Willikin was perfectly suited, so Martin had confidence it would all be fine.

He watched Willikin trudge through the slush and over to the keep before turning his own face to the sky, resigning himself to the fact that it really wasn't the weather for riding out – and besides, he shouldn't stray too far from Edwin. In the absence of the lord earl, Martin had no immediate duties, and he felt the very odd sensation of being at a loose end.

The other three were looking at him expectantly. Fortunately, he was saved from the embarrassment of a long pause by hearing the word 'training' from some of the Brandon men passing out of the hall. It was always a word that made him perk up, and he followed along, the others trailing after him into the outer ward, where a small armoury was situated.

Some of the garrison sorted themselves out with weapons for drill while others were set to helping the grooms lead horses around the ward, it having been decided by the stablemaster that conditions were not suitable for exercising them by riding out. All eyes were naturally drawn to Fauvel, far and away the finest animal in the castle, and Martin basked in the glory of being his owner. He paused for a few moments to admire the courser once again; still, after all this time, hardly able to believe his luck. Some of the grooms were pointing Martin out to each other, and he was amused to see that there was some competition going on among them as to who should be allowed the privilege of leading Fauvel.

The stablemaster's decision about exercising the horses inside the castle walls caused an issue that Martin spotted first and Luke only afterwards; they couldn't train in the middle of a cramped space full of animals, so they all traipsed back over the footbridge again. As he was about to follow, Martin opened his mouth to direct Lambert to remain with their horses, but was forestalled by Tom, who offered to do it. 'Shame for the lad to miss out on his training – I know he's keen.'

'All right,' said Martin. 'And it's not as if he doesn't need the practice.'

Once they were back in the inner ward he stood with Lambert and Turold while the Brandon men, under Luke's instruction, cleared away the snow and slush. He felt an unfamiliar presence at his elbow and looked down to see the squire, Milo. It struck him what a difficult position the boy must be in, his master dead while he still had many years of training ahead of him. 'I'll have a bout with you, if you like?' he asked, by way of introduction. 'You don't want to get out of practice.'

Milo looked mildly apprehensive but agreed; Martin approved. 'We'll borrow some of the blunts, so we won't need proper armour – just fetch yourself a pair of gloves.'

The Brandon men appeared to have split into two groups, one for some quite basic-looking drill and the other comprising the more experienced men. Luke's instruction was very different from Sir Geoffrey's back at Conisbrough: he barked orders and found fault with everything without ever letting a word of praise drop from his lips. Sir Geoffrey could certainly be hard – Martin knew that from many years of experience – but he also knew good technique when he saw it and was a past master at getting the best out of all the men, whatever their natural ability. Luke, on the other hand, seemed to be nothing but a bully. Martin consigned Lambert to Turold's rather more moderate tuition.

Milo returned and Martin found a space for them. He guessed the boy to be about the same age as Adam, so he pitched their activity at the level he would use at home. The world around him narrowed as he focused on every move, watching his opponent and stopping frequently to give detailed pointers on Milo's balance, footwork, wrist technique and the exact angle at which he held his shield, which, of course, needed to be tailored to the height and reach of his opponent.

Martin didn't know how long they'd been working, but eventually he noticed Milo beginning to tire, so he stepped back and told him to rest for a few moments. The squire gratefully dropped his arms before shaking his head in wonder. 'Sir, I've learned more from you in an hour than I have done from … than I have done in months of training.'

'Glad to hear it. You have the makings of being a good swordsman; you just need to—'

Martin belatedly became aware that the group drills around them had stopped, and the men were all watching him and Milo. Most of them were looking on in admiration, but Luke was sneering in a way that irritated Martin. Why had the man taken such an instant dislike to him?

'Oh yes, let's all bow down before the knowledge of a youth still wet behind the ears, shall we?' he asked, with exaggerated deference. Then, to Martin, 'Think you're so good, do you?'

'I know I am,' replied Martin, shortly, reminding himself not to be drawn.

'Well, in my book experience counts for more than fancy footwork. Want a proper bout to settle the question?'

Martin was caught. He didn't want to get involved in anything acrimonious, but to back down from such a challenge was unthinkable. 'Of course.'

Luke smiled, but instead of stepping forward himself he beckoned to another man, a veteran who looked to have a sharp eye in the body of a gnarled tree.

There were shouts and calls from the other men around, plenty of banter aimed at their champion. The man didn't seem fazed at all, evidently confident in his own abilities as he moved to face Martin.

Now, concentrate, came the voice in Martin's mind. *Yes, he's smaller than you, but he looks like he's survived many fights, and you don't know anything about him. The conditions underfoot are treacherous for both of us, but he'll know them better than you. There's no sun, so you can't manoeuvre him to look into it. Sleet is falling. Begin cautiously.*

It was just as his opponent was taking some final advice from his friends that Martin happened to look up and see that Joanna was at the keep's window. Their eyes met. He stood for a long moment before forcing himself to break the contact and turn away. She was watching. Watching *him.* Joanna's full attention was focused on him, Martin, while he had a sword in his hand. There went his heart again, and he knew he had never wanted anything more than he wanted to win this fight.

As they engaged, Martin remained cautious. What did this man have? He circled, keeping his shield up and only allowing himself brief attacks and feints, never overreaching, until he could make a clearer assessment.

The onlookers started to become restless, calling for more action and shouting a few insults. 'Hey!' came a voice out of the crowd. 'The lady's watching you, Hugo – better step it up!'

Martin's opponent took a momentary glance up at the keep window, and Martin forbore from using his distraction as an opening to attack. He wouldn't give any of these men, and especially Luke, the opportunity to say he'd only won by underhand means.

But then Hugo looked away from the window with a sneer, said 'murdering whore' in a voice that was perfectly audible to Martin, if not to everyone else, and spat on the ground. He put his guard up again.

Martin couldn't quite remember what happened after that.

When he returned to himself, he was breathing heavily, still with the unfamiliar blunt sword in his hand, and Hugo was lying sprawled on his back in the mud. Martin stepped back to allow him to rise.

He didn't move.

'Come, now,' said Martin, once he'd got his breath back. 'The bout is over, have no fear.'

Still Hugo didn't move. A murmur started around them.

Luke strode over to the supine man, evidently displeased that his champion had fared so badly against the stranger. He poked him with a foot. On receiving no response, he knelt to examine more closely.

After a few moments, he looked up. 'I think he's dead.'

Chapter Five

Edwin could sense that something was wrong as soon as he entered the gatehouse. The outer ward was empty, the last few men who had been in it now on their way across the bridge to the inner, from where Edwin could hear shouting and commotion.

With Aubrey and Willikin at his heels, he made his way towards the gate in the palisade so he could look over the bridge and see what was going on. His immediate impression was of a swirling group of men, some seemingly only curious but others angry. And – *of course*, thought Edwin with a sigh – the unmistakeable form of Martin right in the middle of it all.

As he made to step on to the bridge, he found himself suddenly unable to move.

Willikin had his thick arms clamped firmly round Edwin's body. 'Sorry, Master Edwin, but my orders is to keep you safe. Stay out of your way while you're talking an' all that but protect you from bodily harm. So that's what I'm doing.'

Edwin didn't bother struggling; there would be no point. 'All right. But what if Martin and the others are in danger?'

'Martin can take care of himself, and the others will have to take their chances. Sir Geoffrey told us all before we set out, you're the important one.'

Edwin didn't know whether to be flattered at being considered important or annoyed at the idea that Sir Geoffrey thought that he needed a nurse. 'All right,' he said, again. 'But let go of my arms, at least. You have my word I won't try to cross the bridge.'

'I'll see if I can find out what's happening,' said Aubrey, slipping past them. Edwin watched as he crossed and made his way over to where Joscelin was standing at the edge of the milling group, unsuccessfully trying to make his voice heard.

They spoke for some time and then Aubrey returned. 'It looks like something and nothing. Luke had the castle garrison in training, and your men came to join in. Your friend there got a bit overenthusiastic and knocked a man out, but he's coming round now.' He paused before adding, 'From what I can gather from Joscelin, both Luke and Martin are riled up and making it much worse than it needed to be. Fortunately, they all seem to be holding blunt weapons.'

Edwin raised his eyes to the wet, grey heavens. Why was Martin making this all so much more difficult than it needed to be?

He looked over at the crowd again. Joscelin had at last managed to calm everyone down, and groups were now separating from each other. He sent away some who were either kitchen men or grooms, leaving Luke and the garrison on one side, Martin and the three Conisbrough men on the other, and two in the middle; a man just starting to sit up, who must be the injured party, and the squire Milo helping him.

Edwin turned to Willikin. 'I need to go and talk to them – there's no danger now.'

Willikin agreed, but stayed so close to Edwin as he crossed the bridge that Edwin could feel the heat from his breath. Edwin wasn't quite as confident as he felt: the absence of a lord of the castle meant an absence of authority, and it was debatable whether the inhabitants would follow the orders – if it came to it – of Joscelin or Luke. Edwin suspected that the servants would follow the steward and the garrison men their commander, and he knew which was more of a threat.

He approached the group, keeping his movements easy and his expression mild. Unfortunately, the natural tendency of people to appeal to an arbiter came immediately to the fore, and Edwin and Aubrey found themselves the centre of attention.

Edwin raised a hand. 'Wait!' he called, with as much authority as he could muster. 'One at a time.'

Astonishingly, the group fell silent, and Edwin was thrown into confusion. *Of course*, he thought to himself, *it's because they think I'm an important man in the service of a great earl, and because I have a sheriff's representative standing beside me. Still, better make the most of it.*

He deemed it wisest not to start with his own party. Instead, he pointed at Luke. 'Please explain.'

'He attacked one of my men,' said Luke, hotly, pointing an accusatory finger at Martin.

'That's not—' began Martin, but Edwin waved him to silence.

He turned to Luke again. 'But I understood that you were all training? An accident?'

'No,' said Luke, with a little less heat, in the face of Edwin's calm demeanour. 'They were sparring, that's true, but he waited until Hugo wasn't looking and then took advantage.'

Edwin was fairly sure that Luke was lying. Firstly, it would be extremely unlike Martin to do that, whatever the provocation, and secondly, many of the castle men were looking at each other in a way that suggested that they knew Luke's words were false but were too afraid to say anything.

After a moment's pause, Edwin turned to Milo, who had succeeded in getting the man to his feet out of the mud and was now passing him over to others to help him lean weakly against a wall. Which gave Edwin an idea to file away for later. But in the meantime … 'Milo, can you tell me any more about what happened?'

The squire looked from him to Luke, and then down at the ground. 'I … I didn't really see, I'm afraid.'

Edwin heard Martin make a sound of annoyance and anger behind him. Much as he wanted to allow Martin to burst out with his side of the story, the most important thing at this point was to keep the situation calm.

'It's not true!' burst out a voice.

Edwin turned in surprise, for the speaker was Lambert.

The boy stepped forward. 'Begging your pardon for interrupting, Master Edwin, but I saw it all. I always watch Martin when he's fighting, if I can, to see what I can learn.' He stopped, his cheeks now a flaming red as he realised how many people were watching him in silence.

At an encouraging nod from Edwin, however, he managed to continue. 'They were sparring. Both of them stopped to look up at the window in the keep. Then the other fellow said something Martin didn't like – I didn't hear what it was – but he definitely waited until his guard was back up before he attacked. And after that …' he waved at the space on the ground when Hugo had been lying, 'it was all over pretty quickly.'

Luke made a furious noise and almost took a pace forward, but Lambert stared at him defiantly, Turold and Tom flanking him. And then Martin moved to place a hand on the boy's shoulder.

That gave Luke pause. 'Well, of course he would say that, wouldn't he?' he managed.

'Just like your men will agree with anything you say,' shot back Martin. 'Even if it's a damned l—'

'Anyway,' interrupted Edwin, hastily. 'Your man there seems to be recovering, and these things do sometimes happen during training exercises, so perhaps we should consider the matter closed?' He looked meaningfully at Aubrey and Joscelin, who had been standing in a most unhelpful silence while he did all the work. They did, belatedly, take the hint, and began to encourage the men to disperse.

Edwin watched them all go.

'That was impressive,' said Aubrey. 'I wish I had your authority.'

Edwin hoped that the other man couldn't see that he was shaking. But, strangely, he did feel a kind of power thrilling through him at the same time. It was most odd. 'I think we managed to avert the danger, at least for now,' he replied, trying to sound as though this was the sort of thing he did every day. 'Though I'm not particularly looking forward to the next part.'

'What? Oh, yes, I see what you mean.' Aubrey looked in some trepidation at the obviously furious Martin, hardly able to keep still.

'Is there somewhere we can go where I can talk to him? Talk to him alone, I mean – not in the hall or the keep.'

Aubrey frowned. 'There are offices and stores and things, but I'd imagine there will be people in there, going about their business and so forth.' He waved a pale hand that had never done a day's manual labour. 'If you don't mind being outside, maybe the best thing is to go out the postern and into the field on the other side. There will surely be nobody working it in today.' He pointed to a small gate that Edwin hadn't noticed before, in the corner of the palisade behind the hall.

'Good idea.' And it was. The last thing Martin needed right now was to be in a confined space.

'Anyway, I'll leave you to it,' said Aubrey, in a grateful tone and already starting to sidle away.

'That's probably for the best.' Edwin turned to face Martin.

Martin hardly knew what to do with himself. He couldn't control his mind; it was furious, confused, jumping all over the place. What he did know was that it could all best be dealt with either by riding somewhere very fast or by hitting something very hard – or both – but neither of those seemed like an option just at the moment. He was not best pleased when Edwin shoved him towards a postern in the corner of the ward. He turned to argue and then smacked his head on the top of the gateway.

That, of course, put him in a fouler mood than ever, as did the fact that he slipped on the slope as soon as he was through and nearly ended up in the stream at the bottom; as it was running water it wasn't completely frozen over. He saved himself by leaping over it just as he was overbalancing, landing safely on the other side and feeling some small satisfaction when he turned to see that Edwin had got his feet wet.

He opened his mouth but was forestalled by Edwin. Martin was taken aback when he realised that his friend was just as angry as he was.

'What in the name of God and all His saints do you think you're doing?' he began, as soon as they were a little further away from the walls and any ears that might be eavesdropping. He was honestly almost snarling – Martin had never seen him this way.

But he wasn't about to back down, even for Edwin. 'He asked for it,' he replied, savagely.

'Who? The man you beat the living daylights out of, for no reason? While we're supposed to be keeping our heads down?'

The fury, the injustice, rose again. 'It wasn't like that!'

'Fine. Then tell me what happened.' He held up a hand. 'Calmly. And let's move over to the edge of the field first – this looks like it's been sown with winter wheat and I don't want us to tread all over it.'

The field ran down to the riverbank, but it was far too wet to walk there so they picked their way round the rapidly thawing ridges and furrows until they reached a grove of trees at the far side.

Some small part of Martin's fury was drained away by the time they got there, and he realised that Edwin had probably done it on purpose, damn him.

'Now,' said Edwin, as they stood under dripping branches. 'Tell me everything.'

Martin poured out the whole story – the training, the squire, Luke, the bout of single combat, what he'd heard the man say, how he couldn't remember the next part, and then Luke again. 'And he knew the man wasn't dead,' he concluded. 'He just said that to rile everyone up.'

Edwin was silent for a moment.

'God's blood,' continued Martin, hardly able to stop talking now he'd started. 'If we can find out that it was Luke who killed Sir Nicholas, I'll be a happy man.'

Edwin had his thinking face on. 'It's a possibility,' he said, at last. 'That is to say, I haven't ruled him out. But we can't just pin it on him.'

'Why not?'

Edwin gave him a look.

'I'm serious. They're all trying to pin it on Joanna, even though she's innocent, so why shouldn't we find a reason to blame it on him? Then he can be executed for it and everyone will be happy.'

'Stop that,' snapped Edwin. 'I'm here to find out the truth, not accuse someone unjustly.'

'But the lord earl—'

'You have no idea what the lord earl said to me.'

Martin was taken aback, again. That Edwin – Edwin! – might have had particular, personal instructions from the earl, which he, his lord's closest attendant, might not know about, almost took the wind out of him.

He was reduced to grumbling. 'But *why* is everyone so convinced that Joanna killed her husband? She wouldn't hurt a fly.'

'People in desperate circumstances sometimes do desperate things.' Martin was about to argue but Edwin continued. 'Oh, I'm not saying that's what happened – not at all. But don't ever say that a person is incapable of harming another, because everyone is if the circumstances force them into it.'

Martin saw that Edwin was in danger of sinking into his own memories. He had to stop that, to keep him focused on Joanna and how they could prove her innocent. 'And it's everyone blaming her – that other woman, for a start.' He couldn't bring himself to say 'sister-in-law', as that would mean acknowledging to himself again that Joanna really was married, and worse, that she had a … his mind shied away. 'Why doesn't Emma like her?'

'Well, I would have thought that was obvious,' said Edwin, coming to himself again. 'As Sir Nicholas's sister, she was the lady of the castle until he got married. Then she was pushed out of that position as soon as he had a wife – of course she didn't like it. Think about what Lady Isabelle would have been like in a similar position.'

Martin winced as he recalled the earl's unbearable sister, whom he had been thoroughly glad to see the back of except for the fact that she had taken Joanna with her. It was true: if it had been the lord earl who remarried first, and Lady Isabelle was still in the same household, the consequences for anyone beneath her would have been dire.

'And of course, it happened to Alys, as well, though she didn't react in nearly the same way.'

Edwin had the smile on his face that always appeared when he thought of his wife, and for one moment Martin was furiously, insanely jealous. Why should Edwin be so happy? Why should *he* have been allowed to marry the girl he loved? He almost wanted to wipe the grin off his face, but then he realised what he was thinking. This was Edwin, for goodness' sake – kind, harmless Edwin. His friend. Martin should be ashamed of himself for such envy, and he told himself firmly he would confess it whenever he next got the chance.

He returned to the subject at hand. 'All right. I can see why Lady Emma might resent Joanna. But the others? And do any of them have any actual evidence, or are they just blaming her because they don't like her?'

'Ah.' Edwin looked awkward. 'I did find out something about that last night, but I haven't had the chance to tell you yet.' He grimaced and looked Martin straight in the eye. 'Brace yourself.'

Martin listened in growing horror as Edwin outlined what he'd heard from Aubrey about how Joanna and her husb— and Sir Nicholas had been found.

'I don't believe it,' he said, flatly, when Edwin had finished. 'Not in a hundred years, not ever.'

'I knew you'd say that. But, unfortunately, what you think is kind of beside the point. It's what everyone else believes, and specifically what the sheriff is persuaded to believe is the truth, that matters.'

Martin shook his head. 'No. I don't care what the sheriff thinks.'

'You will if she's tried and condemned.'

'No,' said Martin, again, aware that desperate thoughts were staring to surface once more. 'If anyone tries to execute her or take her away, I'll fight them all. I don't care if it kills me.'

'We've been through this,' said Edwin, sharply. 'So stop it right now. The only way to sort this out is to find out the truth – the *actual* truth, not just how you want it to be. You need to calm down and control yourself.' He paused, then added, 'Besides, do you think the rest of us would survive long if you tried fighting off the sheriff and all his men? Some of the rest of us have reasons to live, you know.'

Martin knew Edwin was right; he said nothing and stared moodily across at the castle.

After a few moments a thought struck him. 'Do we know if the postern was locked on the night he died? Or who was guarding it? Could anyone have got in?'

'I don't know yet, but it's on my list to find out.'

'It would be much less obvious than someone coming in the main gatehouse, and for a quiet murder like that it need only be one man, not an army.' Martin felt the glimmerings of a new hope. It would be wonderful if they could find out that someone from outside had somehow managed to get in and kill Sir Nicholas. That would solve all their problems.

Edwin was silent for a while – thinking, no doubt, so Martin left him to it. From where they were standing he could see across to the church, with the village behind it, smoke from the cottages drifting up into the grey sky. The wet sleet had stopped again, and Martin did wonder if the fresh breeze coming across the flat ground might herald the start of a proper thaw.

He shivered. Edwin was wearing his cloak, but he had none; he'd been training just in his shirt and tunic, and Edwin had dragged him out here before he'd had time to put anything else on. Now he'd cooled down after the exercise he was feeling the chill.

Edwin noticed. Of course he did – Edwin noticed everything. 'Perhaps we'd better go back in, if you're feeling calm enough. Don't forget, we're invited to the evening meal in the solar again, so I'll need you to be … composed.'

Martin felt the wrench inside of his body as he thought of spending the evening in Joanna's company in the present circumstances. For a moment he wanted to cry, but that wouldn't do at all. He pushed the feelings down. 'I will.' He took a deep breath. 'I promise.'

'All right.'

They made their way back across the field, Edwin recounting as they went his visit to Sir Nicholas's concubine that morning. Martin didn't have the leisure to think through it all properly, concentrating as he was on picking his way through the crops and the puddles, but he wasn't as angry as he might have been. Of course, noblemen could have liaisons however they liked – the earl had a bastard son down in Lewes – so that didn't shock him, although it was more usual in men who were single or widowed. That Sir Nicholas had kept this woman and fathered children with her before his marriage was neither here nor there. That anyone could even look at another woman when he had Joanna as his wife absolutely beggared belief, and did threaten to raise Martin's ire, but on the other hand it did support his own view that Sir Nicholas had in no way been worthy of her and that his death was not worth mourning.

As they neared the swollen stream that broke off from the main river to encircle the castle's palisade, Martin looked down carefully, but of course they'd trodden and slipped all over it themselves earlier, which would have obliterated any existing marks, and besides it had snowed several times since the night of the murder. There was no hope of finding any clue as to whether anyone had come in that way.

He passed through the postern, remembering to duck this time.

———— • ————

The atmosphere was awkward.

Well, of course it is, thought Edwin to himself as he looked around the candlelit group. *It's not exactly a friendly family gathering, is it?*

It was Twelfth Night, which under normal circumstances would mean wassailing, merrymaking and raucous misrule. Some few sounds coming from the direction of the hall indicated that a subdued version of the festivities was taking place over there, but here there was nothing, other than a token effort at spiced ale, and the faces around the table were either morose or rancorous.

Edwin wished he were at home in the cottage with Alys – or even in the loud, boisterous hall at Conisbrough that he usually disliked for that very reason. At least there the animated throng was usually good-natured. But he wasn't in either of those places, and the best way to get back there was to find out the truth here, so he would need to keep his wits about him.

Emma at least had a good appetite, but in between the ingestion of delicacy after delicacy she was casting poisonous glances at Martin as well as Joanna. The reason soon became apparent when she mentioned the afternoon's fight. Had she seen it herself, Edwin wondered? Or had she only heard about it from someone else? The problem with everything about this situation was that all he knew was what people told him – he had no first-hand evidence or experience of anything at all. He had never met Sir Nicholas, did not know anything of the circumstances that led up to his death, had not seen the body. All he had was gossip, and that was a double-edged sword.

Martin, he was pleased to see, was making a heroic effort to control himself under the multiple provocations of Emma's barbs, Joanna's presence and Aubrey's ever more obvious toadying to a lady of higher rank. The food was again excellent, so at least Martin could distract himself with that; it was a treat for him, surely, to be sitting down and served rather than being the hungry server himself. That post fell to Milo, of course, and Joscelin was also floating about, fussing over each dish as it was brought it.

Edwin would have loved to apply himself properly to the pigeons in sauce, but he could see that Martin's veneer of goodwill wasn't going to last forever. How could he change the subject? He remembered Joscelin's enthusiasm that morning as he spoke about his family – one of the few smiling faces Edwin had seen since they had arrived. Maybe that might do.

He waited for a lull in the rancorous conversation before interposing. 'I was glad to hear this morning that your family in the village were well,' he said, addressing the steward but then giving Joanna a significant look, which she happily seemed to understand.

'Oh, yes, how remiss of me not to enquire, when I knew you were going out to see them. How are they all, and especially dear Beatrice?' She turned to the others around the table. 'Joscelin's younger daughter is a talented needlewoman, and has often helped us out when we needed an extra hand, hasn't she, Emma?'

Edwin could see that it was a huge effort for Emma to agree with anything Joanna said, but here she probably had no choice, and certainly not if she wished to avoid offending the steward. 'Yes, indeed, a very good hand for someone so young. What is she now, eleven?'

'Twelve, my lady,' replied Joscelin, with a bow that was tactfully aimed at both women.

'Perhaps she'd like to come up to castle again one day soon?' asked Joanna.

'No, I don't think that will be possible.' The words had shot out of Joscelin's mouth so quickly that he almost interrupted her. 'What I mean,' he added, in an attempt not to seem rude, 'is that, although they're all fine, Beatrice has something of a cold, and I wouldn't want to bring her anywhere near the young lord until she's recovered.' He sighed. 'We all know how fragile such tiny lives are.'

Edwin felt a stab. Here he was, many miles away from home, leaving Alys to manage everything while she was expecting their precious child. What if she had a miscarriage while he was away? What if she carried the pregnancy to term, and then the baby died, as so many did in the first days and weeks of life? How would they ever get over the grief? What if he lived just long enough for them to become attached to him, and then he was taken away?

Edwin must have been lost in his thoughts for a while, because when he came back to the conversation it had turned to a more general one on loss. Aubrey's mother had died when he was a child, he found, and Emma was a widow.

'Yes,' she was saying. 'After my husband died I made sure his affairs were in order, and then came back here to do my duty by my own family. I didn't stay there to be a burden on the new lord.'

'But that was your husband's brother, not a son.'

Joanna's voice sounded a little waspish, and Edwin wondered if the two women had had this conversation before. Chances were that they had, locked up together like this, the one unable to leave and the other refusing to do so in case it looked like capitulation.

Joanna was continuing. 'And the brother had a family of his own. And of course, you had no reason to stay, having borne your husband no children.'

Was there a hint of superiority there? Edwin thought he could detect one. After all, the primary duty of a noble wife was to give her husband an heir, a male heir if possible, and at least there Joanna could claim victory over Emma.

'Unlike you, I suppose,' Emma replied. She was unconsciously touching her own stomach as she looked enviously at Joanna's.

Joanna smiled with sweet venom. 'Of course.'

'Well,' said Emma, clearly and with deliberate malice, 'We're all aware that you've had a child. But whether he's also my brother's son is far from certain.'

Chapter Six

Edwin lay in bed, staring at the darkness. Next to him Martin was fast asleep and snoring, which was both preventing him from dropping off himself and giving him the chance to think while there was nobody else around.

There had been absolute uproar in the solar after Emma's statement. Both Martin and Aubrey had leapt to their feet, and it had been all Edwin could do to keep his friend's temper under control. Emma had sat smugly through it all, and Edwin wondered why she had said such a thing, and why she had chosen that moment and that company in which to say it. Was she simply trying to cause more trouble? Or did she genuinely believe it? Unfortunately, Edwin's attention had been so fixed on Martin that he hadn't been able to gauge Joanna's reaction to the accusation – something that might have given him one piece of first-hand information, at least.

Anyway, he was planning to have a serious talk to Joanna tomorrow – or later that morning, as it probably was by now. Seeing the dazed man out in the ward had reminded him of the story of his own head injury, and he had agreed with Martin that in the morning he would feign some return of dizziness, thus giving him an excuse to miss Mass while everyone else attended it.

The castle was not large enough to have its own chapel, so the inhabitants went out to the village church; a skeleton garrison would be left, but they were unlikely to come into the keep and certainly not up to the solar. Joanna would be there, as she was not permitted to leave the castle enclosure. Her only spiritual comfort was that the priest apparently came up after Mass to see her while he was in the castle for his Sunday dinner. Edwin hadn't been able to explain the whole plan to Joanna last night, but as he and Martin were leaving the solar he had managed to whisper to her that she should find an excuse in the morning to send the wet-nurse out so she would be alone for an hour. He was confident that she'd understood.

He must have dozed, because the next thing he knew was the sound of the shutters being opened in the main room. Martin was just waking up, so Edwin reminded him of the plan. He'd had a hard time yesterday trying to persuade Martin that he had to go out to church with the others; it would look suspicious if both of them stayed behind, and if Martin were to be present when Edwin spoke to Joanna then the chances of him being able to talk swiftly and to the point, and to get the information he needed, were small.

Thankfully, everything went well. Edwin remained in bed as Martin got up and spread the news about the return of his infirmity, which seemed to be accepted. The sounds of the castle lessened as the church bell was heard in the distance; Edwin thought he could make out that one man had been left outside the keep, but that shouldn't be a problem. And then he heard the final thing he was waiting for; Joanna's voice from the top of the stairs bidding Ada to take the baby outside for some air while it was quiet.

Edwin shifted a little in the bed so he could see out the open door into the main room, and was soon rewarded by the sight of Ada carrying a fur-wrapped bundle and going outside. A murmur of voices showed him that he had been correct in his assumption that there was a man outside. But the guard was now distracted – young women of his own class being a rarity inside the castle walls – and in any case, he would be looking to prevent Joanna leaving and anyone other than Ada from entering, not paying attention to those already inside. It was thus safe for Edwin to tiptoe out of the chamber and up the stairs, where Joanna was waiting for him.

She waited for him to enter, then shut the door and leaned back against it in relief. 'Finally!'

'We don't have all that much time,' said Edwin, moving briskly towards the fire. 'How quickly does your priest say Mass?'

'Fortunately, he spends so long railing against sin every week that it goes on for quite some time,' she replied, joining him, taking a seat and gesturing to him to do the same. 'Now, before we start, a question: what happened to Godric, my messenger? I didn't see him come back with you.'

The name hit Edwin in the pit of his stomach, and for a moment he found himself unable to reply.

'Yes, I know,' continued Joanna in a gentle tone. 'Him having the same name as your father – and an unusual one these days – seemed like a good omen. I trusted him, and he was willing to risk the journey for me.'

'I'm so sorry,' said Edwin. He recounted how the man had been found, emphasising that although it had been a lonely death, it seemed to have been peaceful. 'And so we buried him with no name, but as soon as I get back I'll tell it to Father Ignatius and pray for him over the grave – I'm not likely to forget that name in a hurry.'

Joanna had tears in her eyes, but Edwin didn't have time to let her grieve. 'Now, please – tell me everything you can. All I've got at the moment is second-hand gossip.'

'Starting from when?'

'Briefly, from when you arrived here. I know it was a year and a half ago, as I was there when the lord earl received the letter from Lady Isabelle telling him so.'

'Yes. I was sorry to leave her in the end – after her own marriage she was a much nicer person. But duty is duty, so I did as I was told and married Nicholas.'

'And how were you received?'

She shrugged, either from unconcern or in an attempt to make light of some hurt. 'Oh, you know how it is. He wasn't hostile, of course – it was a good match for him and he was no doubt grateful my cousin had consented to it. But he wasn't exactly welcoming, either, and neither was anybody else.'

'Was Emma here then?'

'Yes, and it was clear she was jealous of me. Then she was married herself and I thought I'd got rid of her, but she was only gone a year before her husband died and she was back.'

'In all the time you've been here, have you noticed anyone being particularly hostile to your husband? Did he have enemies?'

'Not any that I knew of,' she said, carefully. 'Although you never know what people are hiding, do you?' She thought for a moment. 'No – honestly, no. He'd grown up here, you know; it was his family's only residence. Not like the earl travelling round all the time. Everyone knew him, and everyone liked him.'

'So, everything had been going along a familiar path for years, and then when you arrived, it was different.'

'Yes, I suppose so.' She fidgeted, and then burst out, 'But that was hardly my fault, was it? I never *asked* to be sent here, and I did try – I wanted to be friendly with everyone, I wanted to fit into their lives, to his life, like a married woman was supposed to. But the more I tried, the worse it got. I was stuck here with no friends, nobody to help me, nobody to talk to …'

She seemed on the verge of weeping. Edwin felt sorry for her, but they just didn't have the time, so he forced himself ruthlessly on. 'But your husband … I'm sorry, I know this is awkward, but I'm just trying to find out as much as I can. He didn't mistreat you? Beat you?'

She shook her head. 'There was no violence, and believe me, I'm thankful for that mercy at least. And as to mistreatment … not really. He always made sure I was spoken to with the respect due to his wife. Although, that's almost the wrong word. He didn't want a "wife", not in the sense of a companion, anyway. He wanted an alliance with a prestigious family, and he wanted a legitimate heir. And I was just the means for him to attain both of those things. He had no interest at all in me personally.' Then she added, in a more bitter tone, 'As to any other type of "mistreatment", I suppose it depends on whether you count him keeping that woman in the village.'

'Ah. Yes, we'll come back to her in a while. But first I need to get some more practical details. What were the sleeping arrangements here in the keep? Who would usually be in here at night?'

With an effort, she composed herself. 'It changed over time. Nicholas and I used the bedchamber, of course. Before I arrived, Milo had his pallet on the floor in there as well, but I didn't like him being in the same room, so he slept in the solar, still within calling distance. But then when John arrived,' she unconsciously patted her stomach, 'and we engaged Ada, she slept up here in case he needed feeding during the night, and Milo moved downstairs. And then when Emma came back, she also slept in the solar. She wasn't best pleased at having to share it with a baby and a wet-nurse, but where else was there? She didn't want a guest chamber or a house in the village.'

Edwin pictured all that in his mind and then pushed it to the back in case he needed to think about it later. 'Now,' he said, gently, 'I'm going to ask you about the night your husband died. Do you want me to pour you a drink of something first?'

She shook her head. 'No. No thank you. I knew we would come to this – after all, it's the reason I asked Martin to bring you if he could.'

Despite her words she was shivering, so Edwin got up to poke the fire and put some more wood on it. There was some kind of fur wrap on a nearby chair, so he picked it up and draped it around her shoulders before taking his seat again.

She clutched it about her. 'Your wife – if you really do have one – is a lucky woman, you know that?'

Edwin thought of Alys, whom he had left alone in the dead of winter while he travelled to take on this task, and how she must be worrying that he'd never come back. 'Yes, I really am married, and trust me, the luck's all mine.'

'One of the village girls?' asked Joanna, her brow creasing. 'I seem to remember …'

'No, she's not from Conisbrough at all.'

Joanna gasped. 'Not – not the girl from Lincoln? I remember Martin telling me at the time …'

'Yes, that's her. Her name is Alys, we're expecting our first child, and I sincerely hope that I may one day introduce her to you. But now we have to get back to the matter in hand. Are you ready?'

She took in a deep breath and nodded. 'Yes.'

'All right. Now, start from the night before, and tell me everything you can remember. Close your eyes if it helps you to see it again, because I want to know *exactly* what happened.'

He watched as she stared into the flames and then let her eyelids droop.

'It was the middle of December,' she began. 'It was dark early and I was up here. I was sitting in this same chair by the fire, sewing clothes ready for when John is old enough to come out of his swaddling bands. A candle on the table beside me. Joscelin's daughter Beatrice had been here helping me during the day, but I'd sent her home before the sun went down. I didn't want her to get too cold – she had no cloak. Godric saw her safely back to the village.'

'And who else was here during the evening?' murmured Edwin, keeping his voice as low and steady as possible.

'Emma was here, of course – she always saw the solar as her territory. She was in Nicholas's chair. He wasn't here, not yet. Ada was in the bedchamber feeding John. Joscelin came up to ask if I knew whether Nicholas would be back in time for the evening meal, because it was nearly ready. I said I didn't know, and asked him to serve it anyway.'

'Was Milo here?'

'No. I don't know where he was – out with Nicholas, I suppose. So Joscelin had one of his men serve it once it was laid out. He didn't stay – he had to see to something in the hall.'

'And what did you eat?' Edwin didn't think that was important, but he wanted to keep Joanna's memories flowing through the evening.

'It was Advent, of course, so no meat … yes, a fish dish. It was more flavoured than usual and Emma said she was going to complain to the cook about using too many spices, because they're expensive. She still seemed to think she was in charge of the household stores.'

'When did Sir Nicholas come back?'

'Just as we were finishing. He was angry that we hadn't waited, and I did answer him back – I said if he couldn't let us know whether or not he'd be here for a meal, it wasn't our place to starve.'

'And how did he react to that?'

'He – he raised his hand as if to hit me, but he stopped.'

As she spoke, Edwin noted that she put a hand up to touch her cheek, but he said nothing.

She continued. 'Then he sat down. Milo was with him, and he started to serve Nicholas even though he hadn't yet washed – his hands were dirty and the hem of his tunic was splashed with mud. And Nicholas was treading dirt on the floor, but I didn't say anything.'

'Was it wet outside?'

She paused for a moment, still with her eyes closed. 'I hadn't been outside since the morning, but … oh yes, when Godric came back from the village after taking Beatrice home he said the rain was turning to sleet, and the old men reckoned there would be heavy snow before long. And there was, of course – by the time Godric set off for Conisbrough it was deep, and I thought it might be even worse further north.' She opened her eyes. 'Poor Godric.'

Damn it, she'd come out of her memories of that night. 'We can mourn Godric later – we'll pray together if we have time. But just now …'

'Yes, yes of course. Where was I?' She closed her eyes again.

'Sir Nicholas ate his meal.'

'Yes. Then he began speaking to Emma about plans for another marriage for her. I was very tired – I have been since John was born – so I excused myself and went to bed.'

'And your husband joined you there later?'

'No, I don't remember anything at all after that. I must have been very fast asleep, because the next thing I remember is—' her eyes shot wide open and she started back with a shock of remembrance that Edwin didn't think could be faked. Or could it?

'Steady, now.' He put out a hand but did not touch her. 'Calm yourself, and talk me through that – again, everything you can remember and as precisely as you can. I truly am sorry, but if I'm going to help you, I need to know.'

She nodded once more, clenching her fists into the fur wrap.

'I woke up very gradually, like you do from a really deep sleep. I was fatigued – dizzy – for some while, in fact; I just couldn't shake it off or clear the sleep from my head. I could hear sounds from outside and smell smoke, and bread baking – the usual sort of thing in the early morning. Or, not quite usual … there was a strange scent, but I was so thick-headed that I didn't recognise it straight away. Anyway, once I was properly awake, I realised I needed to use the garderobe – there's one at the end of the bedchamber, where the outside corner of the keep is over the ditch. I sat up. It was cold. I reached out to take one of the furs off the bed to wrap round me. And then …'

Her breath was coming in shallow gasps. 'And then …?' prompted Edwin.

'Nicholas was lying there, and there was blood *everywhere*. He was dead, I knew he was dead – he was cold and his eyes were open, and his throat was—' she swallowed a couple of times and buried her face in the fur.

Edwin hated himself, but he had to know. 'I'm so sorry to make you go through this,' he repeated, 'but I still need more. His throat was cut? That's what had killed him? He had no other wound?'

'Well, I didn't exactly examine the rest of him, if that's what you mean,' came her voice, muffled by the fur. She looked up. 'But no, I didn't see any other wounds. And his throat … it was certainly enough to kill him.'

'Was the weapon still in the room?'

'Yes. His own eating knife, would you believe. Just lying there on the bed next to him, with the blade and the hilt covered in blood.'

'And you picked it up?'

'Yes. I don't know why – I wasn't thinking clearly. Almost … just to see if it was real. It was like I wasn't really there. I think I thought that I must be dreaming, that it would all disappear if I reached out to touch something. But it was real, and I *was* there, and *he* was there, and the knife was in my hand … and that's when Milo walked in and my nightmare truly began.'

There was silence for a few moments while Edwin took in and digested everything he'd heard. Then, in a businesslike manner that he hoped would help move her on from the contemplation of her husband's dead body, 'And Milo? What did he do?'

'He went completely white. Honestly, it was like I could see the colour just draining out of his face. Then he turned and ran, without saying anything. And before I knew it the room was full of people – Luke, several of the garrison, Joscelin; even Emma came in, which didn't do her any good. Thank the Lord Ada stayed out of the way, or the sight of it all might have turned her milk sour.'

'And everyone jumped to the conclusion that you must have killed him.'

'Yes.' She looked over at him. 'But I didn't, I swear on my life, my *son's* life, that I'm innocent.'

If she was a liar, she was an exceptionally good one. But Edwin had met good liars before. 'Was there anyone – anyone at all – who seemed to exhibit doubts about your guilt? Anyone who you felt was on your side?'

She shook her head. 'Nobody stood up for me, or at least not straight away. Dear Godric said he believed in me when I saw him later on. He tried to get himself posted as the guard outside the keep door, but Luke knew he was sympathetic to me so of course he picked someone else.'

'And then what?'

'Well, there was chaos for a while, but then Joscelin said there were laws, and someone should be sent for the sheriff. Emma wasn't best pleased – I think she'd have had me executed out of hand if she'd had her way – but she agreed. Aubrey arrived a couple of days later; there was some snow by then, but it wasn't all that deep, and he only had to come from Warwick.'

Edwin nodded. 'And I suppose everyone thought he would cart you off straight away, and that would be that?'

'Yes. But, thankfully, the one advantage of being the means to a prestigious alliance is having powerful relatives. So he was under strict instructions to investigate properly. But, as you've seen, he's not very good at it. Seeing him asking questions reminded me of you, and of course I often think of … so I wrote. Partly it was because I wanted you; I didn't know if you were even still in the earl's household, but if you were then I knew you would be the best person to find out the truth, and get us all out of this terrible limbo we seem to be stuck in.' She sighed. 'And as to Martin … was it so wrong of me to want, in my hour of need, to have here the one person in all the world I knew would be on my side?'

'It wasn't wrong,' said Edwin, 'but it was dangerous.'

'It certainly was for poor Godric,' she said, the bitterness rising to the surface again. 'And I'm responsible for *his* death, regardless of anything else.'

'He undertook his mission in good faith,' Edwin reassured her. 'No, I meant it was dangerous to have Martin here. He's like a wild bull, knocking over everything in his path. He's never stopped thinking about you for one day since you left, did you know that? I was there when he found out you were married, and I watched all his hopes and dreams crumble into dust.'

That, finally, was the thing that made her cry.

Time was surely running out by now. 'Before everyone comes back, can we speak of the woman in the village? Sir Nicholas's concubine?'

'Oh, *her*.'

There was no mistaking Joanna's tone. 'Obviously, you didn't like her, and I get the impression she doesn't appreciate you much, either.'

'You've spoken to her?'

'Yesterday. I did want to talk to you first, but I just couldn't arrange to see you alone any sooner than this, so I thought I might as well get on with other enquiries while I was waiting.'

'And she will have had nothing good to say of me.'

Edwin thought he'd better not repeat what she'd said. Besides, he couldn't be quite sure he'd heard it correctly anyway. 'She's been in her relationship with Sir Nicholas a long time? Those boys are all his?'

'Yes. Or so she says – a woman like that, how do we know she hasn't been with other men as well? But certainly not her husband's; he was old and infirm, chosen for her deliberately by Nicholas. Anyway, Nicholas acknowledged the boys as his, so that was that. Would you believe, in the autumn he said he was going to bring the eldest into the castle, to find him a position here? Right under my nose.'

'And did you raise that with him?'

'I did. And it's the one thing I ever persuaded him out of in all the time we've been married. He didn't care about the insult to me, personally, of course, but I told him it was a slight to my family and my connections, and that carried more weight. So the boy stayed where he was.'

'And did he …' Edwin was recalling something Mabel had let slip. 'Did your husband actually agree to stop seeing her?'

'How did you know that?' Joanna was looking at him in surprise.

'You asked me here to find things out.'

'Yes, yes he did say he would. It took much longer to persuade him of that, but I talked about our son and heir, and how he had to be put first now, and I think that swayed him. By the time Advent came around he *said* he would tell her, though I don't know if he ever did.'

'Hmm. And if he had done, that would have made her very angry.'

A spark of hope lit up her eye. 'Of course!' But then her face fell. 'But that's no good, is it? She would have killed me, not him.'

'In theory, though, would she have been able to get into the castle? Did she have a right to come and go?'

Joanna shook her head. 'No. Not since I've been here, at least. Before that I gather he used to summon her here sometimes – she's no doubt been in my bed.' Her lip curled. 'But since our wedding he did at least have the decency to go out to see her.'

'But she's known by the garrison? They're local, and so is she?'

'That's true. But unfortunately I do know she wasn't here on the night Nicholas died. The one thing Aubrey did manage to do was to check with the gatehouse guards whether or not anyone came or went after the gates were shut.'

'And?'

'Nobody. So he must have been killed by someone in the castle.'

'Which means that the murderer is still here.'

'Yes. So can you blame me for wanting to have Martin here? And you, of course.'

He sighed. 'No, no I can't. And I wouldn't have made it here by myself, anyway.' He held off, for now, from telling her that the lord earl himself had actually ordered him to come. If he told her that, it would be difficult to avoid repeating the earl's callous disregard for her in his orders to Edwin.

'You've changed, Edwin,' said Joanna, suddenly.

'Pardon?' He was jerked out of his thoughts.

'When I first came to know you, you were so shy, creeping about and almost too scared to speak to me or to anyone else. And now look at you: you've been bombarding me with questions all morning, telling Aubrey what to do, and yesterday you took charge of all those men outside. I saw you out the window.'

'Well, yes, I suppose I did, but that was only because they all think I'm an important man in the lord earl's service.'

'And aren't you?'

Edwin blinked.

'We've all changed, of course,' she continued. 'But you most of all. Perhaps it's been gradual for you, but don't forget I haven't seen you for a year and a half. I don't know what's happened to you in all that time, what you've seen and done, but you're a different man. You were always clever, but now you have a confidence and an authority that you never had before.'

He still said nothing.

Their silence was interrupted by sounds in the distance; the castle men were on their way back from church, which meant that Edwin's time with Joanna was up. He ran through everything in his mind. Had he missed anything that he might just be able to squeeze in?

Then another sound, closer this time, under the solar window: a baby crying.

Joanna got up and hurried over to look out. 'Sounds like John has woken up. Ada will need to come in to feed him once she's finished gadding about outside.'

She turned away from the window. 'He is my first, my only concern now. My son. For myself I've almost got to the point where I don't care whether I live or die – either would get me out of the purgatory of this room. But I have to fight for my life: I have to live for *him*, and it frightens me that I might not. What will happen to him, if I'm not here?'

'Surely your husband's overlord would—' began Edwin.

'Oh yes, from that point of view, the castle, the estate … but what I mean is, what will happen to John, himself? I already know that he'll be taken away from me eventually – his wardship rights will be sold, he'll have to go as a squire somewhere – but as he's still an infant, I should be able to keep him, to stay with him, for another five or six years at least, to see him turn from a baby into a little boy, even if I'm not there when he grows up. But I want to stay with him until the last possible moment, and let him know that he's got someone who loves him more than anyone else in the world, who will always be on his side, no matter what happens.'

She moved back towards the fire, turning away from Edwin to hide her face. 'He'll laugh that off, when he's older, I'm sure. Womanly softness – that's what all men call it, isn't it? But he's mine, no matter what the law says. I carried him inside my body, and he's part of me. I love him and I'm terrified for him all at the same time. What if he's ill? What if he has an accident? What if he dies? So many things can happen to a child. But what I'm most frightened of is that he'll grow up without me, and thinking that his mother killed his father. That would blight his prospects forever, as well as poisoning his mind.'

She turned back to look him directly in the face, her eyes red as they bored into his. 'I tell you, Edwin, until you have a child of your own, you don't know what love is. Or fear.'

Chapter Seven

Martin let the time-honoured Latin words wash over him. He didn't know what most of them meant but he'd been hearing them every Sunday all his life, wherever he was, and their familiarity was comforting.

He was standing over by a wall, as he always did in church in order to minimise the stares. Naturally it was much worse here, what with him being a stranger; he could feel eyes upon him, glances that were hastily withdrawn as soon as he caught them and glared back. He knew he should be praying, but he couldn't concentrate. All he could think of was Joanna, what she was going through, the way he'd felt as he spent the last two evenings in her company, but without being able to talk to her properly, exactly how she'd looked as he gazed at her in the candlelight … he *ached* for her, like a physical pain. And he could hardly bear the thought that Edwin was alone with her now – assuming all had gone according to plan – and that he would have her all to himself for some while.

Of course, *of course*, it was better in the long run that it should be Edwin who spoke to her, because her best interests would be served by having the truth brought to light and Edwin was the best person to do that. He, Martin, should keep reminding himself that he was Joanna's devoted servant from afar, like the lovers you heard about in those minstrels' stories, who worshipped ladies unattainable to them.

But still, he was envious that Edwin should be with Joanna for as long as the rest of them were stuck here. He wondered how close together they would be sitting. He wondered if they might speak of him at all.

Martin sighed, loudly enough for some of those around him to resume their stares. He wouldn't find out what Edwin and Joanna were saying any time soon, as it seemed his imprisonment in the church would go on for quite some while. It was the Feast of the Epiphany, which meant that Mass was longer, and Father Clement didn't seem to be in any hurry to get through it. Indeed, part of the way through he broke off from the Latin, switched to English and embarked on a thundering sermon about sin, the wages of sin, and how all the assembled congregation were going to hell if they didn't mend their ways.

'Cheerful,' Martin murmured to Turold, who was at his shoulder. 'Remind me to appreciate Father Ignatius more whenever we get back to Conisbrough.'

Plenty of others in the church were also whispering or outright chatting by this stage. Martin, of course, had a good view of all of them, and he spotted even Emma ignoring the priest to say something into the ear of a village woman. Juicy gossip, evidently, for the woman took on an expression of surprise and immediately turned to the neighbour on her other side to repeat it.

Eventually the Latin resumed, and Martin let it slide over him again until he heard *Ite, missa est*, always his favourite part of the Mass as it was the signal that the service was over.

He waited until the church was cleared, unwilling to wade through all the curious villagers, and then had an odd moment of stillness. He wasn't a particularly devout man, he knew that. Of course, he heard Mass like everyone else, but he didn't spend hours on his knees like some others did, and nor did he feel the need for additional fasting and penances. But now he experienced … something.

He walked forward to the rood screen so he could look past it at the altar. It was just a plain altar, nothing special, but there was a candle burning on it and Martin stared into the flame. He wasn't eloquent enough to form the words of a proper prayer, but somewhere within him it all distilled itself into *Help me, please*. He was going to need strength for everything that was to come, and having the Lord on his side would be a great help. And Joanna was innocent, he knew it, so surely the Almighty would find a way to bring that to light?

Then he shivered and realised he was standing on his own in a cold, empty church. Foolishness. He walked briskly to the main door and stepped out, unsurprised to see that most of the villagers and garrison were still there, milling about and glad of the company of their fellow men during these short winter days. The weather was definitely warmer than it had been for a while, a watery sunshine breaking through the clouds, and extended families stood to chat, children playing round their feet and throwing wet slush at each other.

Martin sighed as he saw most eyes turn to him, a few conversations pausing, and he wandered over to the little knot of Conisbrough men.

Turold, who always kept his eyes and ears open, nodded and murmured, 'I'm not sure I like the look of that.'

Martin followed his gaze to see that Emma and Luke were engaged in what looked like quite an intense conversation, and that they were drawing interest from others, one woman in particular. 'Who's she?'

Turold shrugged, but Willikin broke off from the surreptitious snowball fight he'd been having with a couple of youngsters. 'Oh, that's her who Master Edwin went to see, yesterday morning.'

'Sir Nicholas's concubine?' Martin stared at her. So this was Joanna's rival. He shook his head, unwilling to believe that any man could prefer this woman, who must be nearly thirty. She had the comfortable dimensions of one who had borne several children and who had plenty to eat without having to work for it.

The gossip over there seemed to be getting nastier, if the expressions on everyone's faces were anything to go by. Martin couldn't get any closer himself for fear of drawing attention, but he gestured to the more anonymous-looking Tom, who drifted over and joined the edge of the crowd.

He returned after a short while. 'They're talking about Lady Joanna,' he said, confirming Martin's fears.

'And?'

'The lady from the castle seems to be trying to say that the baby isn't Sir Nicholas's.' Tom put out a hand to Martin, who was already on the move. 'She's not said that right out loud, mind, just … well, you know how women can say things without saying them when they're gossiping.'

It was at that moment that Luke looked up and caught Martin's eye. Addressing the group round him, loudly enough for the words to carry over to Martin, he said, 'Well, we don't know anything about her, do we? She might have been a whore before she came here for all we know.'

That set Martin's mind on fire again, and before he knew it he was striding over, calling for Luke to retract his comment. People scattered out of his path and he found himself facing the smaller man in the middle of a circle of onlookers. 'Take it back right now.'

'Why?'

'Because she's never been immoral in her life.'

Luke made a derisive noise. 'Anyone could say that.'

Martin couldn't stand the man anyway, but these insults were just too much. 'Well, I'm saying it, and if you want to argue about it—'

'And you'd know, would you?'

'Of course I—'

Martin stopped dead, realising too late what he'd said as Luke and Emma both crowed with triumph.

'I knew it!' she screeched. 'I knew you knew her already! I could see it.' She turned to Luke. 'Told you.'

'You did,' he replied, warmly. 'You're cleverer than her – than all of them.'

Oh no you're not, thought Martin. Yes, you've outwitted me, and I'm an idiot who should have kept his mouth shut. But if you think you're cleverer than Edwin then you've got a shock coming.

But he was uncomfortably aware that he'd just made Edwin's task, and Joanna's situation, infinitely more difficult.

———•———

Edwin lay back on the truckle bed in the solar. He'd been about to leave when he realised he would meet Ada coming up; she would no doubt wonder why he'd been there, and he couldn't risk her mentioning it to anyone else. He'd quickly agreed with Joanna that they would use the illness excuse again, and by the time the wet-nurse arrived with the baby he was groaning and feigning dizziness.

'The poor man came up to plead for help,' explained Joanna. 'Here, give John to me a moment and pull out that bed. He needs to lie down until I can find someone to tend to him, and he's better up here near the fire.'

Once Edwin was stretched out, Joanna sent Ada off to feed the baby, telling her not to come out the bedchamber while the priest was present – 'If he catches sight of you feeding, we'll never hear the end of it' – then moving to tuck a blanket round Edwin. 'Stay there and stay quiet,' she whispered. 'It might be useful for you to hear Father Clement when he comes.'

'But I can't listen if it's time for your confession!' Edwin was appalled.

'It's all right,' she said. 'I won't say anything I don't mind you hearing. Boredom, anger – you've heard all that already. I might throw in gluttony as well.' She stood up with a grim expression. 'None of those are what he actually wants me to confess to.'

It wasn't long before the door opened and the priest swept in without knocking.

'Father,' said Joanna. 'Do come in.'

Edwin could see the priest opening his mouth, then stopping as he noticed the bed. He came over and Edwin closed his eyes, feigning a restless unconsciousness.

'Who is that?'

'A traveller. He arrived the other day with a party of men, having fallen off his horse and hit his head.'

'It's your Christian duty to offer hospitality, of course, but here? A strange man, here in the solar?' His tone was disdainful. 'Still, I would have expected no better, not from you.'

'He's in the service of one of the realm's greatest earls, Father, so all care needs to be taken. We wouldn't want it to be known that we hadn't extended every courtesy.'

The priest only sniffed, and then Edwin could hear him moving away again. 'If he looks like to die, send for me and I'll hear his confession.'

'I shall.'

'Now, as to confession … are you ready to save your immortal soul?'

'As I've told you many times over the last weeks, Father, I cannot confess to something I didn't do.'

'Nonsense!' came the loud reply, momentarily confusing Edwin. Did the priest honestly want her to …? But he was continuing. 'Of course you did it. There is no possible other explanation, and you're a wicked, murdering woman, all the more evil because you refuse to tell the truth.'

'I am telling the truth.'

'All women are liars and deceivers. Temptresses. Sinners. Eves in the Garden of Eden. But at least some of them try to strive against it. You, on the other hand …'

He sounded as though he was almost spitting with contempt. Edwin risked opening his eyes a fraction and caught a glimpse of a twisted face, ugly in its ferocity. Thank the Lord Martin wasn't here. He'd have lost his temper by now, and if he were to strike a priest then the ramifications would be very serious indeed.

Edwin lay back as Father Clement raged on and on, pouring out his bile against women. All women, but Joanna in particular. Edwin wondered that she could put up with this, but what choice did she have? She couldn't exactly leave.

After one particularly vituperative rant, the priest came back to his principal subject. 'Confess.'

'I will confess to anger, Father – anger with you and with everyone else who is accusing me unfairly. But I will not confess to killing my husband, because I did not.'

He almost howled. 'Liar! Whore of Babylon!'

That brought a whip-fast response. 'I was properly married to my husband, Father, by the laws of the land and of the church. So how can that possibly be true?'

'All women are whores, tempting men, lying with them, taking men's attention away from God. The only decent women are those who recognise their innate sinfulness and seek to assuage their guilt by remaining chaste all their lives, like the Blessed Virgin.'

'If that were the case,' she replied, tartly, 'then there would soon be no men left to worship God. Or do you claim that your own birth was a miracle? Are you not the result of your mother and your father lying with each other?'

Joanna's words had a veneer of confidence, but Edwin could hear her voice beginning to falter, and the priest's fury was only growing. Edwin was seriously starting to wonder at what point he would have to give up his pretence and rise to defend her from physical attack.

After spluttering in incoherent rage – for surely he must realise that her words were true, no matter how angry they made him – Father Clement summoned up a modicum of dignity and played his best card. 'You are a sinner,' he boomed, 'and as such you will hear no Mass from me, take no sacrament, until you confess. Do it now, and perhaps the flames of hell will be less hot for you.'

'If I confess to something I did not do,' she said, her voice now cracking, 'I will be committing the sin of falsehood. Moreover, I will be condemning myself to flames here on earth.'

'Better those than the eternal fire that never goes out,' he raged, 'but you will suffer both, and the torment will be richly deserved. I have done with you.'

Edwin heard him stamp across the room. Then came the noise of the door opening and closing, and silence.

And then the sound of weeping.

Edwin opened an eye and looked about him. He could hear a soft singing coming from the bedchamber, so he assumed the wet-nurse was still feeding the baby, or perhaps rocking it to sleep. He risked getting up and moving over to where Joanna was sitting by the fire, her head in her hands while she sobbed and sobbed, tears dripping on to the rushes of the floor.

He drew a stool near to her.

'I'm sorry,' she managed. 'I try to stand up for myself while he's actually here, so I don't look weak, but being spoken to like that all the time … it's *horrible*. And I'm scared that one day he'll shout at me so much that I'll end up confessing, just to make him stop.'

Edwin looked at her in sympathy. He knew he was supposed to be keeping an open mind on her guilt or innocence, but he couldn't help it. 'We'll get you out of this,' he said, softly. 'Martin and I, we'll do everything we can.'

That brought a fresh bout of weeping. 'I know, and I'm sorry I've dragged you into this, I really am. Martin – I didn't realise how much he – I get the feeling he'd fight them all for me, and then he'll get himself killed and I never meant that! I was just so afraid and I wanted someone here who would be on my side. But now I see what I've got you both into.'

Edwin made a soothing noise.

'I didn't do it, I didn't kill him – it was all exactly like I told you, I just woke up and there he was. But if I can't convince everyone else of that, they're going to kill me too.' She looked up and her reddened eyes met Edwin's. 'They're going to *burn* me, Edwin, and you're the only one who can stop them.'

He leaned forward and took both her hands in his. 'I will do everything I can, I swear. I'll find out the truth.'

It was just as they were sitting thus that Emma walked in.

———— ◦ ————

Martin hurried away from the church, cursing himself all the way for his stupidity. He was hoping to get back before Emma did, so he could warn Edwin and Joanna, but he was brought up short as he crossed the bridge by shouts for help.

Between the river and the castle's outer wooden palisade lay a kitchen garden. It seemed that a cow had managed to break in, laying waste to some of the winter vegetables that were still in it, but then getting itself stuck in the mud of the sodden riverbank, where it was currently half submerged. Several men were trying unsuccessfully to shift it.

Martin clicked his tongue in annoyance, torn as to whether he should stop to help or hurry on, but one of the struggling men caught his eye. 'The bull calf kept from last spring, sir, for breeding – belongs to the castle – we'll have to get him out or there'll be hell to pay – they'll say we didn't take good care …'

Well, that settled it. The loss of such a valuable animal would be a blow to Joanna's estate, and he couldn't pass by, not when his size and strength might make all the difference.

Martin turned to the others, who had by now caught up with him. 'Willikin, with me. The rest of you stay here in case we need pulling out ourselves afterwards.' He took off his cloak and handed it to Lambert. 'Here, look after this.' Then he looked down at the slush and the mud and took off his boots as well, while Willikin did the same.

They made their way off the bridge and through the garden, slipping and sliding as they approached the riverbank and then sinking into the freezing mud when they neared the men and the stricken animal. These were having little success so far, but their faces brightened at the sight of the two mismatched but strong-looking newcomers.

The bullock's hind quarters were sinking deeper and it was bellowing in distress, scrabbling with its front legs and throwing its head around. 'Reckon he's hurt a hind leg,' said one of the villagers. 'Twisted it, or something. That won't make it any easier – he can't push himself up.'

'Has anyone got a rope?' asked Martin, eyeing the animal's jerking head and horns.

'My lad should be fetching one now.'

'Good. While we wait, let's stop it sinking any further.' Martin turned to Willikin. 'You go round behind and get your arms underneath.'

Willikin waded good-naturedly deeper into the mud, crouching down and wedging himself under the animal's hind quarters. It stopped sinking. Martin chose his moment and then lunged forward to catch the horns so nobody would get gored while they were working.

'That's got it,' said the man whose son had been sent for rope. 'We'll get him out of here before he drowns, you see if we don't.'

'Drowns?' Martin looked in surprise at the river, which was several yards below them.

'Always the same, when the thaw starts. That field'll be underwater before we can get to it tomorrow, and you have to be careful – the river comes up fast once it starts, you don't want to get caught in it.'

Martin grunted, concentrating now on keeping his grip on the horns to keep them still and to hold the head and face out of the mud so the bullock could breathe. It was growing quieter – tired and cold, no doubt – and he could feel himself sinking. The mud was well over his knees, and it was *freezing*. 'Where's that rope, damn it?'

Willikin's voice came from the other side of the animal's body. 'Wait, I think I've got my feet on something more solid now – a big rock or something. If I can just …' His muscles bulged and Martin could see the veins beginning to stand out on his neck.

There was a heave, a movement, a sucking, squelching noise, and the bullock – to the astonishment of all and the sound of cheers from the bridge – came suddenly free of the mud as Willikin single-handedly lifted it. The men managed to push, pull and slide the animal further up the bank, but it was so wet underfoot that they were all in danger of sinking again.

'I'm here, Pa!' came a piping voice from the bridge. 'Shall I bring it down?'

'Wait!' called Martin. He turned to the men around him. 'No use him coming down, he'll just slide in with the rest of us.' He looked up at the bridge. 'Turold, Tom!' he shouted. 'Take that rope and make it fast around something solid, then throw me the end.'

Once he had it, they were able between them to get the rope round the bullock, which was by now exhausted and quiet. Martin and Willikin stayed with it to push, while the rest made their way up to pull. Water was coming up fast behind them, and Martin urged them all to hurry. With much effort on both sides they eventually had the animal safely up into the garden, to the cheers of the now packed bridge.

Willikin had pushed so hard that he'd nearly sunk himself, but between them he and Martin managed to slither and stagger out until they could reach the many willing hands ready to help.

'Well, this wasn't how I planned on spending my Sunday,' panted Martin, when he could get his breath back.

'We're grateful to you, sir – to both of you,' said one of the men, to general agreement, while Willikin had his back patted by everyone within reach.

'Will it survive?'

'I hope so sir, though he looks lame – see how he won't stand up? Still, it's not for us to say. We'll get him up to the castle so they can warm him up and have a look, and then it's up to them.' He began to organise men into building a litter to drag along.

'We'll leave you to it, then.'

'Aye, sir, and thank you again. And I'm sorry about your fine clothes.'

Martin looked at himself. He'd have to change as soon as he got back … the castle! Damn it – in concentrating on the task in hand he'd forgotten what he was supposed to be doing. Of course, it was too late now: Emma wasn't among those lining the bridge, and she had surely already entered the castle and reached Joanna.

He left the villagers to it and made his way to the gatehouse with the others. He was so filthy that he declined having his other clothes back and chose to enter the castle barefoot and shivering as he splashed through the slushy remains of the snow. Perhaps this was the penance he needed to do in order to have the Lord on his side in what was to come.

When Martin reached the keep, he went first into the guest chamber, wiping himself down as best he could and changing into the dry shirt and hose he'd brought with him before donning his spare tunic and boots. He was about to leave the room when he paused, came back and buckled on his sword belt. Never mind incivility; Joanna's safety – and Edwin's – were more important. The familiar weight gave him confidence, and he checked that both sword and dagger were loose in their scabbards before he loped up the stairs.

It was worse than he thought. Not only was Emma angrily confronting Joanna, but Edwin was still there, standing upright and not looking even slightly like a man who'd been struck down by the recurrence of a head injury.

'… both of them, is it?' Emma was screeching.

'My lady, please, moderate your tone and listen to what you're saying.' That was Edwin, as ever trying to be conciliatory.

'I knew as soon as she came here she was trouble,' continued Emma, stabbing a finger at Joanna and then turning to her again. 'You're a liar, a murderer and a wh—'

Martin strode to place himself between her and them. 'You will stop this,' he said, firmly, allowing himself to loom over her.

Emma was so angry that even his physical presence didn't intimidate her; she merely turned the tirade on him. 'And as for you – staring at her like a lovesick puppy ever since you've been here. An old friend? Or maybe more – how well did you know her, exactly?' she sneered.

Martin felt a cautioning hand on his arm, Edwin's. But he wasn't – yet – about to draw his sword on a lady.

There was a loud sound of dogs barking from downstairs, and the door opened to admit Aubrey, Luke and Mabel, the woman Martin now knew to be Sir Nicholas's concubine. A boy of about eight trailed after her; Martin assumed it was one of her sons. The dogs came in too, still barking, and Luke aimed a kick at one of them.

Now it was Joanna's turn to erupt. 'How dare you bring that woman in here?'

Luke sneered. 'You don't give the orders around here, not any more.' He moved to stand by Emma, staring belligerently at Martin, who felt his hand tighten around the hilt of his sword.

'Oh yes I do – this is my son's castle, and until we hear more, I am responsible for him and for it.'

Luke gestured at Edwin and Martin, and at Aubrey, who was hovering at the edge of the room – *Damn the man*, thought Martin, *he's supposed to be the representative of the sheriff, of law and order; why doesn't he do something?* – and jeered again. 'You? With all your fancy men around you? How many of them have you lain with? And which one is the brat's father?'

Martin might not have wanted to draw his sword on a lady, but he certainly had no such qualms when it came to Luke. Again, he was prevented by Edwin, now gripping his sword arm quite firmly. Of course, Martin could have shaken him off, but the touch brought him a little to his senses, and he held off for now.

'Your accusations make no sense,' Martin heard Edwin say, coolly. 'Lady Joanna's child is what, four months old? and thus must have been conceived not long after she was married to Sir Nicholas. None of us were anywhere near here, or near her, at that time.'

Ha, thought Martin to himself, *not so clever now, are you?*

'Once a whore, always a whore,' said Luke, dismissively. 'If she'll lie with any of you, she'll go with anyone. Could have been anyone in the garrison, any time Sir Nicholas was away.'

'I did not!' shouted Joanna. She stepped forward to face Luke down with a courage that only made Martin love her more. 'I was a good wife, a faithful wife, to my husband. More so than he was to me, creeping off to see *her*.' She gestured at Mabel, who was seemingly enjoying the spectacle before her. 'If you want to call anyone a whore, start with her.'

To Martin's confusion, both Luke and Mabel only smirked.

'Oh, I knew him a lot longer than you, little girl,' said Mabel. 'And he talked to me about many things, including you.'

Joanna's fury was by now so visible that Martin wondered she didn't burst into flames. But she was prevented from replying by the sudden hurried entrance of Joscelin, Milo and Father Clement.

The steward addressed Joanna and Emma. 'My ladies, the river has burst its banks. It's coming up fast, so we've had to close the gates and sandbag them – and the postern.'

'I told him,' interrupted the priest, 'to let me out before he shut us all in, but he wouldn't.'

'It was too late for that,' replied Joscelin, again aiming his remark at both ladies equally. 'You know how fast the water rises once it starts. We're only just keeping it out of the ward as it is.'

A thought was dawning in Martin's mind, but Edwin was quicker. 'Does that mean we're all trapped here?'

'I'm afraid so,' said Joscelin, apologetically. 'We can't open the gate or the postern and judging by previous experience, the water will get higher before it starts draining away.'

'How long?'

'I beg your pardon?'

'How long will it be before the gates can be opened?'

Joscelin made a helpless gesture. 'I can't say, exactly, but I would think at least two or three days.'

Martin looked around the overcrowded solar at all the angry faces as they took in this information.

Mabel was the first to react. 'My younger boys!' she exclaimed. 'I sent them home after Mass. I can't stay in here for three days!'

She was already making a panicked move for the door when Luke caught her arm. 'You heard what he said. The gates are shut – what are you going to do, jump over the wall and swim?' She pulled against his hand, but he held firm. 'Anyway, you came here to say something, and you haven't said it yet.'

'Never mind that now.' She wrenched away from him. 'I have to go and see.' She ran out of the solar.

Everyone else started shouting at once, or so it seemed to Martin. Joanna was admonishing Luke again for bringing Mabel into the castle, and he was answering back. Emma, her face ugly with hate, was yelling something at Joanna. The priest was still angry with Joscelin, who was defending his actions. The dogs were barking. Ada came out of the bedchamber looking bemused and carrying the baby, which added to the din by crying. Edwin was trying to talk over everybody to get their attention. The only quiet people in the room were Martin himself and Milo, who was sensibly staying out of all the arguments and banking up the fire.

Martin drew his sword.

Edwin heard the unmistakeable rasp of a blade being drawn and turned in horror to Martin. Thankfully, he soon realised that his friend was calm and that the action had done what nothing else had succeeded in doing: it made everybody fall silent.

'That's better,' said Martin, in a level tone, as Edwin saw Luke clutch at a non-existent hilt by his own side. 'Now, you will all, of your goodness, remain quiet and listen to Edwin.' He turned. 'I'm sorry, but the cat's out of the bag. They know half of it already, so you may as well tell them the rest, especially if we're all going to be stuck here.'

'You mean …'

'Yes. About why we're here.'

This was not what Edwin needed just now, coming on top of all the different strands of conversation in the room that he was trying to disentangle, the scene with the priest that he'd witnessed and the long discussion with Joanna before that. He hadn't yet worked his way through everything in his mind. But they were all staring at him, so he'd better get on with it.

'We … I was sent here to find out the truth about Sir Nicholas's death.' Out of the corner of his eye he saw Joanna start into movement, and he made what he hoped was a surreptitious gesture for her to keep quiet. There was no need to bring in her appeal for help if they could get away with it.

'On what authority?' It was the sort of question that should have come from the sheriff's representative, but actually it was Luke who had spoken. He was, Edwin noted, standing very close to Emma.

'I work for Earl Warenne. Not as a steward, but as … a seeker after truth.'

'Well, that's not a position I've ever heard of,' said Luke, his tone a cross between dubiousness and belligerence.

'And have you ever been in the close household of one of the realm's most powerful earls?' snapped Edwin, before he could help himself. 'The king's own cousin? No? Then perhaps you don't know what sort of positions he employs.'

That seemed to silence Luke, for a moment at least, so Edwin pressed on. 'He is the overlord of Lady Joanna's cousin, who is the head of her family. He received a message expressing concern about the situation and sent me to find out what happened. It's something I've done for him before.'

'I didn't realise our little castle was of such importance to someone so far away,' said Joscelin, looking a little shaken. 'But for someone as mighty as Earl Warenne to send a member of his close household …'

'Two members,' said Edwin. 'Martin is his senior squire.'

There was a general gasp, which Edwin heard most clearly from Milo, who was nearest to him.

'Lady Joanna was once companion to the lord earl's sister, so she lived in the household too, which is how we know her already.'

'And if anyone thinks …' began Martin in a rumble.

Edwin held up a hand to stop him. 'And that is the *entire* extent of our acquaintance, do you hear? That's all.'

Emma recovered her voice. 'So, you're here to let her get away with murdering my brother, just because she has powerful connections?'

'No.' Edwin was surprised at the firmness of his own voice. 'No, that's not what I'm here for.' He could sense that Martin was staring at him, but Edwin didn't want to meet either his eye or Joanna's. 'I'm here to find out the truth, one way or another, not to point the finger at – or away from – any one person.'

He noticed Aubrey standing with his mouth open. 'As you know,' Edwin continued to the room in general, 'the sheriff of Warwickshire has already sent his representative here to investigate the matter, so I propose to work with him – I have no wish to override local authority.' *But I will if I have to*, was the subtext he hoped they all understood, as Aubrey shut his mouth again and tried to look like a man who had the slightest clue what was going on.

'So, to go back to Luke's question, that is my authority. If you wish to question it, you can do so now, or we can send a message to the lord earl as soon as we can open the gates and send a man out.'

Even Emma wasn't about to quibble with that level of power and influence; the room remained silent.

Edwin surveyed them all. 'Good. Now,' he continued, more briskly, 'I will need to talk to you all as we go along – together with Aubrey, of course – but for now we had better concentrate on our immediate situation. Joscelin.'

The steward jumped, having been sunk in his own thoughts. 'Yes?'

'Are there enough stores to feed everyone, and the horses, while we're locked in? Even if it goes on for more than a few days?'

'Of course.' Joscelin sounded slightly offended. 'You might not be a steward after all, but surely you would know we keep adequate supplies for the winter, like any well-run place. Now, let me think.' He took a breath. 'Yes, the kitchen garden will be out of use, which will cut down on the fresh food – we'll have to see if the rest of the leeks survive – and we won't be able to get to the mill, but we have plenty of dried goods. Peas, beans, flour, salt meat and fish ...' He broke off in the middle of enumerating on his fingers. 'And it looks like we'll have fresh meat, too: the bullock that was brought in earlier has a broken leg, so it will have to be slaughtered. The smoke-house is outside the walls, unfortunately; we can salt some of it here, but the rest may as well be eaten straight away.'

'Not one of those we kept from this spring, to rear to replace the old bull?' asked Joanna.

'I'm afraid so, my lady. But there's nothing to be done. We kept two, as you know, so we'll have to make sure greater care is kept of the other.'

'Yes, perhaps we should—'

Edwin felt they were getting a little off track. 'Thank you, Joscelin. Now, as to where to put everyone. I see already that some extra guests will need to be accommodated.' He looked at Father Clement, but he was staring in pop-eyed horror at Ada, who hadn't quite laced her dress up properly after feeding the baby. She noticed the priest's gaze and gave a huge and guilty start, hastily tidying herself and pulling the laces tight.

Edwin continued. 'That is to say, Father Clement, Mabel and her son. Are there any others we know of? Or is there anyone from the castle who is trapped outside and can't get back in?'

'I'll check. Some of the villagers might still be—'

'All the garrison should be accounted for,' broke in Luke. 'At least *I* know how to keep track of my men.'

Edwin ignored the jibe and hoped Joscelin would too. This was hardly the time for internal household rivalry. Now, the new situation would pose dangers of its own, so perhaps some re-ordering was necessary …

'Here's what I suggest,' he said, after a moment's thought. 'Our men will move from the hall to the keep. There's only four of them so there should be room, and it will make a little extra space in the hall in case you have to put others in there. Aubrey, have you got any men with you?'

Aubrey seemed startled at being addressed. 'I, er …'

Edwin didn't have the time or the patience for his confusion. 'Have you or haven't you?'

'Yes, two,' he managed.

'Good. I propose they move in downstairs as well. Then either you or we will need to move out of our guest chamber so that Father Clement can—'

'Stop!' thundered the priest. 'I will not sleep under the same roof as *women*.'

'I'm not asking you to share the solar with them, Father,' explained Edwin, attempting to keep his temper with the priest, who was already low in his estimation after the morning's events. 'They'll be up here and you'll be down there.'

'Unacceptable!' Father Clement seemed strangely over-annoyed, even judging by Edwin's limited experience of him. 'Women are inherently sinful and should be kept away from—'

'Then you can sleep in the hall with the others,' retorted Edwin. He remembered to whom he was speaking and added, 'Or perhaps Joscelin could make you up a bed somewhere on your own.' He threw the steward a sympathetic look, conscious of the extra work he was creating.

He'd saved the most unpleasant bit until last. 'And finally,' Edwin added, trying to make it sound like a matter of no moment, 'I think Mabel will have to join the other women in the solar.'

'What! How can you—'

He needed to cut off Joanna's anger. 'I know you don't like it, and I understand that, of course. But to have a lone woman sleeping somewhere in the castle – it might not be safe.'

'Ha – not if some of my lads have anything to do with it,' interjected Luke, who seemed to find the prospect amusing. 'If they're going to be locked in, they could do with a bit of fun, and who could blame them? And with her reputation …'

'That woman is a *whore*!' Father Clement had been set off again. 'If she were to be assaulted it would be her own fault, for she has no shame.'

Edwin was really losing his temper now. He hadn't asked to be put in charge here, but nobody else seemed to have the wit or the will to take it on – Joanna angry, Joscelin overwhelmed, Aubrey examining his fingernails – and he'd felt pressured into doing something, simply because it needed to be done. But he could feel himself sweating, feel the distress rising as he tried to gauge and control everyone's reactions.

Strangely enough, the interruptions from Luke and Father Clement seemed to have swayed Joanna; Edwin wondered if perhaps she disliked these two men even more than she despised Mabel. 'Yes, Edwin,' she said, talking over Emma's attempt to cut in. 'I agree, it's safer for any woman to remain in female company, with all these *undisciplined* men around.' She might have been looking at Luke as she emphasised the word, Edwin couldn't say. 'Mabel and her son are welcome to sleep up here until she can go home, and with you and your trusted men downstairs we will all feel more secure.'

'Thank you, my lady,' said Edwin, in some relief. 'Now, I suggest we all get about our business. There is much to do, so I'll leave talking to people about the murder until tomorrow.' He mustered one final effort. 'But, be in no doubt – I will need to see all of you, and I *will* get to the bottom of what happened. It's my duty to my lord earl.'

With varying degrees of dissatisfaction everyone except Joanna, Ada and Martin left the chamber, and Edwin sagged with relief.

A huge clap on his shoulder nearly sent him flying. 'Wonderful!' said Martin. 'Absolutely superb. The way you shut that priest up, and Luke …' he laughed as he sheathed his sword.

Edwin met Joanna's eye. 'Like I said,' she murmured. 'You've changed.'

'Thank you, my lady. But … could I please go into the garderobe in the bedchamber? I think I'm about to be sick.'

Chapter Eight

The food was excellent once again, and Edwin decided to focus his attention on the partridge in wine and the meat pie while he let the tense atmosphere wash over him.

In truth, it wasn't quite as bad as it could have been. Father Clement was not present, thank the Lord, for he refused to sit at the same table as the women, and Mabel had not yet returned – although Edwin doubted whether Joanna's change of heart would extend to allowing Mabel to eat with them anyway. Surrounding Edwin at the table were Martin, Joanna, Emma and Aubrey, with Milo serving and Joscelin fussing in and out every so often. Through the gloom of fire and candlelight Edwin could make out Ada in the far corner, tucking heartily into her own meal while she rocked the baby's cradle with her foot. On the other side of her was Mabel's son, who had appeared from somewhere when the food arrived.

As he chewed, Edwin considered the position of wet-nurse. Ordinary women didn't employ them, of course; they fed their babies themselves or, if they couldn't, they were normally able to find a friend or relative who was in milk herself to help out. Noble ladies, on the other hand, could pay to find the best sort of girl available so they didn't have to tie themselves to the baby and could have more children more quickly. It was a good position for a village girl, for it meant being fed good food in order to produce better milk; Ada was certainly enjoying something. It also meant living in at the castle, with constant fires in the winter, although sleep was presumably in short supply. But Ada had been there, in the background, all this time. What had she seen and heard?

The other obvious thing about wet-nurses, it now occurred to Edwin, was that they had to have a baby of their own – they wouldn't be producing milk otherwise. So where was Ada's? He hadn't seen a sign of any other infant, and although he'd only been here a few days he knew she'd have to see it often, several times a day, to keep it fed. Perhaps she had passed her own baby on to a sister or something in order to devote herself exclusively to the lord's child and earn money for her family.

There were nuts and pastries to end the meal, and then the group broke up into separate parties. Edwin saw Joanna and Martin move to the window seat; it would be cold over there, but it afforded more privacy than the chairs round the fire. Being forced to reveal their identities and background was not, Edwin was sure, going to make his life any easier in terms of finding the truth, for everyone would be wary and suspicious of him, but the one positive point was that they no longer had to pretend that they didn't know Joanna. Martin could at last speak to her openly.

Emma had moved away from the table to the most comfortable chair by the fire. Initially she sat on her own, but the sound of the dogs from downstairs prompted Edwin to look at the solar door and, sure enough, Luke soon entered to sit near her. Edwin would dearly like to know what they were saying, but if he moved any closer it would be obvious he was eavesdropping – and all the more so given that they now knew what he was here for. The sight of Luke reminded Edwin of the interaction with Mabel earlier: what was it that Luke had been trying to get her to say?

Anyway, that would have to wait. Edwin was about to turn his attention away from them when he saw Joscelin moving to pass a cup of wine to Emma and heard Luke, in a more audible tone, ask Joscelin about his family. Joscelin's immediate reaction was startled, almost fearful, but he hid it so quickly that it would have been barely noticeable if Edwin had not been looking that way already. But, of course, he would be worried if he was going to be separated from them for several days. Edwin certainly knew that feeling – he hated being parted from Alys, and he knew he'd hate it even more once there was a baby in a cradle to leave behind as well.

He allowed himself to daydream for a few moments, imagining the peace of the cottage, a winter's night when they had full bellies, a warm fire and a child of their own. It would be nice and quiet, maybe just his mother or aunt dropping by, and he would keep them all safe.

Mabel entered the room, and Edwin's eye turned involuntarily to Joanna. However, she was engrossed in her conversation with Martin and barely spared a glance. Mabel took a seat with Luke and Emma, and Edwin wished once more that he could hear what they were all saying. But he could not, so he turned his attention to the one other person still sitting at table with him: Aubrey. The sheriff's man had been awkward and fidgety throughout the meal, and Edwin could guess the reason.

Might as well get straight to the point. 'I expect you were surprised by what I said earlier.'

'Well, yes,' replied Aubrey. Then, after a pause, he burst out, 'And you're sure that it was your own lord who sent you here? It wasn't Sir Philip, the sheriff, asking you because he thought I wasn't doing a very good job?'

It was difficult to see in the candlelight, but Edwin thought Aubrey's face was red. 'Is that the sort of thing he would be likely to do?'

'It wouldn't surprise me,' mumbled Aubrey. 'And he'd be right, really – I've been useless. I like it here because the food and the company is better than at home, but I haven't done much and I can't stay indefinitely.' He sighed. 'I don't think I'm suitable for my position at all, to be honest, but I'm a younger son so my father thought it would be a good opportunity for me.' He waved his arm. 'It's difficult. You go have to go out and talk to people, and find out about nasty things, and I don't enjoy it. And that's not even including the executions.' He shuddered.

Edwin tried to encourage him. He felt the irony of giving advice to a man who was older, richer and of higher status than himself, but he needed Aubrey to pull himself together if he was going to be of any use. The sheriff's man needed to stop feeling sorry for himself and get to the matter in hand.

'So, let's go through what you learned before I got here,' Edwin concluded, forcing himself to sound more hopeful than he thought. 'You might find it's more than you think.'

Aubrey made a helpless gesture.

Edwin tried not to grind his teeth. 'Let's start with the body, for example. From what I gather, there must have been a great deal of blood. Lady Joanna was obviously stained with it, but that doesn't offer us any proof one way or the other – it might be because she killed him, or merely because she was in the same bed when he was killed.'

Aubrey sighed and looked over to where Joanna and Martin were sitting in the window seat, deep in conversation. 'That's exactly what I mean,' he said. 'Everything is so difficult – how am I meant to find out which one of those two things is true?'

'By looking at other things,' explained Edwin. 'Surrounding events.' He sighed as he saw Aubrey's confused face. 'In this case, surely the question must be, was anyone else in the castle observed at that time with blood on them?'

Aubrey brightened a little. 'Actually I did ask that. But the problem was that they were slaughtering some pigs that morning, to have the meat hanging ready for Christmas, so there was a lot of blood around and many people were splashed with it.'

'And?' prompted Edwin.

'And what? How does that help?'

Edwin's eyes rolled, despite his best efforts. 'Did you then make a list of those people, and look to find out where each of them was at the time of the murder, and whether any of them could have been in the keep?'

Aubrey's face fell even further. 'I didn't think of that.'

This was hopeless. Edwin allowed himself to lapse into silence.

'Perhaps,' began Aubrey, tentatively, 'perhaps if I stay with you while you talk to people, I might be able to learn more about this sort of thing.'

'Perhaps.'

'It might help me to get promoted in future. A sheriff has the opportunity to bring in a great deal of money, you know.'

After a few moments, Aubrey seemed to realise that he was not going to receive an answer to that. He began to fidget and look about him, then rose and drifted over in Joanna's direction.

Martin won't like that, was Edwin's thought, but he made no move to prevent it. Some time on his own now would be useful, as he had a lot to work through after all he'd seen and heard that day. He moved his stool over to the wall so he could lean back, then stared at the flame of the candle on the table and allowed himself to sink into his thoughts.

First had been his conversation with Joanna. If – *if* – he assumed she was telling the truth about the morning after Sir Nicholas's murder, then she had woken to find her husband's body, which meant that someone else had previously entered the bedchamber to kill him. They must have come through the solar, as there was no other way in – Edwin had taken the opportunity to check the chamber's garderobe while he was in there, and the chute was far too narrow to allow access. That person had then slit Sir Nicholas's throat without waking either him or Joanna, or anyone else on the upper floor. Edwin could see how people had thought that impossible and dismissed Joanna's protestations of innocence. But, assuming for now that it had happened, how would it have come about?

There were several possibilities, each of varying levels of complexity. Starting with the most unlikely, someone from the village might be the culprit, but they would have had to get inside the castle, inside the keep, through the solar and into the bedchamber. This would not be feasible without help from someone on the inside, which he would not rule out for now.

Next to consider was a murderer already inside the castle walls; again, they would have to get through the lower room of the keep before they could get upstairs. It seemed that only Milo had been in there, and if he was a sound sleeper, as boys of his age often were, that might not have proved very difficult. But wait – had Sir Nicholas's dogs been in there with him? Or had they only started sleeping there when they had lost their master? That would need checking. The final options, and perhaps the ones that were *physically* the most likely, were that the culprit had been Milo himself, creeping upstairs, or one of the two women who were already in the solar.

But, as Edwin remembered being told all those years ago, think not just of who and what and when, but also of *why*. He smiled sadly. The remembrance of Father's face was slowly fading, but his words would always remain in Edwin's mind. So, why would Milo, Emma or Ada wish to kill Sir Nicholas?

Ada seemed the least likely candidate. She had been employed to feed the baby and could have had little contact with the lord of the castle, except in passing; dealing with infants was women's work. There was perhaps a possibility that he had been cruel to her in some way, but it seemed implausible, to say the least, that this could have resulted in her slitting his throat in the middle of the night.

Milo, as a squire, would naturally have more familiarity with bladed weapons, which would make him physically the most capable of those in the keep on the night in question. But, again, why? Why kill the master on whom his livelihood depended? As Edwin knew, a squire whose master died was put in a very difficult position, as it was not easy to find a new one: lords and knights tended to take on boys who were much younger and who could be trained up; if they wanted a more experienced lad in his teens, they already had one. So, if Milo had murdered Sir Nicholas, he would need an exceptionally good reason to have done so.

Emma, now. She was a different matter entirely, and he certainly wouldn't rule her out simply because she was a lady. Her accusations about the baby not being Sir Nicholas's were an obvious display of her ambitions: if her brother died leaving no legitimate children, she would be the heiress to the estate. But this thought brought to mind a more disturbing one – was the infant itself in any danger?

No woman would harm a baby, surely. The fact that Emma had chosen to insinuate illegitimacy rather than attempting to get rid of the child more permanently was a point in her favour here; but, as Edwin knew, if people got desperate, they could resort to desperate actions. Which led on to another very obvious question. Just how desperate was Emma? How badly did she want the castle and its estate? Enough to kill her brother for it?

Up until now, and for many years of her life, Emma had been the heiress to the estate. Then Sir Nicholas had married. This was not necessarily a problem on its own, but he had started a family within months, which certainly was. His wife was proved to be fertile, and was young; she would expect to have more children and possibly many more over the course of the next few years. If Emma intended to make a move to ensure her position as the next in line, now would be the time to do it, when there was just one child, a baby who was young enough to be susceptible to all kinds of ailments that could result in its death.

Edwin broke off his stare through the candle flame to look over towards the fire, where Emma was sitting. Some very dark thoughts indeed were now running through his head.

———

Martin was in heaven. Well, not quite, but nearer to it than he'd ever been. Even back when Joanna had lived at Conisbrough and he'd seen her every day, their actual interactions and conversations had been brief or stolen. After she'd been taken away, he hadn't seen her at all. Then he'd come here and had to suffer the torture of having to stay away from her, pretend not to know her. And now here he was, sitting with her – alone with her, sort of, or at least as alone as anybody ever got inside a castle – able to see and speak to her as much as he liked.

To start with he'd been almost overcome. Stuttering, falling over his words, heart racing, convinced at any moment that some figure of authority was going to appear to separate them. But as the evening wore on, he was able to relax more, to enjoy her company, to remember more clearly all the things about her that he loved. She hadn't really wanted to talk about her experiences, brushing off his questions and saying she'd already told it all to Edwin and that she didn't want to ruin their time together by remembering it again. She'd changed the subject by asking him all about what he'd been doing since she last saw him – listening to him, exclaiming at the right moments and making enquiries after various Conisbrough folk whom she still remembered with fondness.

As Martin spoke to Joanna, some of his irritation with Edwin ebbed away. He didn't quite know what he felt about it all anyway – whether to be angry or confused or something else at the thought that Edwin might have a different aim from himself, and that he might hide it – so the best thing to do was just to suppress any thoughts and feelings. Instead, he moved on from his toned-down description of the battle at Sandwich to tell Joanna all about Fauvel, his reward for it.

She sighed. 'I'd love to come and see him – he sounds like the finest horse in the world. But until I'm allowed out of this solar …'

Martin scowled as reality intruded on him once more. 'We'll get you out of here, one way or another. By cleverness if Edwin can, and by force if not.'

She laid a hand on his arm, and he felt the shock of the unfamiliar contact run through him. 'Please, Martin – don't do anything foolish. You have great prospects ahead of you, and I would never forgive myself if I ruined them.'

He desperately wanted to lay his own hand on top of hers. But he couldn't: although it felt like the two of them were alone there were others in the room, some of them enemies of hers, and he wouldn't give them the ammunition.

He lowered his voice. 'I would do *anything* for you.'

'I know you would,' she whispered, 'but what I most want you to do at the moment is not to endanger yourself, or my son.'

He recoiled at the mention of the thing he'd been trying to block out of his mind. A dismissive remark made it all the way to his lips, but he stopped it falling out, seeking instead to change the subject.

He glared at Luke, still sitting by the fire with Emma and Mabel. 'I'd like Edwin to find out that he was responsible, and that's for sure.'

Joanna shook her head. 'So would I, of course, but I'm afraid it can't have been him. It was one of the few things I managed to find out: he was on wall duty that night, and he was at the top of the gatehouse the whole time.'

'That's a shame,' said Martin, really meaning it. 'But if we try hard enough, I'm sure I can find another reason to give him a good drubbing.'

He was pleased to see Joanna smother a smile, and then much less happy to see that Aubrey was approaching them. Martin longed to push him away, like the annoying puppy he was, but Joanna was smiling and welcoming him.

They began to speak of this and that, and Martin tried to ignore them so that he wouldn't end up doing or saying something he'd regret later. He turned his attention back to the group at the fire, safe in the knowledge that they were by the light and he was almost in darkness, so they wouldn't be able to see that he was watching.

He strained to hear their conversation. They were whispering, which meant that he couldn't really catch any individual words, but it did remind him of the other night in the stable. In the time since then, and in the absence of any attack, he'd almost convinced himself that he'd imagined it, but now it all came rushing back to him, and he could hear the two mysterious figures while he smelled the familiar scent of Fauvel next to him.

He concentrated harder. Was Luke's one of the voices he'd heard? It was possible … but after some while, Martin didn't honestly think that Luke had been the one to say, 'Kill them all.' But if that were the case, and he had been the other speaker, who could possibly have been giving him orders?

⸻

'About what you said earlier.'

Edwin had hoped to get away without being too closely questioned by Martin this evening, but it seemed not. Martin had spoken almost as soon as they were alone in their guest chamber.

'Yes?'

'What exactly did the lord earl tell you, before we came here?'

'Are you sure you want to hear it?'

'Yes.'

Edwin took a deep breath. 'He said, and I quote, "I don't care whether she did it or not. If she didn't, and you can find another culprit, all well and good. If she did then she'll have to face the penalty, but make sure you keep me well out of it and deflect as much as you can away from de Lacy. Paint her as some kind of abomination, not as a member of his family, and play down any link to me."'

There was a deep, dark silence.

'And those were his exact words?'

'They were.'

'He … he actually said that about a young woman, a girl who'd been in his close household all that time?'

'He did. I'm sorry.' Edwin had never been under any illusion about the earl: he was ruthlessly dedicated to his own self-interest, and to him all others were expendable. Edwin had assumed that Martin shared the same knowledge, but evidently he hadn't, which was why this came all the more as a shock.

'But now,' said Martin, eventually, and with what Edwin thought was some effort, 'but now at least you know the truth, because you've spoken to her, so we can count on working on that first bit – finding another culprit.'

'Well … sort of.'

'What do you mean, "sort of"?'

Edwin tried to find a way of phrasing it so that his friend would be less hurt. 'Everything I know about this whole situation is just what people have told me about it. I wasn't here when it happened, I don't know anything at first hand.'

'And?' Martin hadn't got it yet.

'And yes, I did have a long talk with Joanna this morning. But what she told me isn't necessarily "the truth", it's just … what she told me. I can't count it as any more the truth than what anyone else has told me – not until I have some firm evidence.'

There was a long, long pause.

Then, rumbling out of the darkness, 'Edwin?'

'Yes?'

'You don't want to make me angry with you.'

Martin turned over and went to sleep, leaving Edwin staring at the ceiling.

He slept only fitfully and was wide awake again long before dawn. He thought he might as well get started with the tasks of what promised to be a long day, so he crept out of the chamber without waking Martin. The main room was crowded, with his men and Aubrey's all sleeping in there as well as Milo, but he managed to make his way over to the outer door without anyone stirring, though one of the dogs by the fireplace raised its head to give a low warning growl.

Outside it was still dark, but there was enough of a moon for Edwin to see a little way and there was already light coming from the kitchen and from a few braziers around the palisade's wall walk. The inner ward was a wet, slushy mess. Instead of crossing it, he went around the keep and was glad to find a stair so he could go up to the wall walk and look out towards the church and the village.

Water surrounded the whole castle, evident even in this light by the splintered reflections of the moon as it lapped in waves across the field. It was Plough Monday, the day for returning to work after the twelve-day Christmas feast, but nobody would be working in the field in which he and Martin had walked the other day. He couldn't see as far as the village just yet, other than a distant smudgy glow from household hearths, but he thought he remembered it being on ground that was a little higher than the castle. Hopefully people's homes were safe and they would be able to get into the fields on the other side of the village to check on their crops.

He looked down over the wall. The castle stood – for now – proud of the flood, being situated on its two earth mounds, but it would not take much more of a rise for the water to come oozing under the palisade and into the wards. And until it ebbed away, they were all well and truly trapped, guilty and innocent alike.

Edwin descended and made his way over to the building next to the kitchen, guessing – correctly as it turned out – that this would contain the steward's office. Joscelin was within, sitting at a table and looking as though he hadn't slept all night. He looked up as Edwin entered, putting his finger to his lips and pointing at a recess where the sleeping figure of Father Clement could be discerned.

Edwin nodded to show that he understood and moved quietly to the pool of light cast by the rush on the table. 'Ah,' he said, quietly, meaning to open the conversation in a general way, 'you have an exchequer board.'

Joscelin looked surprised. 'I thought you said you weren't really a steward?'

'I'm not, but I know what one of these is. My uncle – who was the steward at Conisbrough for many years – didn't use one, but the new man who came last year swears by his.' He glanced at the exchequer, marked out in dark and white squares like a chessboard, on which Joscelin had placed various counters. 'It does make things easier to see as you're doing your accounting.'

'Yes,' said Joscelin, putting down the pen with which he had been writing on a stack of second-hand parchment sheets and stretching his ink-stained fingers. Then he yawned. 'Your pardon – there has been so much to do that I …' he gestured at it all.

'You probably shouldn't do it when you're tired,' said Edwin, in sympathy. 'Look – I think you've made a mistake there.'

'What? Have I?' Joscelin rubbed his eyes as Edwin pointed at the board and at a corresponding entry in the figures on the parchment. 'You're right, I have. Good thing you spotted it.' He looked out of the open door, through which dawn was beginning to enter. 'No point in trying to get some sleep now – may as well get going. And yes, I'll leave this until I'm feeling more alert.' He blew out the rushlight and swept up the sheets of parchment.

The dawn light reached the recess, waking Father Clement. He stretched and then started as he saw the others. Edwin waited for the inevitable tirade, but the priest merely rose with as much dignity as he could muster and declared that he would say morning Mass in the hall before stalking out.

Edwin risked a conspiratorial smile. 'I think we got away with it.'

'I think we did. Which is one less thing to worry about.'

'You seem to have plenty on your plate at the moment.'

'What do you – oh, I see, yes. Sir Nicholas dying in any circumstances would have been difficult for all of us who work here, of course, but what with …' he waved his arm vaguely, '… *everything*, it's worse. Some of it is purely related to the tasks that need carrying out; should I keep ordering in wine and spices when I don't know how long it will be until there's a new master, or when I don't know what my budget is for doing so? And some of it is personal.'

'How so?'

'Well, you've no doubt seen the tension between Lady Joanna and Lady Emma. One or other of them is going to win out in the end, and the other will be gone. And the one who stays won't look kindly on anyone she thinks sided against her during this period.'

'And your problem is that you don't know which is going to be which.'

'Correct. So we – or most of us – are trying not to take sides, but it's getting more and more difficult as the weeks go by.' Joscelin rubbed a tired hand over his face. 'Everything is.'

'And of course, you must be worried about your family.'

Joscelin's head jerked up. 'What do you mean?'

'Being separated from them while everywhere is flooded – you stuck here and them in the village.'

'Oh, yes, that. Yes, yes, of course that's an additional worry. You'll have to forgive me – I'm very tired.'

He was, thought Edwin, but tiredness didn't really account for the strange expression that had come over his face when he talked about being separated from his family. He had seemed almost *relieved*.

'Anyway,' said Joscelin, changing the subject, 'I'd better get out and oversee the slaughtering.' He grimaced. 'Not my favourite thing.'

'You don't like all the blood? I'm certainly with you on that.'

'No, no I don't. But I didn't attend the last one and I'm fairly certain some of the meat went missing between the carcass and my stores. So it's my duty to supervise to make sure that doesn't happen again.'

He had almost reached the door when the sound of a commotion was heard. 'Oh, what *now*?' he said, at exactly the same time as Edwin.

They moved outside to be met by the rather unexpected pairing of Father Clement and Mabel. They were storming across the ward with a number of shouting, gesticulating or merely curious onlookers trailing behind them. They seemed to be heading in the direction of the keep, so Edwin hurried to cut them off.

He managed to get between them and the door and held out his arms. 'Please tell me what's going on.'

That gave them pause, but Edwin suspected it wouldn't be for long. 'Wickedness and sin!' began Father Clement, and Edwin groaned inwardly.

But it was Mabel who stepped forward, waving a finger in Edwin's face. 'You let us past so we can see justice done!'

'If you mean Lady Joanna, there is no justice to be done until we get to the bottom of the matter. As I said last night—'

'Oh, not because of killing Nicholas, though she should burn for that too. It's because she's a witch!'

'A *what*?' Edwin was stupefied. 'How can you possibly …'

Once more he was cut off in mid-thought by a distraction. This time it was an unearthly howl, a scream of loss and rage and pain that made Edwin's blood turn to ice and shocked all those around him into silence. It came from the outer ward.

Chapter Nine

Martin awoke with a stiff neck and in a foul temper, one that was not improved when he turned over to find that Edwin was not in the room. Damn the man! Of course, he couldn't get out of the castle, but nevertheless he should say where he was going so Martin could keep track of him.

It was no good staying in bed – that would only give him time to brood. He got up and went into the main room, poking the Conisbrough men with his foot to wake them as he went, and then sat at the table while he watched Milo take down the window shutter to let in the morning air. It was raining.

Martin's mood deepened when he remembered the pitiful way the squire had acted the other day. When the boy stowed the shutter and happened to meet his eye, Martin came straight out with it. 'Why did you lie?'

'What?' Milo was startled.

'The other day, at the training. You knew perfectly well that I waited until he had his guard back up before I engaged, and yet you said you hadn't seen.'

Milo hung his head.

'You were scared, is that it? What of? Honestly, even young Lambert stepped up to speak the truth, and yet you wouldn't.' He looked around. 'Where is Lambert, by the way? He was here a moment ago.'

'He's gone to the stable to check on the horses,' replied Turold. 'He thought that's what you'd want.'

'He's turning into a good lad.' The brief moment of cheerfulness soon passed, however, and Martin turned back to Milo. 'I know you're young, but you can't let the men intimidate you. You'll be a knight one day – you need to learn to command.'

'Easy for you to say, when you're a head and half bigger than anyone else. And besides, you haven't lost your lord.'

'No, I haven't, that's true.' Martin was painfully reminded of last night's conversation with Edwin. 'But I know a boy who did, and he got a new position by being keen and brave. Can you say the same?'

Milo mumbled something and then looked up as footsteps sounded overhead. 'I'd better go up and see if they need anything,' he said, sliding away.

Martin now found Aubrey at his side, poking around at the plates on the table. If he was looking for leftover food he was going to be out of luck, for the perpetually hungry Willikin had already swept up all he could find. But it seemed it was mere absent-mindedness on Aubrey's part. 'He's gone out without me,' he said at last.

'Who, Edwin? Yes, he does that from time to time. It's annoying. I'll go and find him in a moment.'

'He said I would be able to come with him, to see what he does and how, so I could learn.' He sounded mournful.

Martin had no patience with all this self-pity, not now. Aubrey needed to pull himself together; either that or someone should pick him up and give him a good shaking. In order to avoid the temptation to do just that, Martin decided he would go and find Edwin and give him a talking to instead.

He was just pushing himself to his feet when Lambert burst in.

'Steady, lad,' joked Tom. 'You look like you've seen a …' he tailed off.

Lambert's face was completely white, his eyes starting from his head in terror. He was shaking, and there were a few flecks of vomit on the front of his tunic.

Martin felt a surge of mingled fear and energy. 'What is it?' He strode over and grabbed hold of the boy. 'What? Is it Edwin?'

'N– no,' stammered Lambert. 'It's … you need to come. The stables.'

The fear triumphed as Martin felt a wave of cold and dizziness wash over him. He gave it a moment to clear, and then ran out of the door as if the devil was behind him.

Edwin hurried into the outer ward, the crowd at his heels and the rain in his face. The immediate sight that met his eye was a wooden frame on which was strung up the carcass of the slaughtered bullock, various men working on it to drain the blood – with which some of them were splattered – and remove the innards. Joscelin was there, fastidiously trying to stay away from the worst of it. None of these men looked particularly panicked; the noise had not come from them. One or two were throwing concerned looks at the stable, from which Edwin could see men leading a group of very skittish-looking horses.

'In there,' said one of the slaughterers, ripping out a long section of guts as he did so.

There was a very strong smell of blood, and Edwin wrinkled his nose as he passed the frame and the buckets dripping with it. But strangely the scent grew more, not less, pronounced as he moved away and neared the stable. A feeling of foreboding came over him and he slowed to a walk, and then stopped, unable to force himself over the threshold.

Outside the door stood a stable lad, about eleven or twelve years of age. He was crying. He couldn't bring himself to speak, merely pointing inside. The rest of the crowd stood back in a kind of horrified silence as Edwin stepped through the door.

The sight that met his eyes would stay in his nightmares for a very long time.

At first it was so horrific that he couldn't really take it in, and instead he focused on the huge swarms of buzzing flies.

Eventually, he forced himself to look again.

Martin was kneeling on the floor of one of the stalls, next to the most enormous pool of stinking, congealing blood that Edwin had ever seen – enough to fill a barrel. Lying in the gore was the body of Fauvel, his throat slit so deeply that the severed ends of internal tubes were grotesquely visible.

But that wasn't the worst.

As Edwin stepped forward and the shadows moved, he could see the horse's head more clearly, and he gagged. As he turned to retch, the smaller items lined up neatly against the stall partition caught his eye: Fauvel's eyes, ears and tongue.

Edwin had to take a moment to compose himself before he could look at his friend, knowing just how deeply he would feel this – and how incapable he would be of expressing it. The scream of loss and pain that Edwin had heard from so far away must have come from Martin, but now he was completely silent, unmoving, rigid.

Edwin reached out a hand to touch Martin's shoulder, but the voice came before he had made contact. 'Who's done this, Edwin? Who?'

'I don't know,' replied Edwin. The waves of pain emanating from Martin were so strong they were almost physical. 'But I'll find out, I swear I will.'

'Yes,' came Martin's voice, still sounding like it came from far away. 'Yes, you will. And when you've found him, you tell me, and I'll deal with him. I'll tear his insides out.'

'Martin …'

'I'll cut off his ears and gouge out his eyes.' Martin now stood up, unfolding himself until he loomed over Edwin in the semi-darkness. 'I'll make him confess, and then when he's done it, I'll rip out his tongue and make him eat it.'

'Martin – stop!'

'In fact, why don't we start now? Someone must know something.'

Edwin tried to stop him, tried to stand between Martin and the door, but it was no good; he was swatted to one side like a fly, crashing into the partition with the breath knocked out of him. It took him a moment to recover, so he was two steps behind Martin as he reached the door.

'You!' Edwin heard Martin roar, reaching the entrance himself in time to see that the person addressed was the stable boy. Unsurprisingly, given the huge, furious and bloodstained figure erupting at him, he did nothing but squeak and attempt to run away. Martin lunged after him.

'Willikin!' shouted Edwin, seeing his face in the crowd, and was relieved when the Conisbrough man reacted straight away, throwing his bulk at Martin and shortly followed by Turold and Tom. Edwin joined them, but even so it took all four of them to push the raging squire back against the stable wall. As they struggled to contain him, Edwin was uncomfortably aware that virtually the entire population of the castle was watching them. 'Help me get him inside,' he said to the others, under his breath, 'and then shut us in. Bar the door.'

'Are you sure?' Turold's eyes met his as they continued the struggle.

'He won't hurt me,' replied Edwin, with a confidence he wished he felt.

'All right. But we'll be just outside.' Between them they bundled Martin back inside, then Willikin gave him enough of a shove to put him off balance, allowing the three Conisbrough men to dart back out and shut the door.

As soon as he recovered his footing, Martin began to hammer furiously on the wood, bellowing incoherently.

'It's no good,' said Edwin, from a safe distance. 'They've barred it, and Willikin is standing right there. Even you couldn't get through that.'

Martin roared – almost screamed – in frustration and turned his attention to pounding on one of the stall partitions.

'Is injuring your sword hand really going to help?'

Within half a moment Edwin found himself almost off the floor, Martin grasping a handful of the tunic under his chin. 'Don't tell me what to do.' His voice was hoarse and his eyes were wild.

'All right. But let go of me.' Edwin was dropped, and put a hand to his throat. He often suffered nightmares about his neck being constricted and was more shaken than he would like to admit.

He focused on the task in hand. 'Martin. This is a terrible, terrible thing, and we will get to the bottom of it. But that's for later. Just now you need to take some time.' He cast a glance at the slim shards of light coming through the boards of the door. 'There's nobody in here except us. If you want to … grieve, nobody will see, nobody will hear.'

Martin had moved back towards the nauseating mess in the stall. He fell to his knees and put out a hand to stroke the dead horse's face. 'He was mine. He was just for me, my companion. We were going to spend years together.' His face started to crumple.

'I know he was. He was a fine steed, like the ones you hear about in stories.' Edwin risked taking a step closer.

'He was. So why did this have to happen? Why?'

Upon the last word, Martin collapsed and began weeping. Edwin knelt beside him and held his head as he shook and sobbed, crying into the front of Edwin's tunic like an abandoned child.

They stayed like that for quite some while, giving Edwin a chance to look more closely – however much he wanted to avoid it – at the carcass of the horse.

Eventually Martin's storm of weeping subsided, and he looked up. 'Sorry.' He stood up and turned his back. 'Sorry.'

'It's all right,' said Edwin, gently. 'Now, do you think you could bear to look at Fauvel again? I don't know much about horses, so I'd like to check some things with you – it would help me.'

'Yes,' replied Martin, still with his back to Edwin as he scrubbed his sleeve over his face. 'Yes.' There was a pause, and then, slowly, he turned.

Edwin forced himself to keep his voice level. 'It looks as though he was killed by having his throat cut.'

'Yes.'

'Would that mean … he died quite quickly?'

'Yes. I've seen it done once before and heard about others. If you cut deep enough it stops the breathing as well as causing the bleeding. The horse just stands there for a few moments and then collapses.'

'And that causes a lot of blood, like this.'

'Yes.'

Edwin looked at the huge, congealing, sickening pool. 'This didn't happen very recently – it must have been overnight.'

Martin nodded. 'They found him when they came in this morning.'

'All right. Now, as to the …' Edwin pointed to the ears, eyes and tongue.

Even in the dim light he could see Martin's face tighten. 'Anyone who could do that to a—'

'It's cruel. But I think at least it was done after death. See how there is very little blood around the ear wounds?' he pointed.

Martin bent. 'I suppose so.' His voice was shaky. 'That's one thing to be thankful for, I suppose. Poor Fauvel.' He stroked the lifeless neck with tenderness. And then, after a pause, 'But why?'

'I think someone is trying to send us a message.' Edwin pointed. 'Don't hear anything, don't see anything, don't say anything.'

There was a long moment of silence. 'I tell you, Edwin, when I find out who's behind this …'

'You will control yourself and act within the law, I hope.'

'Yes, but—'

'Please. I'm asking – no, I'm *begging* you, please just leave this in my hands for now. There's … an awful lot going on, and I need to sort through it all.' Edwin hoped fervently that Martin would not hear of the witchcraft accusation against Joanna while he was still in this state, or it might tip him over the edge.

Or maybe that had been somebody's aim all along.

'Look,' said Edwin, in reply to Martin's silence. 'I'm going to go out now, to start asking some questions.'

'Take Willikin with you,' was Martin's immediate response. 'It's too dangerous for you to be anywhere on your own.'

'Only if I can safely leave you here without him.'

Martin made a helpless gesture. 'I won't cause violence, I promise. Or at least not yet.'

'You're sure?'

Martin took a deep breath, then choked, spitting out a fly. 'Yes.'

'Will you stay here?'

'Just for a while.'

'All right. I'll ask them to leave you alone for the time being, but we'll open the door.'

He left Martin to stare and to mourn alone, and made his way to the entrance.

He knocked softly. 'It's me, Edwin. You can open up now.'

The door creaked open and Edwin was met by the sight of the Conisbrough men and, behind them, a slightly smaller crowd than there had been earlier.

He looked about him until he spotted the stable boy. 'Can I talk to you? I mean no harm,' he added, hastily, as the lad looked set to flee again. 'I just want to ask you a few questions about what you might have seen and heard.' The boy looked fearfully at the open stable door. 'And we can do it away from here, if you prefer.'

The boy nodded and went over to an older man, tugging at his sleeve and asking him something. The man looked over at Edwin and then nodded.

'Good,' said Edwin. 'How about we sit over there under cover?' He pointed to a space on the other side of the ward, under the wall walk and away from the stable, the slaughtered bullock carcass and the horses being led round in an attempt to calm them.

'Now,' he continued, when they were safely perched on a barrel, Willikin standing at a discreet distance. 'There's no need to be scared – none of this is your fault at all, and I just want to find out as much as I can about what happened. Is that all right?'

'Yes. And anyway, I'm not scared.'

'Of course you're not. What's your name?'

'Matthew.'

'And you work in the stables, do you, Matthew?'

'Yes.'

'For how long?'

'Since last year. Before that I was too small.'

'And you enjoy it?'

'Oh yes – I like horses. Much better than working out in the fields. Except …' his lip began to wobble.

'You saw a terrible sight this morning,' said Edwin, gently. 'And it might take you a little while to feel better about it. But you will.'

Matthew said nothing, merely folding his arms tight across his chest.

'So, do you actually sleep in the stable at night?'

'No. There's no room, so we sleep in there.' He pointed to one of the buildings in the outer ward. 'It's where we store the bran and such. You don't want to keep it in the stable itself.' His boldness returned as he showed off his knowledge to a stranger.

'I see. And you were in there last night? Just like usual?'

'Yes.'

'And did you hear anything?'

Matthew nodded. 'I heard some kicking around, so I woke up Mark – that's my brother, he works here too – to tell him. But he said it was probably just the horses getting restless, like they have been a lot recently, and to go back to sleep.'

'Why have they been getting restless?'

The boy looked at him with such scorn that Edwin had to suppress a smile. 'Because they've had no exercise,' he spelled out, as though talking to someone of slow wits. 'And because with all the snow and wet around, more rats than usual have come in the stable.'

'Because it's dry and warm there?'

'You know something, then.' He sniffed.

'So this wasn't the first time you've heard horses kicking about in their stalls at night.'

'I just said, didn't I?'

'Do you have any idea what time it was? Soon after you went to bed? Or nearer to dawn?'

Matthew thought for a moment and then shrugged. 'Don't know. It was dark and it was in the night – that's all.'

'And you didn't hear anything else – no men talking, no horses screaming?'

'No.' The boy went quiet for a moment, his brashness ebbing away again. 'Would it have screamed, then? The horse? When …'

'No, not at all. I've spoken to my friend – he knows all about horses – and he said it would have been over very quickly. Fauvel wouldn't have known much about it.'

'Fauvel? Was that the horse's name?'

'Yes.'

'Finest one I've ever seen. And it belonged to him – that great tall knight?'

'He's not a knight, not yet anyway, but yes, it was his horse. He's very upset.'

'He's scary, that's what he is.'

'I suppose he is. He didn't mean to frighten you – he'd never hurt anyone who didn't deserve it.'

'Yeah, but who gets to decide who deserves it?' asked Matthew, making Edwin pause in surprise at the unexpected philosophical question. 'Anyway, I'd better get back to work.' He jumped down off the barrel.

'I wonder,' said Edwin, a thought striking him. 'I wonder if they might spare you just for today or a couple of days – I could do with a lad to help me out, to run errands and fetch people. A bright boy who knows his way around the place.'

Matthew puffed out his chest. 'That's me, that is.'

'Who would I ask?'

Matthew pointed to the man Edwin had seen him speaking to earlier.

It was soon arranged; the gossip about who Edwin was and why he was there had evidently got around. Edwin found himself heading back to the inner ward with Matthew striding proudly behind him, looking around in a superior manner at those less fortunate mortals who were busy with their usual tasks, and Willikin bringing up the rear.

Edwin headed for the steward's office, unsure if it was because he genuinely thought it the best place, or whether it was simply that the aroma of spices reminded him of home and of a time when things were simpler.

'I'm just on my way to the kitchen,' said Joscelin, a list of some description in his hand and a harried look on his face. 'Did you need me?'

'Actually I was wondering if I could use your office. It's as good a place as any for me to talk to people in confidence – more so than the keep or the hall.'

'Yes, yes of course – help yourself. I'll be on my way.'

With Matthew's help, Edwin made some small rearrangements to the furniture. Anyone he was talking to would sit in the best light from the door and the window, while he himself stayed further back in the shadow. 'And your job,' he said to Matthew, 'will be to run and fetch people for me, and then to stay outside with Willikin and make sure we're not disturbed. Like a proper guard.'

Matthew's pride swelled even further.

'Now, I think I'll start with a woman called Mabel. She normally lives in the village, but she's here in the castle at the moment. Do you know her?'

'Course I do. And her sons.' His tone dripped with scorn. 'Her eldest, Nick, he thinks he's so much better than me, because Sir Nicholas was his father, but he's nothing but a bastard, that's what I say.'

'Well, try not to say that to Mabel when you find her, or you might get your ears boxed. Off you go now.'

The boy rushed out the door so fast that he created a draught, and some of Joscelin's parchments fell to the floor. Edwin collected them all up, placing them back on the table next to the exchequer board and looking about him for something to use as a weight. As he put a candlestick down on them, he glanced at some of the figures. Startled, he looked at the board, and then back at the parchment. Well, well.

His thought was interrupted by the arrival of Mabel, announced with a blunt, 'He's in there,' by Matthew.

Edwin quickly took his chosen seat and waved Mabel to the one he'd set out for her. She seemed to be a mixture of anger, defiance and nervousness.

He decided to go on the attack straight away. 'Why are you accusing Lady Joanna of witchcraft? And what specific evidence do you have?'

'Might have known you'd stand up for her.'

'That's not what I'm doing. I'm here to find out the truth, and the fact that you seem unable to answer my question makes me think you might be making it all up.'

'She's a witch, I tell you. Should be burned for it.'

'And your justification for this is …? Otherwise it's just slander, for which you could find yourself up before the manor court yourself.'

'That baby isn't Nicholas's.'

'So I've heard from several people, and not very convincingly. She can't have been near another man at the time the child was conceived, so early in their marriage.'

'But that's why she's a witch!' exclaimed Mabel, in evident triumph.

'I'm not following you.'

For the second time that day, Edwin found himself being spoken to very slowly. 'She wasn't with another man. She's conjured that baby up out of thin air.' She leaned forward, her eyes sparkling. 'Witchcraft. Like I already told you, the other day.'

The assertion was so ludicrous that, for a moment, Edwin could hardly believe it. He paused, waiting for more, waiting for *something*, but Mabel merely sat back, satisfied that she'd made her point.

'And Father Clement agrees with you on this, does he?'

'He thinks she's a witch, too. You saw him with me this morning, and you can't argue with a priest on something like that.' She gave him a triumphant look.

'He really believes that Lady Joanna gave birth to a child that has no human father.'

'Yes.'

'Like the Blessed Virgin Mary, whom he admires so much.'

'Yes.' She realised what she'd said. 'I mean, no. I mean—'

'I know perfectly well what you mean,' snapped Edwin. 'You mean that you've made this whole pathetic story up in order to whip up feeling against Lady Joanna. Which you hardly needed to do – opinion seems to be against her all round.'

'No, I—'

'But what can you possibly hope to gain? Trying to say that the child is illegitimate so he can't inherit is one thing, but that wouldn't help you or your sons in any case – it wouldn't make them any less illegitimate.'

She mumbled something that might or might not have been, 'We'll see about that.'

This reminded Edwin of something. 'Of course. When we were in your cottage the other day, I thought you'd called Lady Joanna a "bitch", so I ignored it. You actually said "witch", didn't you? And when I didn't protest, it led you on to continue with these accusations.'

She opened her mouth to reply, but he forestalled her. 'What I want to know is, how did you manage to persuade Father Clement to back you up? I know he doesn't like her, but from what I've heard he doesn't think much of you, either. I'm surprised he should go along with it.'

Her mouth set in a thin line.

'Anyway, surely if you loved Sir Nicholas, as you say you did, your first concern should be finding out who killed him? Everything you're doing is just muddying the waters and preventing that from happening.'

'My first concern,' she said, rising from her stool and pointing a finger at him, 'is, and always will be, for my children. Now, if we're quite finished …' she swept out.

Edwin sat for a moment, thinking. Then Willikin poked his head through the doorway. 'Was I supposed to stop her? You said to make sure nobody came in to disturb you – I wasn't sure what to do about someone coming out.'

'It's all right,' Edwin reassured him. 'I might need to talk to her again later, but it's not as if she's going anywhere.'

'Nobody is,' piped up Matthew. 'The water's rising again and it's starting to come under the fence.'

He pointed to the other side of the ward, where Luke was supervising a group of men piling sandbags up at the base of the palisade.

'I've never seen it this bad,' continued the boy, cheerfully. 'Do you think we'll all have to sit on the roof?'

'Let's hope not,' said Edwin, but he was worried. A flooded castle, with the associated panic and potential loss of stores, was the last thing he needed. 'Anyway,' he said briskly, 'the next person I need to talk to is Lady Joanna. We won't be able to ask her to come here, so we'll go to the keep.'

'The keep?' Matthew's eyes were round. 'Me? In the keep?'

'Don't worry, lad,' said Willikin, cheerfully. 'I won't let anyone eat you.'

Once they were inside Edwin wasted no time in making his way up the stairs to the solar, the others following. Inside were Joanna, Emma, Ada and the baby, and Milo.

'I need to talk to Lady Joanna alone,' announced Edwin.

'Well, I'm not leaving,' declared Emma.

That put Edwin in a quandary. He did need privacy, but he could hardly send women and a baby outside in this weather. 'Very well,' he said. 'We'll go into the chamber.' He hesitated, aware that yet more rumours might start. 'We'll leave the door open so you can see us talking, but Willikin will stand by it to make sure nobody gets too close.'

Emma, unsurprisingly, seemed offended at this implication that she might eavesdrop, but she dared not respond to Edwin or the hulking presence at his side. Instead, she turned to the person she could bully with impunity, slapping Matthew sharply around the back of the head. 'I'm not having this filthy stable brat in my solar, though – get him out.'

Matthew was on the point of making a retort, which was not a scene Edwin wanted to create. 'You go downstairs, Matthew. There's a fire there; you can sit by it while you wait for me. If anyone comes in the keep, tell them I said not to come up here.'

The boy gave Emma a poisonous look and marched towards the door.

'Right,' sighed Edwin. He followed Joanna into the chamber, where she seated herself on the bed and he remained standing, careful to ensure that both of them were visible to those in the solar.

'I heard about Martin's horse,' were her first words, spoken in a low voice. 'Is he …?'

'He's as upset as you'd expect him to be.'

'What a horrible, cruel, *spiteful* thing to do. But surely whoever killed the horse would be covered in blood? And it must have been someone who's still in the castle.' A shiver ran through her.

'Unfortunately, it's coincided with the slaughtering of the bull calf, so there's blood everywhere in the outer ward – lots of men are splashed with it.'

'Oh.'

'I've promised him I'll get to the bottom of it, but just now I need to talk to you about something else.' He filled her in on Mabel's allegations of witchcraft, his own belief that they were entirely spurious, but also the danger of others believing the gossip.

She listened in silence, and then gave a hollow, despairing laugh. 'Being burned for one crime I didn't commit is no worse than being burned for another, I suppose.'

'Nobody is going to burn you – not if I have anything to do with it. And besides, I can spread a bit of gossip of my own, seeing as that's how everything seems to work round here.'

'How so?'

'Our men have moved in downstairs – a few words can be dropped in here and there about how fearsome they are and that challenging them would be foolish. Nobody would try to get past them and get in.'

'Well, yes,' said Joanna, eyeing Willikin as he stood outside the chamber door. She raised her voice a little. 'I recognise your friend there from my Conisbrough days. I'm sorry I can't recall his name, but I'd feel as safe as the queen of England with him guarding me.'

Willikin didn't move, but Edwin saw his ears redden.

'Now, on to something else. I want you to tell me about Ada.'

'Ada?' Joanna frowned. 'Surely she can't have anything to do with all this?'

'Nevertheless.'

'Very well. What do you want to know?'

'How did she come to be your wet-nurse? She must have had a baby of her own – where is it?'

Joanna sighed. 'She did, but it died.' She crossed herself.

'She's married?'

'No; that's one of the odd things about it. She's not married, and she refused to tell anyone – even her own mother – who the child's father was. Of course, with morals like that she's not the sort of girl I would normally have chosen to nurse my baby, but it's a small village and she was the only one in milk at the time, so Nicholas insisted. There have been several more births since, of course, but we got used to having her around, and John seems content with her, so there didn't seem to be any need for change.'

'As a matter of interest, what did everyone else think about her situation? Was there gossip?'

'Plenty. And of course, Father Clement wanted her driven out of the village, but her family protested and Nicholas supported them. They're good workers and they don't cause any trouble.'

'And you?'

'Well … look at her. I know she sinned, but surely she's foolish rather than wicked? Some boy in the village or a soldier of the garrison took advantage of her and left her to face the consequences on her own.' Her voice hardened. 'As often happens to women, of all stations.'

Edwin was just taking all this in when yet another disturbance occurred. Mabel, her son and Father Clement entered the solar, with Aubrey trailing along behind them.

Matthew darted in, ran past them and over to Edwin, hovering by the door of the bedchamber. 'I'm sorry. I told them not to come up, that you'd said so, but they told me to get out the way, they were coming up no matter what, and he's the *priest*. I couldn't—'

'It's all right,' Edwin reassured him. 'It's not your fault.'

Matthew retreated, he and Nick aiming a reciprocal kick at each other as he passed.

With a feeling of overwhelming fatigue, Edwin turned to the little group. 'What *now*? And don't start again with those ridiculous accusations of witchcraft.'

Mabel sniffed. 'I still say that brat isn't Nicholas's.' She gestured over to Ada, who had picked up the baby and was turning away from the newcomers in a defensive gesture. 'But it doesn't matter, because it's a bastard anyway.'

Edwin was genuinely puzzled. 'I don't follow you.'

'Nicholas was never married to her at all.'

Joanna pushed past Edwin. 'He most certainly was. There are records and witnesses.'

'Oh, yes, you stood there and said the words, but they meant nothing. Nicholas couldn't marry you, because he was already married to me.'

There was a moment of absolute, stunned silence.

It was Emma who broke it. 'Liar!'

'It's true!' Mabel pushed the priest forward. 'Tell them!'

'Yes,' said Father Clement, distantly, keeping his gaze straight ahead and not meeting anyone's eye. 'Yes, I married them some years ago in a secret ceremony.'

'So,' said Mabel, triumphantly, 'This castle and everything in it belongs to my boy Nick.' She placed a proud and possessive hand on the bemused child's shoulder.

Emma and Joanna both began speaking at once, with Aubrey ineffectually trying to stop them.

Edwin broke through the noise, addressing the priest. 'Father,' he warned, 'You of all people should be aware that lying about such a matter endangers your immortal soul.'

'Many things endanger one's chances of entering heaven,' was the slightly cryptic reply.

Mabel shot him a hard glance. 'And your enjoyment of the life we have now on earth.'

There was definitely something not quite right here, but Edwin couldn't as yet work out what it was. He did have one certainty, though: 'That's not what you said when I spoke to you the other day at your cottage. Back then, you said, "I knew we could never be married".'

'Well, of course I said that then,' she replied, in an obvious attempt to buy time while she thought of something better. 'But I needed to be here, in the castle, to make the claim properly, didn't I?' She prodded the boy forward. 'So all of this is Nick's, and my two other sons next in line.'

'I don't see them,' said the still seething Emma, looking pointedly past Mabel to the door.

'They're not here just now; they're safe in the village. I had one of the garrison shout across, and Joscelin's wife has taken them in for now until I get back. Anyway, of course they're not here – you know as well as I do that nobody can get in or out while the flood lasts. It doesn't make a difference to my claim.'

'Nick's claim, surely?' interposed Edwin.

'Well, I'm his mother, so while he's young it's my claim too. He'll need me to help him push *her* and her bastard brat out of the way.' She turned to Joanna. 'Didn't do you much good, did it, killing Nicholas?' she goaded.

Joanna lost even the veneer of calm – not only furious at the accusation but also panicking, Edwin guessed, about the threat to her son. 'It's all lies! Nicholas would never have married you! And he went out to break it all off with you just before he died!'

Emma joined in – also worried, no doubt, about the inheritance that had seemed like it might be hers. 'A village slut like you? He would lie with you, to be sure, but *marry*? Never!'

The noise got louder. Edwin wasn't quite sure how to intervene in a dispute between women: he could hardly wade right into it, or order Willikin to separate them physically. But the situation was becoming more intense. The baby started crying, causing Ada to walk up and down with him in an anxious way that did nothing to calm him, while Father Clement stepped away from her as though he feared being contaminated. Matthew had sidled over to hide behind Willikin. Aubrey was just standing there with his mouth open.

It was that last which caused Edwin's temper to snap. 'STOP!' he shouted, surprising them all enough to cause a brief lull, into which he dived. 'Stop it, all of you. Aubrey, for the love of God will you *do* something – take Mabel and Father Clement somewhere and get to the bottom of this claimed marriage.' Aubrey's face was blank. 'Names, dates, witnesses – every single detail.'

Father Clement recovered enough to speak. 'You dare question my word?'

'Yes, Father, I do. I don't know why, but you're lying to me. And if Mabel wants to claim a whole estate, she's going to have to do better than stand here and make wild accusations – you both will. There will be legal enquiries, and no doubt your bishop will have something to say about how you've acted.' Edwin was really angry now – all this was just throwing hurdles in his path and making everything more difficult. 'I don't think he'll be particularly pleased with you either way: either you carried out a clandestine marriage ceremony, kept it secret and then allowed Sir Nicholas to take later, bigamous vows, or you did nothing of the sort and you're telling a pack of lies now for reasons of your own. How do you think that's going to look to your superiors?'

Sweat broke out on the priest's forehead and he cast a nervous glance at Mabel, who returned a look as hard as flint.

Edwin said nothing more, but his mind began to work, and with Willikin's help he shepherded Mabel, Nick, Father Clement and Aubrey towards the door to the stairwell.

Once they were safely through Edwin shut it with relief and turned to Joanna and Emma. 'Well, for once it looks like you have a common cause.'

Neither of them looked particularly thrilled at the prospect.

Edwin rubbed his face. 'I'm going to go and talk to as many castle men as I can – garrison, servants, grooms, everybody. Seeing as every single facet of this whole situation is based on gossip and what people say about other people, I may as well fill myself up with it.' He beckoned to Willikin and Matthew. 'We'll go back to the steward's office.'

He was on the point of leaving when he remembered. 'Which reminds me,' he said to both ladies, 'Does either of you have any idea why Joscelin is swindling the castle accounts?'

Chapter Ten

By the middle of the afternoon Edwin was about ready to give it all up and head back to Conisbrough, even if he had to swim there.

Every single man in the castle had an opinion about his lord, his lady, his fellow servants or soldiers, everything. Edwin could substantiate none of it, but he sat and listened to it all, nevertheless, making brief notes on a scrap of parchment whenever he felt something might be worth pursuing, or if several men all said the same thing.

It was just as he was dismissing the fourth groom in a row to lament the loss of such a fine horse and the additional work it would cause to clear everything up and make the stable fit to put the others back in, that Joscelin entered. Edwin raised his eyebrows at Matthew, who sped off on his agreed errand.

To fill in time, Edwin engaged the steward in chat about the kitchens and thanked him for sending over bread and pottage for them, the remains of which still lay on the table. He hadn't wanted to go to dinner either in the keep or in the hall.

'Have you picked up anything useful from any of the men?' asked Joscelin.

'I've heard a great deal, but whether or not any of it is actually useful, I can't tell.' Edwin sighed. 'I have men willing to swear both that Father Clement was in the castle that night and that he wasn't. The same of Mabel. Reports of dubious strangers lurking about; suspicions that Sir Nicholas was the father of half the children in the village; and so many tales about Lady Joanna that it's hardly worth going through them.' He poked his notes. 'Plus a few about Lady Emma. I'm not sure some of the men around here like any women at all.'

Matthew slipped back in the room and nodded, and Edwin saw shadows outside the door. Turold, Tom and Lambert should all now be standing outside with Willikin, in case the situation got difficult, as it probably would; Joscelin was hardly likely to just confess out of hand. Edwin had considered trying to have Martin fetched as well but had decided against it – he was just too volatile at the moment, and besides, the other Conisbrough men would be perfectly sufficient to subdue one civilian steward if it came to it.

It was time. 'By the way, when I was in here this morning,' Edwin began, with deceptive mildness, 'these all fell on the floor.' He indicated the lists of accounts. 'So I picked them up and weighed them down so they didn't blow away.'

'Oh … my thanks,' replied Joscelin, moving towards the pieces of parchment like a protective father.

'I couldn't help looking at them, especially as I was right next to your exchequer board. Tell me,' he continued, conversationally, 'how long have you been falsifying the accounts?'

Joscelin gaped, his mouth open like a fish. Then a hint of something Edwin couldn't quite interpret appeared in his eye, and he sat down abruptly. 'Yes, yes I am. I admit it.'

Edwin couldn't hide his surprise.

'I've been doing it for some time,' continued the steward. 'All my own idea, and all to enrich myself.' He folded his hands in his lap and stared straight ahead.

Edwin was so taken aback that he couldn't, at first, work out what to say. 'And … nobody else was involved?' he managed, eventually.

'Nobody,' came the firm reply.

'Hmm. And what did you spend it on?'

There was the slightest pause. 'Oh, you know.' He made a vague gesture. 'Fine clothes and possessions, that sort of thing.'

Edwin looked pointedly at Joscelin's faded and patched tunic.

'For my wife and family,' he added, hurriedly. 'Obviously I didn't want to appear too gaudy here in case suspicions were raised.'

'Hmmmm,' said Edwin, again, drawing the sound out longer this time and leaving Joscelin to recall that Edwin had seen his shivering, badly dressed children in the village.

'I deeply regret what I've been doing – actually it's a relief to confess to it – and I'm ready to take my punishment, whatever it may be. After that my family and I will leave here and I'll start a new, honest life somewhere else.'

Edwin was flummoxed. Something was evidently not right here, but he couldn't put his finger on what it was. 'Turold,' he called.

Turold put his head round the door. 'No trouble?'

'None, oddly,' Edwin replied, his forehead creasing as he looked at Joscelin sitting serenely.

'He's confessed? What are we to do with him?'

Edwin turned to Joscelin. 'For now, I'm going to let you retain the freedom of the castle. You can't get out, and to be honest I don't think anyone will eat properly if you're not available to organise the meals. *But*, my men will be keeping a close eye on you, so don't attempt anything foolish.'

'You're not going to lock me up?'

'No more than we're all locked up for the foreseeable future.'

'Are you sure?' That was Turold.

'Where could he go? Unless he's going to jump over the wall into freezing water and swim for it. Besides,' Edwin added, an idea beginning to form in his mind, 'I'm sure he wouldn't flee and leave his family behind him.'

He was watching Joscelin as he said the words and saw him flinch. Yes. Edwin's idea would be worth pursuing.

'In that case, may I go and check on the salting of the meat?'

'You may. But remember what I said. Oh, and give me your keys.'

Joscelin rose, untied the bunch of keys from his belt, laid them on the table and left, all without saying another word. After a murmured conversation between the men, Tom broke off from the others to follow the steward at a discreet distance.

Edwin sat down and drummed his fingers on the table. So much information had come his way in such a short space of time today that it was all jumbled in his mind. He needed some time and space to think.

The fact that he was in a steward's office should help. The spice chest in the corner was giving off scents familiar to him since childhood; he closed his eyes and inhaled. Cinnamon, his favourite. Some sugar was just about discernible among the sharper aromas of ginger and pepper. And … something else.

Edwin opened his eyes again. What was that odd smell? He wrinkled his nose. Certainly no spice he'd ever encountered. Or maybe it wasn't a spice – there was a tang of bitter herbs, reminding him of some of the remedies made up by his aunt Cecily, who tended the sick and dressed all the bruises, blains and cuts in Conisbrough.

Joscelin's keys were right in front of him. His curiosity piqued, Edwin moved to the spice chest, found the right key and opened it. The usual packets and jars were there, but the other aroma was stronger … ah. He pulled out a small, stoppered clay vessel. He sniffed. Yes, that was definitely it.

He took it back to the table, wary of removing the stopper. Could it be poison? But if so, how and when had it been used? Sir Nicholas had been murdered with a knife, and there had been no other fatalities except the horse, killed in the same manner. Or was it for future use? Or … oh, of course. Well, there was one way to find out.

He called out to Matthew and the boy bounded in. 'Did you say there had been many more rats than usual in the stables recently?'

'Yes.'

'Think you could catch me one?'

'Why do you want a rat?'

'Never mind that. Can you?'

'Of course I can.'

'Good. Go there now, find one and bring it back to me – alive, I mean.' He recalled the scene in the stable that morning. 'Lambert? Are you still there? Go with him, please, and if you run into Martin, tell him you're there on my orders. Hopefully he should have calmed down by now.'

Lambert went pale at the thought of returning to the stable, but he lifted his chin. 'Of course.'

The boys set off and Edwin returned to his thoughts, trying to unpick the tangled threads so he could weave them into a logical pattern.

Lambert and Matthew seemed to return very quickly; or perhaps it was just that Edwin didn't know how much time had passed. They were carrying between them a squeaking, rattling bucket over which they had placed a piece of wood as a makeshift lid. They put it on the table and stood back to watch, Turold and Willikin also hovering to see what was going on.

The plate containing the remains of that morning's dinner was still on the table, and Edwin found a crust of bread. Then, at arm's length, he unstoppered the earthenware jar and dripped some of the contents on to it. Interestingly, although the smell coming from the vessel was strong, it dissipated a little once it soaked into the bread; only someone with a nose as good as Edwin's would really notice it. Swiftly, he lifted the lid of the bucket, dropped in the bread, replaced the lid and stepped back.

The squeaking noise immediately turned to chewing. Edwin waited, listening. After some while all movement ceased and he risked opening the lid. They all peered in to see the rat lying on its side.

'Poison?' asked Matthew. 'Have you killed it?'

'I may have done, which is why I wanted a rat. But if I'm right …' gingerly Edwin put his hand into the bucket and touched the rat. It was warm, breathing and had a heartbeat. 'I thought so.'

Turold grasped the significance first, and gave a whistle. 'A sleeping draught?'

'Yes,' replied Edwin, making sure the jar was firmly sealed once more.

'And in here?'

'Yes, though that doesn't necessarily mean it was Joscelin who used it.'

More thoughts were starting to order themselves in Edwin's head. 'Right,' he said. 'It's getting dark already, so it won't be long until your meal is ready in the keep. You all head over and get something to eat. Check with Tom, though I have no doubt Joscelin hasn't been doing anything suspicious now he knows we're watching him, and then maybe swap over.'

Willikin shook his head. 'I'm to stay with you.'

Edwin hesitated. 'All right. But please just stay quiet.'

It was an unnecessary injunction, he knew – nobody was less likely to ask questions than Willikin. Edwin listened as the others moved away and across the inner ward, Matthew's high and excited voice the most prominent. 'Can I come with you? And eat in the keep instead of going into the hall? Oh, wait until I tell Mark …'

Edwin settled down again. He finally had one real, solid piece of evidence. He was not merely being *told* that there was a sleeping draught in the castle; he had it right here in front of him. If it had been administered to Sir Nicholas and the others, either by Joscelin or by someone else – and he was keeping an open mind on that at the moment – then it would explain why Joanna had slept so soundly that she didn't wake when someone crept into the bedchamber, and also why Sir Nicholas had been killed without a fight. Of course, it also caused a problem in that it widened considerably Edwin's pool of suspects. If all those in the solar were fast asleep, anyone could have come in from outside. And, of course, to slit the throat of an unconscious sleeper was much easier than trying to kill a man – a knight – who might rouse in an instant and fight back.

The next obvious question was: Why a sleeping draught? If someone could successfully doctor Sir Nicholas's food, why not simply poison him? Why go to the bother of drugging him and then cutting his throat, which had its own risks even under the circumstances? But another moment showed Edwin an equally evident answer: the food eaten in the solar would be shared by everybody, and the culprit only wanted to kill Sir Nicholas. He (or she?) needed Joanna to remain alive so that she could be set up to take the blame. And there might be other reasons, too.

Thinking of the word 'she' turned Edwin's mind again to Mabel, and also to Emma and Ada. Mabel was clearly taking advantage of the confused situation to make a concerted play for power – nominally on behalf of her son, but also for herself. She claimed that Sir Nicholas had remained faithful to her, but Joanna thought that he'd intended to break off the illicit relationship, or indeed that he had actually done so.

Which brought matters back to the question of Mabel's claim that they had actually been married, which would make Joanna's later union invalid – and would make Mabel's sons legitimate and Joanna's not. Was it true? And, crucially, had Joanna known of the claim before Sir Nicholas died?

When the truth of the matter finally came to light, one or other of these women would see her son lose out. Which raised yet another obvious question in Edwin's mind: how far would either of them go to protect the rights of their children?

⸻

Martin didn't know how long he'd been in the stable, but he suspected it was many hours.

After Edwin left, he'd slumped down on some straw, initially in Fauvel's own stall, but the buzzing clouds of blood-gorged flies had got too much, and he'd moved into the next one. The smell was also overwhelming, but he didn't object to that – the constant reminder of what had happened to his beloved Fauvel helped to fuel his anger.

The hot, lightning flash of incandescent rage of earlier had faded, along with the shock and panic. Now what he felt was an immense, slow-burning fury that would hold steady until he could let it all out; preferably at the right person, but if not then at anyone who got in his way. He would try, for Edwin's sake, to keep the fire dampened until he was told the identity of the culprit, but Edwin would be patient forever if he needed to be. He just didn't understand. He was a clever man, a pleasant man and a good friend. But he wasn't a knight, and he had no idea of the way in which knights were supposed to think and to comport themselves. In particular, he had no idea of the depth of feeling that could exist between a man whose whole life was geared around being a mounted warrior, and his horse.

Every so often, the stable door would open a crack and one of the grooms would poke his head round. But Martin wasn't ready to come out or to be disturbed, so he growled at them until they went away. Towards what he judged to be the later end of the morning it all went quiet; the men heading up to the hall for their dinner, no doubt. Martin was hungry himself, but he couldn't bring himself to stand up and walk out, not yet.

As the afternoon wore on, he realised that the men really would need to enter so they could clean up before allowing the other horses back in. Martin still didn't want to move, but the thought that the horses might still be outside in the rain after it got dark persuaded him – it wouldn't be good for them.

He got to his feet and stood over the body of Fauvel for a few moments, swearing to himself that the death would be avenged. Then he moved to open the door wide so he could face the world.

Almost the first sight that met his eye was Lambert, along with the stable boy Martin had seen earlier. The lad started back, but Martin held up a calming hand. 'It's all right. I'm sorry if I frightened you earlier.'

'I wasn't afraid,' said the boy, stoutly but from a pace behind Lambert.

'Good lad,' replied Martin. 'A few others in this castle could do with your spirit.'

As the boy's face brightened, Martin turned to Lambert. 'Were you looking for me?'

'No, or at least, not exactly. Edwin sent Matthew here to fetch him a rat, and I was to come with him to explain that to you if you were still here. So you didn't send him away, I mean.'

'A rat? Why in the Lord's name does he want a rat?' As Lambert opened his mouth to reply, Martin went on. 'No, never mind – I'm sure it's a very long story, and you're best off just doing as he says. Is Willikin still with him?'

'Yes.'

'Good.'

Martin rubbed his face as he watched the boys disappear into the stable. The grooms were looking at him warily from their scattered positions around the ward, and Martin noticed that one or two of the horses looked a bit cold. His fault. He caught the eye of the stable-master, nodded to him without speaking and walked off.

But where to go, and what to do? Edwin was no doubt holed up somewhere working on matters of great detail, and Martin just couldn't face that just now. Normally his default position if at a loose end would be to train or ride, but of course neither of those things were possible. And he had no horse to go and see to.

He crossed the bridge, now only an inch or two higher than the water, and reached the inner ward. Why was everyone staring at him?

Martin was about to send the curious onlookers about their business when he noticed for the first time that he was caked with dried blood. Ah. That would probably do it.

He directed his steps towards the keep, remembering as he did so that his other clothes, the ones he'd been wearing when he was in the river, were screwed up in a ball in the corner of the guest chamber. He cursed himself – what had he been thinking of? He would never have done such a thing with the lord earl's garments. But damp and muddy was probably better than bloodied, so he would change anyway.

He was surprised, on entering the keep, to find that his shirt, hose and tunic were draped over stools near the fire, having apparently been cleaned.

Milo looked up from where he was sorting through another pile of clothes. 'I saw them on the floor in the chamber,' he explained, his voice hovering on the edge of nervousness. 'Sir Nicholas often did the same, so it seemed natural to pick them up.'

'So it should, for a squire. I don't know what I was thinking when I threw them there. And now …' he looked down at himself.

Milo drew nearer. 'Hmm. The mud was one thing – that brushed off quite easily once it was dry. But this is another; that tunic will need a proper wash, and I'm afraid there are no laundry women inside the castle at the moment.' He hesitated. 'I could see what I can do with a bucket of water, at least, if you like?'

'My thanks,' said Martin, unbuckling his belt and beginning to work his way out of the stinking, stiffened garment. 'I haven't looked like this since we were at Sandwich last year.'

Milo gasped. 'You were there? What – actually on one of the ships?'

'Yes. You know of the battle?'

'It didn't take long for tidings to reach us, though I didn't hear many details about how the fighting was actually carried out. You were on foot? On a ship out at sea?'

As he got changed, appreciating the dry, warm shirt, Martin sketched out some of what had happened on that fateful day. He hadn't known it at the time, but it had been the engagement that brought the war to an end. Prince Louis and the regent had reached terms not long afterwards, and the would-be usurper had sailed back to France.

Milo wasn't overly interested in the grand political situation; he wanted to hear about the combat. As he spoke, Martin felt some thawing of his feelings towards the boy. He was in a difficult situation, no doubt about it, and squires should stick together. As he recounted his part in the battle, he remembered the energy and the rage that had coursed through his veins – and how it had both frightened and exhilarated him at the same time. When would he ever experience that again?

After some while he felt the need to change the subject. 'What are those?'

Milo glanced at the jumble on the table. 'My lord's clothes. Lady Joanna kept them all upstairs for a while – as a kind of keepsake, I suppose. Who knows what women are thinking? But now she's decided to get rid of them. She said if there was anything I particularly wanted, I could have it, but these are all too fine for me, and besides …' he held up a tunic, and Martin could see that Sir Nicholas had been rather a fat man. If Milo tried to put that on, it would be about the right length but it would go round him twice.

'Is Lady Joanna upstairs now?' asked Martin, before realising that the question was unnecessary. 'Sorry – yes, of course she is. Where else would she be?'

He was starting to move towards the stairs when he stopped and turned back to the squire. 'It was you who found the body, I gather.'

Milo was immediately wary. 'Yes. I went into the chamber just as I usually did first thing in the morning, and …'

'I know what you saw,' said Martin. 'Edwin told me what you said. But tell me – are you really certain, in your heart, about what happened?'

'I – I don't know,' said Milo. He sat down. 'To start with my lady's guilt seemed certain; how else to account for what I saw? But now, with all these confusing things going on … but I just can't work out what else might have happened.'

That was a start, at least. Martin said no more and made his way up the stairs.

Inside the solar he found, as he expected, Joanna, Emma and Ada. No doubt the child was there somewhere as well, but Martin didn't bother to look for it.

Ignoring the others, he walked over to Joanna, who was in the window seat making the best of the fading light for some sewing she had in her hand. She smiled up at him and indicated that he should sit.

'I'm so sorry to hear about Fauvel,' were her first words. She laid down her work and gave him her full attention. 'I know how much he must have meant to you.'

Martin felt a sting in his eye, but he refused to give into it. 'Yes. Like I said yesterday, he was a gift from the lord earl after the battle. We'd been together a year.' He allowed himself a sigh.

'Edwin will get to the bottom of it.'

'So he said to me. But …'

'What?'

He leaned forward and lowered his voice. Emma looked as though she was concentrating on some embroidery or something, over by the fire, but Martin couldn't be entirely sure she wasn't trying to listen to them at the same time. 'What if he doesn't?' he whispered.

'Do you mean the horse, or …'

'I mean everything. Look, as soon as the flood subsides, we could be out of here. You and me. Together.'

'Don't be ridiculous.'

'I'm not.' He glanced over at Emma, who had not given any sign that she had heard. 'We could take two of the Conisbrough horses and be out of here. Nothing simpler.' He felt the energy surging within him at the thought of it. To be riding away, at speed, Joanna by his side, to a new life …

But she was shaking her head. 'And where would we go? How would we live?'

'Does it matter?'

'Of course it matters. You'd be thrown out of the lord earl's service for sure, and that's if you got off lightly. We couldn't go to either your family or mine.'

'Well …'

'And what about John?'

'Who?'

She looked pointedly at the cradle that Ada was rocking with one foot.

'Oh.' Martin was confused. 'But the baby is part of your old life, here – part of the husband you didn't like.'

'Are you,' she said, with what he thought was a note of incredulity, 'saying that we would leave him behind?'

'Of course. He belongs here.' Martin looked at her face and realised his mistake. 'But,' he added hastily, 'of course we could bring him with us if you prefer.'

She was shaking her head and smiling. 'Martin, listen to yourself.'

He began to feel the first stirrings of irritation. Didn't she *want* to be with him? 'What do you mean?'

She sighed. 'Firstly, the practical implications of riding off with a baby are greater than you seem to think they are. And secondly, I couldn't possibly do that – it would damage his prospects.'

'So, like I said, leave him here! He'll inherit his father's estate and we can be free.'

She was getting angry now, though he couldn't see why. 'I will not abandon my son.'

'Your son? But surely he's just a reminder of—'

'He's my son, Martin. *Mine*,' she said, firmly. 'How can I make you understand? He grew inside of me – all those months, here, under my heart. And it makes no difference whether I liked his father or not – John is my child, and I will never abandon him, never do anything that might harm him. He has a future.' She held up what she had been sewing, and he saw that it was a tiny tunic, the sort a tot would wear when it came out of swaddling bands.

'But—'

'No buts.' She glanced over to where Ada had just lifted the baby out of its cradle. 'I'm a mother now, Martin, and that's more important than anything. You would fight and die for many causes, I know, so trust me when I say I would do the same for my son.' She looked Martin full in the face, and the fierce expression took him by surprise – he had never seen anything like it. 'Or kill for him, for that matter.'

He got up and walked out without saying another word.

By the time he got down the stairs, he was absolutely seething. Why was everything so difficult? And why, oh why, had Joanna abandoned him? He'd thought that she loved him with the same intensity that he felt for her. But it was all a lie.

Fortunately, the keep's main room was empty, so Martin kicked over a few stools. But it wasn't enough to relieve his feelings.

He went into the guest chamber that he shared with Edwin and looked at the baggage stacked in the corner. After a moment's hesitation he reached for the heavy, clinking pack that contained his armour.

It was, of course, very difficult to get into it by himself, but he was damned if he was going to call for help. Eventually he managed to fight his way into the gambeson and shrug the heavy hauberk into place, the struggle just making him even more frustrated and angry. Once the familiar weight was in place, however, and he'd belted on his sword, he felt more like himself.

He was going to kill somebody, and soon. He just didn't know who it was yet.

Chapter Eleven

Gossip had been the defining feature of this whole situation so far. Gossip, of course, was strongly associated with women, and Edwin tapped his fingers as he thought of everything he'd heard from those he'd spoken to, and tried to reconcile their differing accounts. Strangely – or perhaps not – he found himself thinking of Alys, and his mind drifted for a few moments in pleasant contemplation.

A conversation they'd had over a year ago came back to him. He'd promised that next time he was thrust into a matter of this kind, he'd make sure that he spoke to women as well as to men, for they often had information that could be overlooked. Well, he'd done that, hadn't he? Alys would be pleased.

There was one woman in the castle whom he had spoken *of* several times but never actually spoken *to*. And she was in a position where she might have seen and heard things that were of importance without realising their significance herself.

'Matthew,' he called, and the boy came in. Edwin noticed that he was shivering. 'I'm sorry, I've been keeping you standing around most of the day when you would normally be working and moving around to keep warm.'

'It's all right.'

'Well, run over to the keep for me now, and up to the solar. Knock on the door, and when you're inside, ask Lady Joanna if she can send Ada to see me, please. Apologise that I won't come to her, but I would like to speak to her without any of the other ladies present. Have you got all that? Repeat it back to me.'

Matthew did, word for word.

'Good. Off you go then. Oh—'

Matthew came back.

'And after you've brought Ada here, see if you can find out where Martin went to.'

He watched the boy splash his way through the mud of the ward in the waning afternoon light.

As Edwin waited, he considered what he knew and what he had heard about the wet-nurse. That she had given birth to a baby of her own must be true, but as to the rest … was it really dead, and who had been its father? Normally the employment of a wet-nurse would be a female matter, but in this case Sir Nicholas had stepped in. He had prevented Father Clement from driving Ada out of the village and had insisted on her being employed. Was there any possibility that he might have been more closely involved in the matter? After all, his relationship with Mabel showed that he had no qualms about engaging in liaisons outside of marriage.

Edwin's thoughts were continuing along this path when Matthew returned, bringing with him not only Ada but also Martin, who was wearing his armour and a grim expression.

'What is it? What's happened?' Edwin was half out of his seat.

'Nothing,' came the abrupt reply, and Martin moved to sit in the shadows at the other end of the room.

Matthew was hovering. 'Why don't you and Willikin both go and find somewhere to warm up,' said Edwin, 'and maybe something to eat? I'll be fine with Martin here.' He watched them as they moved off, then turned his attention to Ada, who was placidly looking about her in apparent unconcern.

'Please, do sit down.' Edwin ushered her to a seat where he would be able to see her face. 'Now,' he began, thinking to put her at her ease, not that she seemed to need it, 'you live in the castle so that you can feed Lady Joanna's baby, don't you?'

She nodded.

'And how long have you been doing that? Since he was born – what, four, five months ago?'

'Yes. Feast of the Assumption, it was.'

'And … you were chosen for the position because you had a baby of your own?'

She shrugged. 'It died.'

Edwin was taken aback by her matter-of-fact tone. But maybe it was something she affected in order not to display her grief openly. 'I'm very sorry for your loss.'

'Like my Ma said, it was the best thing, really. And besides, I wouldn't have got this position and all this food if it hadn't happened.'

'I understand,' said Edwin with delicacy, 'that you're not married?'

'No.'

'Can I ask you some questions about the father of your baby?'

'Why not? Everyone else has. But you'll get the same answer – I'm not saying anything.'

Edwin let the silence develop for a few moments, and then suggested, 'I wonder if some of your reluctance to speak is because the man in question told you not to say anything.'

He received no reply.

'And perhaps also because he wasn't just one of the lads in the village, but … someone else? Someone, perhaps, whose rank was higher than your own?'

She still said nothing, but Edwin was sure that he caught a flicker of alarm.

'If your baby's father had been one of the boys your own age, maybe someone you grew up with, you could simply have married him, couldn't you? I mean, it's not uncommon for a couple to be expecting their first child when they say their vows.'

Her lips remained tightly closed.

'And even if he'd been a bit reluctant, if you'd named him then your family, or his, or others in the village, would have pressured him to do the right thing.'

Was that another flicker?

'So all of this implies to me that you either didn't want to marry the father, or that he was not able to marry you – is that right?'

She almost opened her mouth to reply but didn't. She was definitely getting more uncomfortable, though.

'Let me think of reasons why he might not be able to marry you. The most obvious, of course, is that he was married already.'

He looked at her keenly in the fading light, expecting her discomfort to increase, but strangely his last comment seemed to make her relax. How odd.

He changed course. 'Or maybe you didn't want to marry him because he'd been unpleasant to you. Forgive me for asking, but … did he force you?'

At last she spoke. 'No.'

Edwin let the silence lengthen again, and was rewarded when he heard her murmur 'Well, not exactly.'

'Ada,' said Edwin, gently, 'if someone attacked you, violated you, you can tell me. I can't help what happened to you, or bring back your lost child, but I will believe you, I promise, and if the truth comes out then maybe justice can be done.'

That got a reaction. 'Justice?' she snorted. 'When there's one rule of law for us and another for them?'

Now Edwin felt like he was getting somewhere. 'So, this man – we won't name him for now – he didn't attack you, but he encouraged you, maybe led you to do things you weren't sure of?'

She nodded. 'Always touching me "accidentally", whenever we passed. Making excuses to talk to me alone. Making comments about how much I'd developed over the years. Letting his hands wander and then telling me I was disgusting.'

'And this continued for some time?'

'Yes. And I didn't want to – I told him it was wrong, and that he shouldn't be touching me, but he said it was his duty to make sure everybody was properly looked after.'

'I see.' Edwin recognised a power imbalance when he saw one, and he could guess what was coming next.

'And then one day when we were alone … it's complicated to explain.' She looked directly at Edwin for the first time. 'He didn't hit me, or force me – or not really – but he did things, and he made me feel like it was all my own fault. My doing, my sin. I'd been tempting him, he said, all this time, asking for it. I was wicked, and wicked girls needed to be punished. It was his duty, he said.'

Edwin was initially confused by this – it didn't sound like what he'd heard of Sir Nicholas, who would surely just have offered her money or gifts.

Wait.

Sin. Temptation. Punishment. A monstrous suspicion began to form in his mind. 'Tell me,' he said, 'where were you when this happened?'

'Well – in the church, of course. I suppose that makes it even worse. Not in the actual church, but in that bit behind where he gets changed before Mass.'

Edwin heard a clinking sound from the corner of the room. He'd almost forgotten that Martin was there. He was now leaning forward, his expression ominous. 'Are you saying that *Father Clement* was the father of your child?'

Perhaps it was Martin's tone, or perhaps it was the simple fact of hearing a different voice, but the spell was broken as Ada suddenly realised what she'd said.

Her hand flew to her mouth. 'Oh! I'll be in such trouble! He told me that I'd made him do a wicked thing, that I'd committed a terrible sin, and the best thing was for me to confess it only to him and say nothing.' Tears began to form in her eyes. 'He said I'd go straight to hell if I ever told a living soul!'

Martin was getting to his feet. 'I'll fetch him here.'

'No!' Edwin heard Ada's voice sounding at the same time as his own; she was terrified. He continued. 'I don't want to see him just yet – it might be an advantage not to let him know that we know. Besides, I don't think Ada is quite ready to face him.'

'When you are ready,' rumbled Martin to the girl, 'you tell me and I'll make sure I'm there. And it won't be you going to hell.'

Edwin wasn't quite sure of the exact doctrinal position on that, but now was not the time to consider it. 'You're not a wicked girl, Ada.'

She wiped away some tears. 'Really?'

'I'm sure of it.'

She cheered a little. 'Well, if you say so … and you being an important man, and all.'

He let that pass, given that the notion appeared to comfort her.

'Besides,' she said, a little more brightly, 'lots of people lie together without being married, even the nobility.' She gestured vaguely out the door towards the keep.

'Yes,' said Edwin. 'Yes, Sir Nicholas and Mabel didn't exactly try to hide their relationship, did they?'

'Oh, I'm not talking about them. I meant Lady Emma and Luke.'

'What?' Now it was Martin who had exclaimed simultaneously with Edwin.

'Didn't you know?' Ada seemed confused. 'I thought it was obvious, especially with her expecting a child.'

Edwin gaped.

Ada's puzzlement increased. 'Surely you noticed? Honestly, *men*.' She got up off her stool. 'Anyway, I'd better be getting back – his little lordship will be hungry again.'

She had passed through the doorway before Edwin remembered to shut his mouth.

'But—' began Martin.

Edwin waved him into silence, beginning to pace up and down as his mind stirred. He had noticed Emma and Luke's friendship, of course, but had made the foolish mistake of assuming it was just the remains of a childhood attachment, or one based on long familiarity. Now he knew better; it was something much deeper than that – and something that might drive either or both of them to desperate action.

Edwin stopped his pacing as that thought developed into a sharp thrust. He could add another woman to his list of mothers who might stop at nothing to defend their child's interests.

Martin was still in a ferocious temper, itching to get up and hit someone, and now he had two more targets. He hadn't particularly taken to Father Clement, a dislike that had only increased as the extent of the priest's hostility and cruelty to Joanna became clearer. Finding out now that he was a philanderer who had betrayed his vows and taken advantage of an innocent girl was just the sort of information Martin needed in order to feel that he would be in the right in punishing him.

He was still a priest, though, unfortunately, and Martin had a nasty feeling that Edwin would probably try to use that as an excuse not to allow Martin to strike him. Luke, though: that was another matter. Martin felt his fist clench even as he thought of punching the irritating, upstart fellow in the face. Maybe he hadn't forced himself on Emma, but he'd certainly lain with a lady of noble rank, grounds for punishment in itself, to say nothing of how it might implicate him in Sir Nicholas's murder. Oh, if Edwin could only discover somehow that Luke had been the one wielding the knife! Yes, yes, he'd already tried to say that he knew Luke had been elsewhere at that time, but Edwin had disproved more impossible things than that before now. He could do it again.

The energy was beginning to build up in a pleasing way when Aubrey entered, making him scowl. Such a prancing little man. Edwin had his thinking face on. Aubrey cleared his throat several times but without any success.

'Edwin!' Martin called out, which had the dual effect of recalling Edwin's mind into the room and making Aubrey jump half a foot in the air.

'I didn't realise you were in here,' he said, unnecessarily. 'I haven't had the chance to see you since this morning – I'm so sorry about what happened to your horse.'

As Martin had just succeeded in distracting himself from the horror for the first time, this utterance of Aubrey's did nothing to recommend him.

Edwin was speaking. 'What did you find out about this supposed marriage of Sir Nicholas and Mabel?'

Aubrey made an exasperated sound. 'They're both adamant that it took place, but they have no proof other than their word. Nothing written down, and both the men they say witnessed it are dead. As is Sir Nicholas, of course.'

Martin expected that Edwin would now express frustration, but he merely nodded. 'Tell me,' he said, 'did one of them seem to feel much more comfortable than the other while they were insisting the marriage was real?'

'Well – it's funny you should say that, actually,' replied Aubrey, his brow furrowing. 'I was watching them as well as listening, and I did rather get the feeling that Father Clement was … yes, like you say, uncomfortable. But,' he added hurriedly, 'that was just my impression.'

'Good, good.'

'Really?'

'Oh yes.' Martin knew that look of Edwin's, and within him the seed of hope began to send out a few first shoots.

'Some of this is starting to fit together now,' said Edwin, much to Aubrey's bemusement. Martin had no clue what was going on, either, but he didn't want to lower himself to Aubrey's level of uselessness, so he said nothing.

'Right,' concluded Edwin. 'It must be more or less time for the evening meal, I would think. Shall we go over?'

Martin watched him leave the office with a spring in his step.

———

The meal was probably good, but Edwin was so busy thinking that he barely noticed it. He had a great deal of information to process and filter, and he also needed to plan the action he intended to take after they'd finished eating.

He looked carefully at those in the room: himself, Martin, Joanna, Emma and Aubrey at the table, Milo serving, and Mabel and Ada further off. Mabel's son wasn't there, but that wasn't surprising – the atmosphere in the solar was hardly going to be enjoyable for the child, so perhaps he'd sought out some company nearer his own age.

Edwin leaned over to speak in Martin's ear. Martin was still wearing his armour, which had made the meal a somewhat more sombre and menacing event than it might have been, but which might turn out to be useful if the situation became serious later on. 'I need to have Father Clement in here,' he murmured, 'and Luke *not* in here. Can you organise that?'

'What if he won't come?' Even through all the layers, Edwin felt his friend's muscles flex.

'You can't hurt him – he's still a priest, whatever he's done. But if you could get it across to him that I won't take "no" for an answer, that would be good.'

'He'll be in the hall. I'll take the men over with me, if you'll be all right here while we're gone?'

Edwin nodded. 'And if Luke tries to follow …?'

'I'll stand guard outside the door here. He won't get past me, don't worry. And I'll be close enough to hear what's going on and to come in if you need me.'

'Good.' Edwin returned to his thoughts. He also watched Emma very carefully, satisfied that Ada had been speaking the truth. He was annoyed with himself for not having spotted the signs before: her waist wasn't merely thickening, as women's did with age, but swelling. And she placed her hand on her stomach frequently in the same way that Alys did.

As those around the table began to push themselves back, sated, Martin slipped out.

'Very nice,' said Aubrey to Joscelin, as the latter supervised his men clearing up the dishes. 'Was that beef from today's slaughtering?'

Joscelin looked ill at ease – as well he might, given his conversation with Edwin earlier in the day. 'Yes, yes it was, although really it needed to hang for a little while longer to bring out the best flavour.'

Joanna sighed.

'I'm sorry, my lady,' continued the steward. 'But there was no saving the animal.'

'And no saving the horse, either, from what I heard,' said Aubrey, having made sure that Martin was not within earshot. 'What bad luck.'

'Bad luck had nothing to do with it,' said Edwin. 'Not for Martin's horse, anyway – that was deliberately killed.'

'It must have been an awful sight,' continued Aubrey. 'I caught a glimpse of Martin this afternoon, before he got changed, and he was covered in so much blood you'd think he'd bathed in it.'

Edwin could see that the ladies both had expressions of distaste. 'Aubrey, please.'

But the sheriff's man continued in the same vein. 'There would be no chance of telling who was bloodied because he'd killed the horse and who was bloodied because he'd been at the slaughtering.' He sighed. 'Just like the morning after Sir Nicholas was killed. And that was the one thing I remembered to check up on when I arrived, like I told you,' he said to Edwin.

'Could we maybe discuss something else?' asked Joanna.

Emma saw her discomfort and immediately attempted to make the most of it. 'Well, you were covered in more than anyone, of course, given that you'd just slit my brother's throat. But you're right,' she continued, turning to Aubrey. 'There was blood everywhere.'

'Yes,' replied Aubrey, oblivious to anyone else's discomfort. 'With Joscelin and his men splashed with blood from the slaughtering, and Joanna and Milo from the bedchamber, I suppose it would have been difficult to tell who had been where.'

Joanna was preparing to defend herself again, and Emma to argue, but this was not the direction Edwin wished the conversation to take. He was glad, therefore, to see the door open and Father Clement enter. Martin was behind him. He gave the priest a bit of a shove, nodded to Edwin and shut the door again, remaining on the outside.

There was a moment of surprised silence.

Father Clement advanced into the room, glancing at Ada with a disgust that Edwin now understood, and one that made his anger rise. But that was not the first revelation that he wanted to make.

Emma, perhaps thinking that the priest's arrival heralded more discomfort for Joanna, welcomed him and ushered him towards a seat by the fire. He did not sit, however, and turned to Edwin. 'Why have you asked me here?'

It was time to begin. 'Well, Father, I thought Lady Emma might like you to be here so she could confess.'

There was a general surprise and exclamation. Edwin kept his eyes on Emma; her first action was to put a hand on her stomach.

'Confess to what?' she managed. 'I had nothing to do with my brother's—'

'I meant,' said Edwin, loudly and clearly, 'that you should confess to being with child, out of wedlock.'

Father Clement hadn't been that close to her, but he jumped back as though he'd been burned. 'Sin!'

Emma spluttered as she at first tried to deny it, but she soon realised there was no point; even if it wasn't obvious now, it soon would be. 'How did you know?'

Edwin thought it would be better to keep Ada out of it. She was going to suffer later on as it was. 'It's obvious to anyone with eyes,' he lied, thinking of his own complete inability to see what had been in front of him all the time.

Fortunately, he got away with it, but she was still defiant. 'What has it got to do with you? It's no crime in law.'

'No,' said Edwin, 'but murder is.'

'What?'

She was astonished, enraged, no doubt suffering many emotions, but Edwin still thought he had the situation under control. 'A mother would do anything for her child,' he continued, calmly. 'Which gives you even more of a motive for wanting to have Sir Nicholas's estate for yourself. When did you discover that you were pregnant? Was it round about the time that your brother died?'

She said nothing, but Joanna and Mabel, who had drawn closer, both nodded. 'It must have been,' declared Mabel, appraising Emma's figure.

'And did you then realise that your brother would not let you marry the man in question, or was it that you knew the man had no property of his own? Or both?'

Edwin took a pace forward and Emma stepped back, a hand protectively covering her swelling belly. 'No, I …'

'And did you then realise that if your brother was out the way, and his son disinherited, that you would gain everything – not just for you, but for your child? That you could marry the father before the birth, thus making your child a legitimate heir?'

She was starting to look frightened. 'No!'

'Did you?' Edwin found himself standing menacingly close to her, his finger in her face. If she backed away any further, she would be in the fire.

And then he caught sight of Father Clement, and the truth of what he was doing hit him. He was browbeating a woman into confessing to something she denied, and for which he as yet had no proof, just as the priest had done to Joanna in a way that had angered and sickened Edwin.

He stepped back, and then walked a few paces away from the fire in order to compose himself. What was happening to him? What would Alys say if she were here? This was not the kind of man that he was. He would not threaten or intimidate; he would put together the facts in an orderly way – and until he knew *exactly* what had happened, he would not accuse anyone.

Facts. Yes, that was the way to go. Time to thrust his hand into a different hornets' nest.

As he turned back to the group, Mabel inadvertently gave him the cue he needed to change the subject.

'So, Lady Emma is with child,' she snarled. 'It makes no difference, though – this castle and land belong to my son, because he is Nicholas's legitimate heir.'

'But he's not, is he?' said Edwin, managing now to keep his voice calm. He knew he was on firmer ground with this one.

'I told you – and Father Clement will bear witness. We—'

'Ah, Father Clement,' interrupted Edwin, looking with a contempt he didn't bother to disguise at the priest, who was attempting to stay as far away as possible from all the women in the room. 'I'm sure he would bear witness for you, given that you've threatened to reveal his own secret if he doesn't.'

The horror-struck expression on the priest's face confirmed that Edwin was right, but he didn't think Father Clement would go down that easily. He looked at Aubrey, hoping to God that he'd stand up for himself this time and repeat what he'd said earlier.

The priest recovered himself. 'I don't know what you're talking about,' he blustered.

'Oh, I think you do,' said Edwin. 'And I'm happy to say it out loud.'

'You wouldn't dare! You wouldn't dare make such disgusting accusations against a man of the cloth.'

'Oh, so you know what they are, then? My accusations against you?'

'No … that's not what I … of course I have no idea what might be in your diseased mind.'

'Fine,' said Edwin, feeling himself, strangely, growing calmer even as Father Clement was getting more and more enraged. 'I'll tell you, and everyone else.' He cast an apologetic glance at Ada. 'You coerced that poor innocent girl into lying with you, got her with child, then tried to blame it all on her and have her cast out of her home.'

Edwin could hear the gasps coming from all around him, but – interestingly – not one person in the room tried to declare that it couldn't be true or raised a voice to defend the priest.

'I did not!'

'Ada says you were the father of her child.'

Father Clement laughed, a sound that came out like a bark. 'Then she's a wicked, lying, sinful woman … how could you possibly believe her over me?'

'Because she is quite evidently speaking the truth, while you are just as evidently lying.'

'You disgust me,' spat the priest. 'To even think such a thing.'

'I agree with him.' Aubrey stepped forward to stand at Edwin's shoulder. 'When I spoke to you and to Mabel earlier, it was perfectly clear to me that you were lying when you confirmed her so-called marriage. The only logical reason for you to lie on her behalf would be if you had something to gain – and this explains it all perfectly.'

'You?' Father Clement's voice dripped with contempt.

Aubrey drew himself up. 'I am the representative of the sheriff, and of the laws of the kingdom, and you would do well to remember it.' Edwin could feel that Aubrey was shaking, but his voice remained level.

Edwin's own sense of composure was, remarkably, still there. He was furious, but in a cold manner that he could control. 'That poor girl.' He shook his head at the priest.

As he had intended, this brought the poison spewing forth. 'Her! She's nothing but a wicked Jezebel, like all women. Flaunting their bodies to tempt good men.'

'Even if that were true,' said Edwin, noting that the priest had more or less confessed and everyone else in the room had noticed that too, 'a good man would have resisted temptation.' His voice hardened. 'You are a disgrace to the Church. You have no morals, you abused an innocent girl, then doubled your sin by trying to punish her and doubled it again by creating a lie to support someone else's attempt to break the law.' He turned to bore his gaze into Mabel, and she shrank back.

Aubrey had gained enough confidence to speak again. 'So?' he asked Mabel. 'What have you to say for yourself?'

She looked like a rabbit cornered by dogs.

Edwin tried to keep his eyes on her while watching Father Clement at the same time. He, however, seemed entirely wrapped up in his own concerns, raving about sin. Then he made a movement as though he was going to dart towards Ada, who was hiding in the furthest corner of the room, and she screamed.

The door burst open and Martin covered the ground between himself and Father Clement in three steps, blocking his way to Ada.

The priest ill-advisedly tried to keep going and literally bounced back as he hit the huge, solid armoured form.

'Keep him there for a moment,' said Edwin.

Martin didn't draw his sword, but he didn't need to.

Edwin turned back to Mabel. 'Well? Aubrey asked you a question.'

Her face bore a look of calculation.

Edwin's almost inhuman patience continued. 'You have no witness, nobody to back up your claim, no way to prove it. I'd give up now, if I were you, and save yourself and your son a whole lot of trouble.'

She wavered.

'Think of him,' said Edwin, soothingly. 'Do you want him in trouble with the law? Or in danger?' He looked around, but Nick had still not appeared; he wouldn't be able to get out the castle, of course, but Edwin thought he'd better send someone out to find him before too long, or Mabel would worry.

Mabel's shoulders slumped, and she mumbled something.

'I didn't quite hear what you said. Out loud, please, so Aubrey and these other witnesses can hear you.'

'I withdraw my claim,' said Mabel, sullenly. 'My sons are Sir Nicholas's, but they were born out of wedlock.'

Edwin exulted to himself. Finally, he knew for certain that one of the four women in the room was telling the absolute truth.

'Three to go,' he muttered under his breath.

It was at that moment that the solar door was flung back and Turold entered at a run. He made straight for Edwin. 'You need to come. There's been … an accident.'

Edwin couldn't help noticing that Turold's eyes slid to Mabel as he spoke, and his blood turned to ice. Dear Lord. Surely not – surely this hadn't all happened too late? It had only been earlier today that Mabel had claimed …

Even as these thoughts were running through Edwin's head, he was following Turold down the stairs and out of the keep. A group of men were gathered at the inner ward's gateway, where the footbridge led to the outer ward, clustered around something lying on the ground.

Something small.

Edwin knew what he was going to see when got there, and his heart revolted. The crowd parted as he arrived, allowing him to look down at the dead child.

'Drowned,' said Tom. 'We were on our way to check the horses, in case …' he tailed off as he saw Martin looming out of the darkness behind Edwin. 'Well, you know. And Lambert spotted him in the water. We fished him out, of course, but it was too late.' He crossed himself.

Edwin automatically did the same. He looked at the bridge. 'Which side?'

Tom pointed. Nick had been in the deep, swollen fishpond off to Edwin's left. If he'd gone in the narrower ditch on the other side, he might have been able to climb out again.

'An accident, do you think?' asked Martin.

Edwin knelt to look at the body. 'Can someone get me a light?' A couple of torches appeared, and he was able to make a quick examination. 'There are no marks of violence on him, as far as I can see, so I agree he drowned.'

'Must have just skidded and fell in,' came a voice from somewhere in the middle of a group of garrison men. 'Slippy on that footbridge.'

There was a murmur of agreement, but Edwin wasn't so sure. 'There's plenty of salt on it,' he pointed out, 'and a boy his age would be sure-footed.' Gently, he closed Nick's eyes before looking up. 'Also, if he'd slipped then he would have had time to cry out, and he would have splashed about for a while before he slipped under or before the cold got to him. Did anyone hear something like that?'

He waited, but nobody spoke. 'Well then,' he continued, with a heavy heart. 'I can't discount the possibility that someone pushed him and then held his head under the water.'

'Murder?' Martin sounded aghast. 'A child?'

'I have my reasons for suspecting so, yes.'

The murmur around him changed in tone: it was angrier, buzzing.

Edwin wasn't sure exactly whom the anger was directed at, but he wasn't about to take any chances. 'Go about your normal business now, everyone. We will get to the bottom of this, I promise. And soon.'

With encouragement from some of the cooler heads, the crowd began to disperse. 'We'll need to find somewhere to put him,' said Edwin to Joscelin, 'until he can be taken to the church. Have you got a cool storeroom or an undercroft somewhere?'

Joscelin had tears running down his face. 'The poor boy. And yes, yes, I can find somewhere.' He paused. 'Who's going to tell Mabel?'

Edwin squared his shoulders. 'I will. You make sure he's laid somewhere with dignity, and I'll fetch her.'

Joscelin made as if to bend and pick up the body himself, but Willikin brushed him out the way. 'I'll do it. He's little enough weight. Just show me where.' Willikin's normally placid face was screwed up in anguish. 'Killing nippers isn't right, Master Edwin. It just isn't.'

'No.'

'I was just playing with him and his little brothers the other day.'

'I know.'

'Well, you find out who did this, Master Edwin, and you just put me in a room with him and shut the door.'

Much as he disliked any form of extra-judicial revenge, Edwin couldn't help feeling that such might be a fitting end for someone who'd used adult strength to overpower and snuff out the life of a small child. *See how they like it.*

They were interrupted by a piercing shriek.

News, of course, didn't take long to fly round the castle, and Mabel was running across the ward, heedless of the dirt and mud splashing around her. 'My boy!' she fell to her knees beside the body and shook it as though to rouse her son from a slumber. 'Nick, Nick – wake up! Mama is here, darling, just wake up.'

When it became clear that the cold little corpse wasn't going to move, she broke down into racking, heart-rending sobs that had tears running down Edwin's cheeks as well as Joscelin's and Willikin's.

Edwin took a few paces back to give her space to mourn, his resolve hardening as he looked on. He *would* find the killer, and in the name of God and all His saints, he *would* see justice done.

He stood in silence, unable even to pray while the horror was still in front of him. It was a sight he'd seen a number of times before, but one he never, ever, wanted to see again: a mother weeping over the body of her dead child.

Chapter Twelve

Edwin lay in the darkness, listening to Martin's snores and those of the men in the keep's main chamber. Several things were now starting to come together in his mind, and he didn't want to go to sleep until he had straightened them out. Besides, the guilt of having caused a needless death – a *child's* death – by not working more quickly had begun to gnaw at him, opening an old wound. He must get to the bottom of this soon, so nobody else had to die.

That Mabel had finally told the truth about her relationship seemed plain. Part of her story had been true all along, of course: nobody had ever doubted that Sir Nicholas was the father of her three sons. No, the lie had been about the boys' supposed legitimacy, and that had now been comprehensibly disproved. Too late for poor Nick, of course. Edwin had no doubt that he'd been killed because of his position as a potential inheritor of the castle and estate.

Once he'd recovered from the initial shock of seeing the body, Edwin's thoughts had turned to the other, younger boys. He had immediately circulated the news that Mabel had retracted her claim and that they were genuinely illegitimate, hoping that the gossip would fly around as quickly as it normally did and that this would keep them out of danger. They were, moreover, as Mabel had said, safe in the village, while the killer was here. *Safe in the village.* Why did that phrase resonate with Edwin, and why was it linked to something else at the back of his mind?

He couldn't quite catch hold of the thought, so he left it to stew and turned his mind back to Mabel. She would have to live with the guilt of her eldest son's death. But just how deep was her guilt in other matters? Had she come up with the tale of a marriage simply in response to events – that is, had she reacted to Sir Nicholas's death by seeing a chance and taking it – or had she set the whole chain of events in motion by murdering him after he visited to say that he was breaking off the relationship? For it now seemed clear that that was where he had been on the evening of his death. It was a plausible motive for the crime, although it was very difficult to see how Mabel could have carried it out in practice.

Ada, now. Edwin had said 'three to go' to himself earlier, but events had proved that she was also speaking the truth, at least in relation to Father Clement and her baby. The poor girl. But there was something else still nagging away that he couldn't put his finger on – was it something she'd said, or something he'd seen her do? The darkness around him had no answer, so he left that question as well for now.

As for Joanna and Emma, they were locked in a power struggle so intense, the one a mother and the other a mother-to-be, that nothing could be put past either of them. Edwin still favoured Emma as the culprit, but she had shown no sign at all of guilt or of giving into his demands that she confess. So now he wondered if he had been wrong, and if his personal feelings were clouding his judgement.

Had he been too quick to clear Joanna in his mind because he *wanted* her to be innocent? But, of course, it was she who had asked him to come here, and she surely would not have done that if she was guilty herself. Edwin was not a conceited man, but he did flatter himself that his previous experience indicated that he was likely to find out the truth of the matter. Joanna calling him in to investigate her husband's murder as a blind to cover her own guilt would be audacious in the extreme.

Old church sermons about the duplicity of the female sex started to come back to Edwin, as he lay in the dark, but fortunately thinking about women and mothers led his mind back to Alys and to his own mother, and they were the more pleasant image before him as his eyes closed.

Edwin slept only fitfully, plagued by thoughts and dreams. There was blood everywhere. That was a familiar nightmare, for it had happened to him in real life more than once. Why was he destined always to be surrounded by death and destruction? And Father was here amid it all, too, trying to say something. But that was strange, as he had died in his bed – one of the few people Edwin had lost in recent years to a cause other than violence.

He tossed and turned. The blood would not recede. It was all around him, rising like a flood, oozing under the fence, and he would need to set sandbags down to keep it out. But it was no good. The slaughtering was continuing inside the walls, and that was where the tide of red was coming from, not from outside. Martin's horse was hanging up from the frame with its throat cut. Everyone was watching, and everyone was drenched in blood. But that wasn't right. Why wasn't the horse safe in the village? And why was Father still here, and what was he trying to say?

Edwin woke up. Despite the cold he was sweating, and his breath came in ragged gasps. But as it slowly returned to normal, he smiled into the blackness of the night. 'Yes,' he said to himself. 'Yes, of course.'

———

As soon as he could sense that it was dawn, tiny slivers of light entering the keep through the gaps in the shutter, Edwin shook Martin awake.

'What? What is it?' Martin was already reaching for his sword.

'I know what happened,' whispered Edwin. 'But what comes next is going to be dangerous.'

He couldn't see Martin smiling, but he heard it in his friend's voice. 'You couldn't have woken me with better news. Tell me what to do.'

They roused Aubrey and the men. Edwin did a quick headcount. Only nine of them altogether, which was going to make things tricky: of course, two of them were Martin and Willikin, but that was offset by three of the others being himself, Lambert and Aubrey, in whom he would have little confidence if – when – it came to a fight. Thankfully, young Matthew had been sent back to his usual sleeping place with the other grooms last night, so he could be kept out of any danger. A desperate killer might lash out at anyone, and Edwin did not want to see any more child corpses.

'What's going on?' came a sleepy voice.

Edwin swore under his breath. He had been trying to leave Milo slumbering, but the squire had been woken by all the movement and his eyes now widened as he saw Martin and the Conisbrough men arming themselves.

'Stay here,' said Edwin, curtly. 'And, in as much as I have any authority to order you, that's an order.'

They were almost ready to move out when Martin pulled Edwin to one side. 'What about Joanna, and the others upstairs?'

Edwin had guessed that such a question would be forthcoming, but all he could do was shake his head. 'I can't spare any of the men to stay in the keep. If all goes well, they shouldn't be needed here anyway.'

Martin looked absolutely torn. Edwin knew how much he would want to stay to protect Joanna at all costs, but his presence or absence at the forthcoming scene was going to swing everything. 'Please,' said Edwin. 'Trust me. This way is best for her as well as for us.'

For a brief moment Edwin thought Martin was going to argue, but he said nothing. Instead, he pushed his way through the others until he reached Milo, who was hovering uncertainly near the fire with the dogs by his side. 'Have you a sword?'

Milo gulped. 'Not down here, but Sir Nicholas's should still be upstairs in the bedchamber.'

'Get it,' said Martin, shortly. 'Wake Joanna, but not the others if you can help it. Tell her to be alert and to find something to defend herself with, and to bar the solar door from the inside if she can. You bar the keep door here once we've gone out, then stand ready.' He looked about him. 'The top of the stairs will be the best place – you'll have room to manoeuvre, but anyone coming up will be funnelled into single file, which will make it easier for you to hold them off.'

'But what—' Edwin could see that Milo was terrified.

Martin grabbed him by both shoulders. 'You're a squire,' he said, forcefully. 'Your lord's dead, so your duty is to his son and heir and his widow. I don't know what Edwin's about to do, but if I don't come back then protecting them is up to you. Try to remember what I taught you the other day about footwork.' His eyes bored into Milo's as he gripped him ever more tightly and gave him a shake. 'You're going to be a knight one day, so act like it.'

Milo set his lips and nodded without speaking.

'Good,' said Martin. 'Now, God willing, we'll meet again later.' He clapped the boy on the back and strode back to Edwin.

Edwin checked to see that the others were all ready. 'Right,' he said. 'We all know where we're going. Quietly, now.'

They opened the door and slipped out. Edwin heard the sound of it being closed and barred behind him, and he hoped to God he was doing the right thing and not putting the women in any further danger.

He took in a gulp of the morning air, noting that it had stopped raining, and they set off. The four Conisbrough men and both of Aubrey's peeled off to head for the outer ward while Edwin, Martin and Aubrey crossed the inner ward to the steward's office.

At a nod from Edwin, Martin kicked open the door.

Joscelin jerked up from where he had been asleep with his head on the table. Behind him was Father Clement's makeshift bed, but it was empty.

The steward got to his feet. 'You take financial matters very seriously, I see,' he said, nervously. 'I've already confessed to my crime – what more do you want me to do?'

Edwin lit a candle and shut the door, gesturing to Martin to stand against it. 'Now,' he said, 'we can't be disturbed, and nobody will hear us.' He saw the shadow of fear pass over Joscelin's face and added, 'Trust me, this is for your safety as much as ours.'

'I … I don't understand.'

'You will. Please sit there. Aubrey, over here, next to me.' He almost added *watch and learn*, but that would have been conceited. Besides, he owed Aubrey a great deal, for it was he who had given Edwin the thread to connect the disparate parts of the weaving. 'You're acting on behalf of the sheriff, remember, so take note of everything you see and hear so you can bear witness. You'll no doubt be asked about it later.'

Aubrey pulled up a stool to sit by Edwin's shoulder, still evidently in the dark about what was going on but asking no questions.

'I'm not here to talk about stealing,' began Edwin, directly. 'I'm here to talk about murder.'

'What?' Joscelin paled.

'It was you who wielded the knife that killed Sir Nicholas.'

Aubrey looked at Edwin in surprise, and Edwin could sense Martin doing the same from behind him. Joscelin, on the other hand, had regained some of his composure, and the same look of calculation came into his eye that Edwin had seen the other day when he'd confronted the steward over the exchequer board.

'And what makes you think that it was me?'

'You're the only person who had both a reason to kill him and the practical means of doing so.'

'Really? How did I do it, then?'

'First, you put a sleeping draught in the meal that would be eaten in the solar that evening. That way Sir Nicholas would not wake and fight back, and nobody else would see you enter. You had plenty of opportunity to administer it as you were supervising the food.'

'A sleeping draught? Really? And how did you come to the conclusion that I had such a thing?'

'I found it. And given that you have just looked towards the exact place where it was hidden, there is no point trying to deny that it was there.'

'Anyone could have come into my office – men are in and out of here all day.'

'But only you have the key to the spice chest.' That made Joscelin pause, so Edwin pressed his advantage. 'During the night you slipped into the keep. Even if anyone had seen you, they were unlikely to have remarked on it, for the same thing applies: you're in and out of there all the time. The dogs don't bark at you, as they do at some others.'

Joscelin was looking a little less secure.

'You went up to the bedchamber, picked up Sir Nicholas's own knife, and slit his throat.'

Edwin heard Martin's hiss from behind him.

'Much blood was spilled. No doubt you managed to wash most of it off your hands, but there were still some splashes of it on you the next morning.'

'Yes,' interrupted Aubrey, 'but that was because of the slaughtering, surely? Or, at least, it could have been.'

Edwin patted him on the shoulder. 'It was you mentioning it last night that gave me the vital piece of information. Joscelin was one of those who was splashed with blood the following morning, you said, and he was there when you said it and didn't deny it.'

'Yes, but …'

'However, as Joscelin had already told me that he wasn't anywhere near the slaughtering that morning, how could he have got blood on him?'

Joscelin was starting to tremble.

'And,' continued Edwin, inexorably, 'who ordered the slaughtering to take place that day? The steward, of course.' He turned from Aubrey to address Joscelin directly. 'It was your fall-back position. You knew there was going to be a lot of blood, so you took steps to make sure there was blood everywhere – the best place to hide is always in plain sight.'

'But why,' came Martin's voice in a rumble, 'did he kill Sir Nicholas by cutting his throat? Anyone would know how much bleeding that would cause – why not just a swift thrust to the heart, especially if he was asleep?'

'Ah, I'm coming to that,' replied Edwin, still looking Joscelin in the eye.

The steward's face collapsed. 'All right! Yes, I did it. It was exactly like you just said.'

'But why?' asked Aubrey, in a puzzled tone.

'Why … because Sir Nicholas found out I was stealing from him, of course. I had to get rid of him.' He bit his lip. 'All my own idea, and I acted quite alone.'

'That was suspiciously easy,' came Martin's voice again. 'What shall we do with him now?'

'Oh no,' said Edwin, shaking his head. 'We've barely started yet.'

'Yes, wait,' said Martin. 'He can't possibly have killed Fauvel – you said he was in here all night that night. And what about the boy?'

'Again, we'll get to that,' said Edwin. He turned to Joscelin. 'Are you going to tell them, or shall I?'

The steward's lips were clamped firmly shut, and Edwin suspected that the reason he'd just folded his arms was to prevent them all from seeing that his hands were shaking.

'You're lying to me,' said Edwin, 'just like you lied about the money.'

'Wait, wait.' Aubrey was confused. 'Are you now saying he *didn't* do either of those things? Steal or kill Sir Nicholas?'

'Oh, he did them – or rather, his was the hand that carried out both deeds. But his wasn't the mind behind either of them.'

'No,' said Joscelin, clearly rattled now. 'No, I acted alone, I tell you.'

'I understand,' said Edwin, 'that you're scared for your family, terrified about what might happen to them, as you have been all along. But you have to understand that it's over. And if you tell us the truth – here, now – we can make sure that they're protected.'

'I can't, I can't—'

'You can, and you will.'

Aubrey was still two steps behind. 'You mean, someone has been threatening his family, and that's why he felt forced to steal, and even to kill Sir Nicholas?'

'Yes.' Edwin sighed. 'I should have seen it sooner. I was so caught up in my thoughts about how mothers would do anything for their children that I almost forgot that a good *father* will do anything to protect his family. And I should know,' he added under his breath.

Edwin turned back to Joscelin. 'Look at it another way. If you say nothing, and take all the blame yourself, you'll be executed, and who will look after your family then, with the other culprit still at large? They'll be in even more danger than they are now, and with no protector. But if you tell us the truth, we can bring the other to justice, and your wife and children will be free of that threat, no matter what happens to you.' He sensed a chink of weakness. 'And don't forget that another mother has just lost her child. How long will you let this go on? How many more will suffer and die?'

Joscelin was weeping, his face buried in his hands.

'Tell me.' Edwin was relentless – because this time he *knew* he was right.

'All right,' sobbed Joscelin. He looked up. 'Yes, threats against my family – my wife, my children. My son would be killed, but only after being tortured first. My wife and daughters violated over and over again, and then the bodies burned to cover up what had happened.' His eyes moved from Edwin to the others. 'A chaste, modest woman, a little boy and two innocent girls. My youngest daughter is twelve. How could I let that happen, if there was a way I could stop it?'

He dissolved into tears again, and Edwin took up his tale for him. 'At first it was just money, wasn't it? "Give me all your wages, and your family will be safe." And then maybe, "These wages aren't enough – if you want to save them, you need to come up with more, even if you have to steal it." Is that how it went?'

Joscelin nodded.

'But you didn't steal from us. When our baggage was put in the guest chamber, our money was left untouched.'

Joscelin looked almost insulted. 'I'm not a common thief, stealing for my own ends. Nobody in the castle knew about your money except me, so I couldn't be forced to take it.'

'Yes, you committed your crimes only because you were coerced. And then, finally – an order to murder Sir Nicholas. You didn't want to, but it was him or them. Maybe the threats increased, maybe your wife and children now knew about them themselves, and they were frightened.'

'No, not that – they knew absolutely nothing of any of it, I swear. But as to the rest, yes. And I was not just to kill him, I was to do it in the bloodiest way possible, both to punish me and to sow doubt about who might have done it.'

'Which is why the sleeping draught was just that, and not poison,' added Edwin. 'If they'd all been poisoned then suspicion would have pointed straight at you or the cook – and it might have killed everyone else.'

Martin's rumbling voice came from behind Edwin. 'So, we're looking for another culprit as well as him, then. And it was the other who killed Fauvel?'

'Yes. Joscelin would never have done that. Not with all that blood, and he wouldn't have killed an animal so gratuitously.'

'But whoever did it used the same trick,' said Aubrey, finally catching up. 'Combining it with a slaughtering so any bloodstains wouldn't be too obvious.'

'Yes, although I think it was the other way round this time. When Sir Nicholas was killed, Joscelin arranged the slaughtering deliberately to coincide. This time, our culprit knew it was about to happen so he took his chance. Just as he took it when he saw a little boy on his own, crossing a bridge in the dark.'

'He?' Aubrey was surprised. 'Who?'

It was just at that moment that a pounding came on the door. The latch shifted up and down, but with an armoured Martin leaning on it the door was not going to move. He echoed Aubrey's question. 'Who?'

Luke's voice sounded from outside. 'What's going on in there? Open this door!'

'Martin,' said Edwin, 'I think I have some good news for you.'

———•◦•———

It took Martin a few moments to work out exactly what Edwin meant, but when he did, he experienced a flood of joy, rage and exhilaration such as he had not felt in a long time. 'Luke? Really?'

Edwin nodded.

Within the space of three heartbeats Martin had wrenched open the door, given Luke an almighty shove backwards and drawn his sword as he ducked through the doorway.

'Not yet!' shouted Edwin, from behind him. 'The charges have to be heard!'

Swearing, Martin lowered his sword – though he didn't sheathe it – and instead shot out his left arm to grab Luke by the throat, propelling him into the middle of the ward.

'Quick,' gasped Luke to some of his men in a strangled tone. 'The armoury!'

They ran off, and Martin smiled at the surprise they would get when they reached it. He shook Luke, almost lifting him off his feet, and turned to Edwin. 'What shall I do with him, then?'

'Hold him fast while we assemble as many witnesses as possible.'

Martin was certainly happy to do that, enjoying the sensation of having the smaller man – the man responsible for Joanna's danger, Fauvel's death and probably also the murder of a child – at his mercy. Luke's own hands were ineffectually scrabbling at his, but Martin's mailed grip stayed firm.

Joscelin had staggered out of his office, and Edwin was instructing him to fetch as many men as he could find – from the kitchens, the stables, anywhere – to act as witnesses.

Martin heard the shouts from the outer ward and grinned in delight when Luke's men straggled back empty-handed. 'We couldn't get in,' one of them called to Luke, keeping his distance as he eyed Martin's long sword arm. 'His men are guarding it, and that big fellow just knocked Jack and Simon out cold by smacking their heads together. They're all armed and we had no chance of getting past them.'

Luke made a sort of strangled, enraged noise that only boosted Martin's mood.

Soon they were surrounded by a cautious circle of men. Martin ran a calculating eye over them. Most hung back, sensibly waiting to see what was going to happen before they decided which way to jump. There were a handful – six, to be precise – who looked as though they were poised to take action on Luke's behalf if they got the chance. They wore no armour, however, and carried only eating knives and daggers, so Martin was confident he could handle them if he needed to.

'Martin.'

Martin looked round to see that Edwin had evidently been trying to attract his attention for some small while. 'Yes.'

'He needs to be conscious enough to answer the charges.'

Martin belatedly realised that his grip on Luke's throat might have been a little tighter than necessary. He loosened it and instead clamped his mailed arm around Luke's body, pinioning his captive's limp arms to his sides, holding him tight against his own body while still keeping his sword arm free.

Edwin addressed the crowd. 'We are here to put charges against Luke and to see how he answers. I do this by the authority of my lord, Earl William de Warenne, and Aubrey does so in the name of the sheriff of Warwickshire. Does any man wish to challenge this authority?'

Nobody did.

'Good,' continued Edwin. Then he took on a tone that was a little less formal. 'Rather than beginning with the charges and working backwards as to why, I intend to start from the beginning and tell you all the whole story. You will all bear witness. If I say something that you know to be false – that is, if you can *prove* it to be false in front of everyone – you may speak up. Otherwise, hold your peace.'

Luke was beginning to recover himself a little, breathing again – albeit hoarsely – now that the pressure on his throat had eased. Martin made sure his grip was fast. At the same time, he did want to hear what Edwin had to say; much as he appreciated Edwin's conclusion that Luke was guilty, he had no idea at all how his friend had come to it.

'It all started a long time ago,' began Edwin, in the tones of a story-teller, as he looked around the circle of men in the ward. 'But it came to a head some months ago when Lady Emma returned here as a widow.'

There was a murmur, and Luke's head came up.

'You see, Luke has been in love with her for many years. When she was unmarried and could provide her brother with an alliance, there was nothing he could do, but as a widow she might have a say of her own in the choice of a second husband.'

The hardened men of the garrison were looking at Luke in some disbelief. He made a derisive noise and called to them, loudly, so they could all hear. 'Love? Don't be so soft. As if any real man would be in thrall to a woman like that. Don't believe him.'

'I'm sure she'll be pleased to hear that.' Martin followed Edwin's pointing finger to see that both Emma and Joanna were standing at the keep's first-floor window. Emma's face was a mixture of emotions as she stared at the scene below. Joanna's was pale, but for the first time Martin had seen since he'd been here, her expression was one of hope.

Luke tried to backtrack. 'No, what I meant was—'

Edwin ignored him. 'Anyway, if Luke was going to make a serious bid for Lady Emma's hand, he needed money. By means of terrible, violent threats against his wife and children, he forced Joscelin to hand over all his own wages, and then, when that wasn't enough, to steal from the castle accounts for him.'

Martin looked carefully at the spectators, as he was sure Edwin was also doing. Some were shocked, but the group he'd identified earlier didn't seem surprised. No doubt they knew of the threats and were among those who would carry out the sickening deeds if Luke ordered them to. Martin felt his anger rise as he thought of the innocent woman and children and how these men would have been happy to harm them. God's blood, but he was going to kill them all before this was over.

Edwin was continuing. 'Luke might have been gaining ground, slowly. But then Lady Emma told him that she was expecting his child.' There really was a collective gasp at that. 'So he decided he needed to act quickly. Indeed, he was now even more ambitious, seeing a future not just as Lady Emma's husband, but as the husband and father of the rulers of this estate – which meant, of course, that he would control it himself.'

Martin, having been privy to various of Edwin's other conversations in the last couple of days, more or less grasped that, but he could see that it had gone by a little fast for everyone else.

Edwin saw it too. 'What I mean,' he explained, 'is that Luke saw that only two people stood between him and having everything for himself: Sir Nicholas and his baby son. If he killed Sir Nicholas and found a way to disinherit the child, the estate would go to Lady Emma. If he married Lady Emma, he would rule in her name. And if he did all this quickly enough that they were properly married before their child was born, it would be legitimate and would inherit in due course.' He paused. 'Indeed,' he added, sounding as though he'd only just thought of it, 'once he had a legitimate child, he might not even have needed Lady Emma at all.' He turned to address the keep window. 'You might have been in more danger than you thought, my lady.'

Martin glanced up, but Joanna was there alone. He had only just begun to wonder if Emma had collapsed in some way when she came storming out of the keep and across to them, shrieking like a harpy. Martin wondered at first if she was about to attack Edwin, and tried to shift so he could protect him while still keeping hold of Luke, but it was actually the latter at whom her ire was directed.

'You liar!' she screamed. 'You killed my brother! You let me think she'd done it, but all the time it was you!' She lunged at him, but Milo, who had followed her out, grabbed her arm and pulled her back.

'Sorry,' he said to Martin, 'I couldn't stop her coming out as I didn't want to lay hands on her, but in these circumstances ...' he held up her hand to reveal the small knife she had in it.

'Well,' said Edwin to the waiting crowd, now hanging on his every word. 'I don't think there will be a wedding any time soon.'

He assumed a more serious tone. 'And then, a complication. Mabel made a claim that she and Sir Nicholas had been legally married. If that was true, then her sons were legitimate, and they were in Luke's way too. It was all too easy to push poor Nick in the fishpond – cold, deep water – and to make it look like an accident. That was in contrast to Sir Nicholas's death, which needed to *look* like murder so somebody else could be blamed.'

'Wait,' came a voice out of the crowd. It was one of those whom Martin had identified as Luke's henchmen. He addressed Edwin. 'You said we could speak if we could prove anything false.'

'That's correct.'

'Well then, on the night Sir Nicholas was killed, Luke here was on guard duty all night. I'd be willing to swear he never left the gatehouse, and so would others, no doubt.' There were a few calls of agreement.

Edwin exchanged a glance with Aubrey, who moved a pace closer to Joscelin. The steward was standing despondently with his head bowed, and Martin hoped he wasn't going to be any trouble. He was confident in his own abilities, of course, but there were some limits on how many people he could defend single-handedly all at once. If he shouted loud enough, he could bring the other Conisbrough men running, but that would leave the armoury unprotected, so he would leave that as a last resort.

'Oh yes,' Edwin was saying to the man and his companions, 'I believe you, because I already know that.'

'Eh?'

'Luke wouldn't get his hands dirty committing the murder himself,' said Edwin, drily. 'Just like he wouldn't fight Martin himself the other day – in both cases, he got someone else to do his dirty work if there was a chance the opponent might fight back. All very different from drowning a small boy in a pond. He threatened to torture and kill Joscelin's family unless *he* wielded the knife, so Joscelin crept into the keep and killed Sir Nicholas while Luke made sure that everyone saw him in the gatehouse at the same time.'

All eyes were upon Joscelin, who had by now fallen to his knees. 'It's true,' he wept. 'It's all true.' He looked directly at Joanna, whom Martin was surprised to see had quietly joined the group. 'Please, my lady – I can't ask for forgiveness, because I'm guilty, but if you'd only heard what he was going to do to my children, my son, my little girls …'

'But what about the horse?' came a piping voice. Martin saw Matthew pushing his way through the crowd. 'Joscelin never comes anywhere near the stables.'

'No, that really was Luke, acting with his own hand. He'd taken a dislike to Martin as soon as we arrived, and he was worried when he found I out I was here to try to discover the truth.' Edwin looked in disgust at Luke. 'It was a threat to us not to look into anything too closely, and for that a fine horse had to die.' He allowed his contempt to show through for a moment. 'Luke doesn't know how to be clever – only how to bully and cause violence.'

Martin felt his grip tighten again. Strangely, hearing of Fauvel's awful fate seemed to turn the onlookers against Luke more than anything else that had gone before. The grooms were certainly disgusted, and even Luke's garrison underlings began to murmur and turn away.

Edwin could see that he had the crowd with him now, and Martin guessed that he was about to start winding up. 'And so, these are the charges against Luke: that he threatened torture, rape and murder against Joscelin's family, to force him to steal and to kill Sir Nicholas; that he planned his lord's murder with the deliberate intention of seeing Lady Joanna executed for it; that he pushed the boy Nick into the water and drowned him; and that he killed a valuable animal belonging to Martin. These charges are too serious for any manor court, so he will have to be taken to Warwick to await the next hearing of the king's justices.'

Edwin paused, but not a single voice was raised in protest, despite Luke seeming to expect it. 'You see?' said Martin, bending to whisper in his ear. 'Not one man to stand up for you – nor one woman either. Nobody likes you.'

'The charges against Joscelin are that he stole – albeit under duress – and that his was the hand that killed Sir Nicholas. He will also have to face the king's justices.'

Joscelin raised his face to address them all. 'I accept these charges against me and will submit quietly to the sheriff's man.'

'And you?' Edwin looked at Luke. Everybody looked at Luke.

Luke struggled against Martin's restraining arms and spat out a series of oaths. Then he took a deep breath and bellowed. 'I demand trial by combat!'

Martin felt a warm glow. Those extra moments in the cold church on Sunday had been well worth it, for all his prayers had been answered.

Chapter Thirteen

Edwin had expected something of the kind, so he ignored the shocked buzz that ran around the ward and turned to confer with Aubrey. There were serious implications, and he wasn't sure anyone else in the castle understood them.

'Can he even do that?' whispered Aubrey.

'Unfortunately, yes.' Edwin had learned much about the law in the past year. 'As he wasn't taken in the act, he has that right.'

'Oh.'

'But I just need to … oh, yes, wait.'

Edwin approached Luke, who was still shouting, struggling to be free of Martin's restraining arm. 'What are you saying? Something about Lady Joanna?'

'I still say she did it. She was caught with the knife in her hand!'

'That doesn't count as being caught in the act unless anyone actually saw her stab him. Otherwise, there's nothing to say she isn't speaking the truth when she says she awoke and just picked it up.'

Luke yelled at Milo. 'You were first in there, boy – say something! Tell them you saw her do it, or by God, I'll flay you alive when I get my hands on you.'

All eyes turned to Milo, who was still keeping a wary eye on Emma. He was pale as he raised his voice. 'I did not see Lady Joanna strike any blow. All I saw when I came into the room, and I will swear to this on a Bible, is that he was dead and that she was holding a knife. As Edwin says, that does not mean that she killed him.' His voice wavered a little in the face of Luke's roaring anger. 'I will stand surety for my words if needs be.' He touched the sword at his belt.

'She did it, I tell you!' screamed Luke, addressing the whole crowd. 'One of you say something, for God's sake.'

There was a deep silence.

'I'll kill her myself,' he bellowed, writhing, still having not worked out that he was never going to escape Martin's iron hold.

Edwin thought this had gone on long enough. 'Am I to understand,' he said, loudly and clearly, 'that you are demanding trial by combat in order to press charges against Lady Joanna as well as to defend yourself against your own?'

Luke stopped, perhaps thinking that this was his way out, and thereby neatly falling into Edwin's trap. 'I am.'

'Very well.' Edwin raised his voice. 'Did you all hear him speak?' There was general agreement.

'Edwin, what are you doing?' Joanna had appeared beside him. 'Surely you can't believe there's any truth in Luke's words.'

'Not at all. But I'm not sure Luke understands the import of what he's just said.'

'I'm sorry, you're going to have to explain that.' As ever, Aubrey was perplexed.

'Well, if he'd been defending himself against charges put by the crown, he'd have to fight a representative of the crown.' Aubrey still didn't get it. 'By which I mean you.'

Aubrey gasped and took an involuntary step backwards.

'But, as he's challenged Lady Joanna, and she's a woman, she's permitted by law to choose a champion to fight for her.'

They all turned to look at Martin.

Joanna rose to the occasion. 'Luke has made an accusation of murder against me, and I join in the accusations against him. As I cannot fight him myself, I humbly ask Martin, of the household of Earl William de Warenne, if he will be my champion and fight to clear my name and to prove the charges against Luke.'

Martin finally released his hold on Luke, shoving him into the unsympathetic arms of the grooms who'd been forced to clear up the bloodied stable before stepping forward to Joanna and thumping down on to his knees, heedless of the mud. 'My lady, nothing would give me greater honour.' Dear Lord, he looked like he really meant it – did he think he was in one of those minstrels' tales?

'You have my thanks and my trust.' Joanna put out a hand, and he engulfed it in his own as he got to his feet.

Oh Lord, thought Edwin, again. He knew he'd been right in what he'd done so far: Luke was bound to ask for trial by combat once he knew he would have to face justice, so Edwin's task had been to arrange matters so that he was fighting the opponent who had the best chance of beating him. But Martin was actively enjoying this, and Edwin now started to worry that his friend was overconfident. It was almost unthinkable, but what if he lost? Luke was nowhere near his size, but he was experienced, canny and vicious. What if, by some chance, he were to be victorious? What if Edwin had just condemned his best friend to death? He began to feel nauseous.

But stop. *Think*. If Edwin hadn't acted as he had done, Luke would be fighting Aubrey, a match he would certainly win, which would prove his innocence in the eyes of God, and he would be allowed to go free. Free to carry out his threats against Joscelin's family, free to harm Joanna and her child … would Martin thank Edwin for keeping him safe if that were the outcome? Edwin knew that he wouldn't.

'What do we do now?' Aubrey was still shaken at his narrow escape.

Now that it was inevitable, the best thing to do was to get on with it. 'Have some men mark out a space, a square about sixty feet each side if that will fit in the ward. Mark it off with posts, ropes – whatever they can find.' Edwin beckoned to Matthew. 'Can you go and fetch my men from the armoury now – I'll need them here. Leave Aubrey's there, though, just in case,' he called after the boy's rapidly departing back.

Martin and Joanna were off to one side, speaking privately, so Edwin left them to it for as long as he could. Then he made his way over.

'I'm sorry to do this, to both of you, but once I knew he would opt for combat, it seemed logical to make sure he faced the opponent who had the best chance of beating him.'

Edwin felt his shoulders being grasped. 'Don't apologise. In fact, it's I who should be thanking you – if I'd been deprived of this opportunity, I'd never have forgiven you.'

'I thought you would say that. But just … be careful, won't you? You can't count on him to fight fairly.'

'It won't last long enough for him to cheat,' said Martin, bleakly.

'Martin – I mean it. I've lost friends in combat before, and I don't want to do it again today.'

'And neither do I.' Joanna laid a hand on Martin's mailed arm. 'Please.'

Martin looked down at them both. Then, daringly, he took Joanna's hand in his own and raised it to his lips. 'I won't let you down. Either of you.'

Joanna's voice broke. 'This is the first time I've been outside in weeks. I didn't think it was going to be like this!' She turned away.

Edwin cleared his throat and blinked. 'So,' he said, trying to keep his voice level. 'You have your sword already. You'll need a shield, won't you?'

'Yes. And my helm.'

'I'll fetch that,' said Lambert's voice from somewhere nearby.

'And I'll get a shield from the armoury.' That was Milo.

Edwin looked over to where Luke was standing. He had a momentary alarm as he saw Emma approaching him, but she had no weapon; she merely walked up and gave him a ringing slap about the face. 'I wouldn't marry you now even if you defeated the whole lot of them.'

He laughed in her face. 'Nor would I – no point marrying an old hag like you if your bastard brat isn't going to inherit anything. Now get out of my way – I've got more important matters to worry about.'

Edwin had never really liked Emma, but even he felt that was brutal – and in public, too. He almost went to her but was distracted by being asked to move so a post could be hammered into the ground. When he looked up again Joanna – *Joanna* – had moved over to the other woman and was gently leading her to one side.

Lambert and Milo came back with the helm and shield. Some equipment had also been fetched for Luke, and one of his few remaining supporters was helping him into it.

Edwin realised that one man who had been notably absent for the whole morning was Father Clement. He mentioned this fact to Turold, who pointed silently to the top of the palisade. The priest was silhouetted against the sky, but he was not observing the happenings in the ward; instead, he was gazing out in the direction of the church.

'I suppose it's too much to expect that he's repenting of his sins,' Edwin said, much to Turold's confusion, 'but we'll need him here.'

Turold nodded. 'I'll go myself – he might not listen to the boy.'

By the time he returned with the priest, all was in readiness. The list was marked, with the onlookers squeezed around the edges of the ward. A few of them were very young, and Edwin worried about them witnessing the fight, but he sensed they would be reluctant to leave; indeed, a couple of lads had climbed on to the roof of the steward's office to get a better view, while another swung his legs from a perch up on the wall walk.

Father Clement seemed surprised by the direction events had taken – he really had been deep in his own thoughts all the morning. When it was explained to him, he did not bluster but simply said, 'Very well,' and stood ready to hear each combatant's confession. Martin came to kneel before him and murmur a few words; Luke did not.

While this was going on, Edwin placed his men one at each corner of the list, though he didn't really expect anyone to interfere. Then he stepped into the roped-off area.

'The rules are simple,' he announced. 'The fight is to the death, and the loser declared guilty. Either man may admit defeat at any time by crying "craven", but if he does so he will be judged guilty and an execution carried out. If there is no result by sunset, then the fight ceases until dawn tomorrow.' That last one certainly wasn't going to happen, but it had to be said. 'Do you understand these terms?' he asked Martin and Luke, who were by now inside the list, at opposite ends.

They both indicated that they did, so Edwin stepped back out, and then prompted Aubrey to give the signal to begin.

As the two combatants moved forward Edwin closed his eyes and began to pray, but before he'd even got halfway through his first paternoster Luke was dead.

———◦◦◦———

Energy and rage had been surging through Martin's body since the moment he'd understood that Luke was the culprit they were after. So strongly had it been roaring that he'd barely been capable of thinking of anything else, his head full of violence and killing even as he'd held Luke fast. He hardly remembered his conversation with Joanna, although he hoped it would come back to him later.

All the buzzing had cleared away as soon as he stepped into the list, sword and shield at the ready and Luke the focus of his narrow gaze through the helm's eye-slit. Martin concentrated, allowing the energy and bloodlust to build up inside him so he could channel it, bring it all to bear on the man who had tried to destroy Joanna and who was now in front of him.

He could feel the enormous strength powering his body, just waiting to be unleashed. Choosing a position that was less slippery than the rest of the list, he grounded his feet firmly; he would wait for Luke to come to him. And there he was, the fool, charging across the open space towards his doom.

Martin crouched, secure in his footing, until Luke was almost within reach. Then he braced his shoulder behind the shield and slammed forward, all his balanced weight behind it as he crashed into the moving man. Luke was knocked backwards, off balance, and that was all that Martin needed. He hammered Luke's shield out the way, flinging it wide and leaving his body exposed to the sword that flashed back and then ran him through in one smooth movement. For one frozen moment Luke's astonished, wide-eyed weight hung from the sword before Martin jerked the blade back, spraying hot blood and broken mail links over both of them. He brought the edge slashing down into the base of Luke's neck even as he fell.

Another fountain of red erupted as the body collapsed to the ground. His opponent was dead, but it had been far too easy and Martin was not satisfied. He wanted *more*. He was furious with Luke for not putting up a better fight, for not making it last longer so that he could work off his fury. This wasn't enough.

With a howl of frustration Martin bent, wrenched the helm off the corpse and hacked off its head.

He didn't know any of this yet, could not have described it; he would have no recollection of the combat until after the battle rage had worn off. All he knew at this moment, as he began to come back to himself, was that mingled blood and mud was oozing round his boots and that he was standing in the middle of a wide-open, deadly silent space with a severed head in his hand.

———◆———

The violence had been so rapid, so shocking and extreme, that the entire ward stood soundless and paralysed. Edwin, who'd seen more bloodshed in the last couple of years than he ever believed possible, had thought he was inured to such sights by now but what had just happened could hardly even be called combat: it had been a slaughter more ruthless and efficient than that of a pig.

Edwin had to say something, he had to move. Beside him, both Aubrey and Joanna were white-faced and immobile, Father Clement not much better. But soon, those men in the ward who were most accustomed to violence – that is, the ones most closely associated with Luke – would recover themselves. He had to head off any possible aftermath.

'The verdict—' he began. He realised that his voice was squeaking. He cleared his throat. 'The verdict is clear. Luke is guilty and Lady Joanna is innocent. There can be no further challenge.'

'Just try it,' came Martin's snarling voice, the hollow tone from inside the helm making it even more terrifying. He went so far as to turn to some of the watching men, but they all shook their heads and shrank back. It was over.

Edwin hadn't realised that he'd gone numb, but now he felt the sensation returning to his hands and feet, painfully. He managed to move without falling over. 'Aubrey, Milo, please take the ladies back into the keep and see that they're warm and have something to drink. Turold, Tom – put Joscelin in his office. I don't think he'll be any trouble, or that anyone will try to break him out, but stay outside the door for now.' They nodded and moved to the steward, who was by now in a state verging on utter collapse. They had to take both his arms to support him inside.

Edwin grimaced as he turned to Willikin. 'Are you up to …?' He looked meaningfully at the figures in the list.

'Someone has to,' was the reassuringly solid reply.

'Do you need me, too?' Lambert's voice wavered.

'No, you stay here. You can help Martin disarm when he comes out, but don't worry, I'll make sure he's calm before he does.'

He and Willikin ducked under the rope and advanced, warily, as though they were trapped in a field with a bull.

'Martin,' Edwin called out, softly, as they neared him. 'Can you hear me?'

'Of course I can hear you!' He swung round, the blank, faceless helm making him look less than human.

'Can you please put that head down before we come any closer?'

'What? Oh.' There was a wet thump.

'We're going to come towards you. It's over, and nobody is a threat any longer.'

Martin dropped his sword and reached up to remove his helm. 'That's a shame.'

Edwin wasn't quite sure how serious Martin was, but he erred on the side of caution, holding his hands out in front of him in a conciliatory gesture. 'It's over. You've won, Joanna is vindicated.'

'And he's dead,' said Martin in disdain, kicking the corpse.

'Yes, yes he is.'

'Too quickly. I should have made it last longer. Broken his legs, cut his arm off, made him scream for mercy.'

Edwin thought fast. 'If you'd done that, everyone might have thought the fight was more even, and maybe come to doubt Joanna's innocence after all, and you wouldn't want that. As it is, the verdict couldn't be clearer – it's better this way, surely.'

After a moment, still staring at the body, Martin nodded. 'If you say so.'

'I do.' Edwin breathed more easily. 'Now, why don't you go and get out of that armour? Lambert will help you. And that sword will need cleaning.'

'Yes.' Martin still spoke as though distracted, but the violence seemed to have receded. He picked up his bloodstained sword, made his way slowly to the edge of the list and stepped over the rope.

Edwin exhaled.

'You did well there,' said Willikin, unexpectedly volunteering an opinion. 'It's difficult enough to quiet him even after a training bout, never mind all this.'

Edwin heard a nervous laugh and realised it was his own. 'Perhaps I'm braver than I feel.'

'Happen you are.' Willikin paused. 'It was him that killed the boy, then, was it?'

'Yes.'

Edwin was worried that this might be used as an excuse to mistreat the corpse, which would finally tip him over into the spell of vomiting he was trying to keep down, but Willikin merely poked it with a toe. 'Good thing he's dead, then.'

Edwin looked about him and then pointed randomly to one of the garrison, most of whom were still standing about in little knots. 'You.'

'Me?'

'Yes, you. Go and find something to wrap this body in and organise carrying it to the undercroft where Joscelin had the boy laid yesterday.'

The man didn't dare argue; he and his friends moved off.

Martin, Edwin could see, had been divested of his armour and was trudging over to the keep. What would happen when he got there was yet another thing for Edwin to worry about, but in the meantime, he had to clear up the situation he'd created here. So he waited, standing in the watery noon sun, trying not to look at the headless corpse at his feet.

Chapter Fourteen

A huge wave of exhaustion swept over Martin, despite the brevity of the fight. He wasn't hurt, but somehow all the energy, all the feeling, was draining out of him. He had to concentrate hard not to fall over his own feet as he walked.

He entered the keep to find the lower room empty except for Milo, who had readied a bowl of water and some cloths. 'I thought you'd want to wash,' he said, stepping back as Martin came forward. 'It's cold, but I can have some water heated if you prefer.'

'Cold is fine,' replied Martin. 'And I'm not that bad – it's my armour that wants cleaning.' He did, however, sit down and dip a cloth, the cool water on his face helping to bring him into the present.

Milo was hovering. 'It's all right, I won't bite. You did well, out there, stopping Lady Emma – if she'd killed Luke before I'd had the chance to, I'd have been annoyed.'

The squire shrugged. 'Anyone would have done the same.'

'And you were ready to defend your lady and your little lord earlier.' Martin finished wiping his face and stood up. He'd done it so suddenly that Milo flinched, but Martin merely patted him on the shoulder. 'Good man. You'll make a knight yet.'

The boy brightened. Martin retrieved his tunic and belt from the guest chamber, put them on, and smoothed his hair. 'Will I still frighten the ladies?'

'Not by your looks,' replied Milo, 'but they're all very shaky so you might consider moving and talking gently.'

Martin nodded and started up the stairs.

He paused outside the door and knocked before entering. 'It's Martin. May I come in?'

Joanna's voice, sounding a little more hesitant than usual, replied and he entered.

She stood in the centre of the solar, facing him. He took a few steps forward, noticing in passing that as soon as he was away from the door Emma, Mabel, Ada and Aubrey all slipped past him and out.

As he took another step forward Joanna almost took one back, but she recovered and came to greet him. 'I can't thank you enough,' she said, simply.

'I'm sorry you had to see it.' She was so tiny. He had an overwhelming urge to protect her, to keep her safe from anything and everything that the world might throw at her. If only fighting could solve everything.

'I … I'm afraid I looked away at the end. But only once I knew it was all over and you were safe.' Some kind of uncertain expression came over her face. 'I knew that I'd asked you here, and it was all my fault you were in danger. If anything had happened to you …'

He took her hand. 'I was never in any danger,' he said, firmly. 'From him? From anyone here? No.' He took a deep breath. 'Come away with me, and I'll keep you safe from everything.'

She shook her head. 'We've already had this conversation, and you know that I can't.'

'You can,' he urged. 'It's over now, and you're free.'

'Free of what?'

'Of Luke, of danger, of everything!' He gripped her hand more tightly. 'Don't you love me?'

She had tears in her eyes now. 'Of course I do!' she burst out. 'You know I do! But life isn't about love or being happy – it's about duty. Yours to your family and the lord earl, and mine to my son.'

'Duty! Who cares?' Martin had no idea what was going on. How could he possibly just have said that? He, who lived to serve? What was the matter with him? But he looked into Joanna's eyes and knew that none of it mattered. He would give it all up for her. 'There's a priest in the castle,' he said, suddenly. 'He could marry us now, today. Then nobody could separate us.'

He did recognise the emotion in her eyes now – it was fear. 'Martin, you're hurting my hand.'

He dropped it like it was on fire. 'Sorry.'

'Listen to yourself,' she said. 'Throwing away everything, your whole future. And I won't let you do it, do you hear? Part of me loving you is that I want the best for you, and this isn't it. Do you hear me? This isn't it.'

He let out an incoherent sound, a cry of rage and frustration. This caused a wail to emanate from the cradle in the corner; Ada hadn't taken the baby out with her when she'd left.

'That is my duty,' said Joanna, pointing. She gripped his forearms and looked up at him. 'If we can sort it all out properly – my cousin, your father, the earl – then of course I'll marry you. I never wanted to marry anyone else. But until that time I won't let you throw your life away, or his.'

The wail got louder. Still not quite sure of what he was doing, Martin strode over to the cradle and looked at the tiny bundle in it, red faced and screaming fit to wake the dead.

'Oh, if it wasn't for you,' he rasped.

'Martin!' Joanna sounded properly frightened now, and a part of him didn't mind.

'Stop!' cracked another voice.

Martin froze in the very act of reaching out a hand. He turned, slowly, to see that Edwin was standing in the doorway.

'Step away from the cradle, Martin,' said Edwin, steadily.

Martin suddenly realised what it must look like. 'No, no, I wasn't – I only meant to—'

'Step away. Now.'

Martin dropped his hands to his side and moved back. Joanna rushed past him to pick up the baby and cradle it, crooning and making 'hush' noises.

'I swear, I was only going to pick him up and hand him to you,' stammered Martin. 'Joanna! Edwin! You have to believe me.'

'It's all right,' said Edwin, coming into the room. 'I know you wouldn't hurt an innocent child.' But he exchanged a glance with Joanna as he said it.

A huge sense of shame came over Martin, along with a wave of … he didn't know what, exactly. He made it over to the window seat before he buried his face in his hands.

They both – all – came over to sit opposite him. After a few moments of silence, Martin looked up. Tentatively, he put out one finger and stroked the baby's face, the only part of it visible in the swaddling. 'So, his name's John?'

'Yes.'

'He doesn't look like you. Does he resemble …?'

'I'm not sure. When he was first born I thought he looked exactly like Nicholas, but now he seems to be turning into his own person.' She dropped a kiss on the baby's forehead.

They sat in silence again.

Eventually it was Edwin who broke it. 'Martin.'

Martin sighed. 'Yes?'

'I'm going to say this because I'm your friend. Remember that, even if you don't like it.'

Martin nodded.

'You're on a path to become like Luke.'

'What?' Martin was almost on his feet. 'How can you even—'

'Oh, sit down. You're not there yet, but I worry that you're in danger.'

He stopped, waiting for Martin to reseat himself, which he did. 'Go on, then.'

'He loved a woman who was sent away to marry someone else. He thought it was over, but then she came back because she was widowed. He thought his chance had come at last, and he was willing to do anything – *anything* – to make it happen. But he was a man already prone to violence, and the further down the path he went, the worse he became. And now we've just put his body in one bag and his head in another.'

Martin thought that Edwin shouldn't say such things in front of Joanna – it might upset her. But she was agreeing. Still holding the baby, she reached out her free hand and he felt it touch his own.

'So, what I'm saying,' continued Edwin, 'is that you have to make a choice. You've suffered, but how will you let it affect you? Are you Luke, or are you going to be Martin?'

———⚬———

Edwin didn't know how much more his nerves could take. So far today he'd unmasked two murderers, taken steps to avoid a possible armed insurrection, panicked that he'd put his best friend in danger of his life, watched a display of sickening violence and wrapped up a headless corpse. And all of that, strangely enough, paled into insignificance next to the worry that Martin was at a crossroads in his life and might be about to take the path that led to destruction – his own and everybody else's.

His harsh words, however, seemed to be having the right effect, or at least they gave Martin the *idea* that there might be a different path. Satisfied that the immediate danger was over, Edwin thought that the best and most tactful thing for him to do now was to leave Martin and Joanna in the window seat to talk.

As he stood up to move nearer to the fire he paused and looked down at Joanna. 'Would you trust me to hold the baby until Ada comes back?'

Joanna smiled and passed it over. It was actually quite easy to hold, tightly swaddled so it couldn't squirm and wave its arms and legs about; you had to do that so the limbs would grow straight, he knew. Edwin cradled it – *him* – so that the little head was in the crook of his elbow and took a few experimental steps. No screaming resulted.

'You'll do very well once your wife has her baby,' said Joanna. 'I'm sure you'll be a wonderful father.'

Edwin winced as he saw Martin start in surprise. 'What?'

Joanna immediately recognised that she'd let something slip. 'Oh, Edwin, I'm so sorry – I didn't realise—'

'It's all right,' said Edwin, softly so as not to frighten the baby. He looked at Martin. 'Alys told me before we left Conisbrough that she was with child. It didn't seem right to tell you, as you had so much else on your mind, especially …' he tailed off.

Martin stood up and enveloped the whole lot of them in his long arms – Edwin, Joanna and the baby. 'I couldn't be more pleased for you,' he said, with feeling. 'Honestly. What wonderful news.' He might have had a tear in his eye; Edwin couldn't say.

Edwin took the baby over to a seat by the fire, rocking it in his arms, making soothing noises and wondering what it would be like to hold a child of his own. He wondered how Alys was getting on. He hated being away from her but thank the Lord she hadn't been here in all this danger, and she hadn't had to see the fight – if you could call it that – earlier. Even Edwin wasn't sure he'd ever be able to look at Martin in the same way again; anyone who didn't know him so well, didn't know how kind and gentle he could be on occasion, would be terrified every time he came near them.

Edwin couldn't hear what the others were saying, and he didn't try. The tone was less fraught than it had been earlier, and that was enough.

He was still sitting by the fire, the baby now asleep, almost starting to drowse himself, when the door opened a crack and Ada put her head round.

'Don't worry, it's safe to come in,' called Edwin, softly.

She entered, taking a circular route from the door in order to leave as much space between her and Martin as possible.

'He's quite heavy, isn't he, when he's asleep?'

'That he is, sir.' She took the baby off him, and for a few moments his arm and body felt cold without the warm little weight there. *Soon, God willing.*

Edwin sat in silence, staring into the fire and feeling some of the tension draining away. But, as ever, it was not to last.

Another knock at the solar door heralded the arrival of Matthew. 'Turold sent me up, sir. Said to fetch you and …' he pointed at Martin, too intimidated even to say his name.

'Did he say what for?'

'He says Joscelin wants to talk to you.'

Edwin sighed, reluctant to get up and leave the restful comfort behind. But duty called, so he went to tap Martin on the shoulder.

———◦———

Martin's rage had been replaced by something else that he couldn't quite put a name to. Sorrow? Grief? Emptiness? But dwelling on it wouldn't help, so he tried to gather his wits as he followed Edwin across the ward.

It was no more than mid-afternoon, but the light was already fading. It hadn't rained for a day and a half, and there was talk of the flood receding, but Martin couldn't see that as the unalloyed good news that everyone else seemed to think it was. As long as the water trapped them all in the castle, the rest of his life was paused, and he could stay here with Joanna. But as soon as it disappeared, the world would start again and that meant that choices would need to be made.

But there he was, dwelling on his situation again. He shook his head. *Focus.* He was about to follow Edwin into a room that contained a killer. Not a very convincing one, to be sure – one who had to drug a man senseless before he could strike a blow – but one who might be desperate.

'Stop,' he said, as Edwin put his hand to the door latch. Martin turned to Turold. 'How did he seem when he asked for us? Angry, violent?'

'Not at all. Despondent, if anything. I haven't heard hardly anything from inside since I've been here – I reckon he's just been sitting there.'

'And he didn't say why he wanted us?'

'No – but I thought I'd better send for you in any case.'

'All right. Edwin, wait there.' Martin drew his sword and held it before him as he entered, wary of any trap or missile. But there was nothing: Joscelin was sitting at the table, his hands folded.

He stood up as they entered.

'You wanted to see us?' Edwin shut the door. Martin would have preferred it open so he could see better in case of sudden attack, but he would have to manage.

'Yes. I wish to ask you – or, more specifically, your friend here – a favour.'

'A favour? What sort of favour?'

'I want him to kill me.'

Martin didn't think he'd heard that properly.

'I'm sorry?' Edwin also looked confused.

'It's perfectly simple,' explained Joscelin, in a level voice. 'I deserve to die, and I will die as soon as I've faced the justices. All I'm asking, for the sake of my wife and children, is for it all to end now rather than being dragged out. You have my full confession, in front of witnesses, and I admit my guilt.' He hesitated. 'I could do it myself, of course, though I'm not sure how I would manage it. There's nothing in here I can poison or hang myself with, and although I have my eating knife, if I tried to cut my own throat I'd be bound to get it horribly wrong.'

Martin could see that Edwin was taken aback, and indeed it was an unusual request. 'Suicide is a mortal sin,' Martin heard him say at last.

Joscelin forced a hollow laugh. 'Do you think that matters to me? I've already committed a mortal sin, so I'm going to burn in hell anyway.'

'I … might need some time to think before I can give you an answer on any of this,' was Edwin's only reply.

'Very well.' Joscelin sat down again. 'It's not as though I'm going anywhere in the meantime.'

Edwin led the way out and they found a quiet corner.

'Well?' Martin asked.

Edwin was biting his lip, his face a picture of indecision. 'To be honest, I'm not sure. If he was trying to get himself killed in order to cover up his guilt, then of course I'd say no. But he's confessed and it's all public. All he's effectively asking for is to be executed now rather than later.'

'So how would that protect his family? He's going to die either way.'

'Yes. Perhaps he thinks to save them the shame of seeing him brought before the justices. What we have to remember is that although he's guilty, his wife and children are innocent; they know nothing about it and shouldn't be punished for his sins.' He took a few paces. 'If he rots in a cell for a year before his case is heard, if it's a constant reminder, if people here won't talk to them or employ them …' he spread his hands. 'A quick end to it all might be preferable.'

Martin thought for a moment, wishing his mind could operate as fast as Edwin's. 'The suicide idea might work,' he said, slowly.

Naturally Edwin grasped the idea straight away once it was raised. 'You mean, that would emphasise that he'd acted alone, that he took responsibility?'

'Yes. Although he didn't act alone, did he? That bastard forced him into it.' Martin felt himself almost wanting to laugh. 'From my point of view, Joscelin's done me a favour – he got Joanna's husband out of the way for me, while doing it for the best of motives rather than greed or hate. I'd be tempted to let him go.'

'That's enough of that.' Edwin rapped out the words. 'Joscelin knowingly murdered a fellow man, and he was happy for Joanna to take the blame, or had you forgotten?'

That brought Martin up short. 'You're right. And he has to lose his life for that. But how?'

'You're asking me?'

'Of course. You know me – I follow orders.'

Edwin was shaking his head. 'Not in this case. I can't order you to kill a man, or that would make me as bad as Luke.' He paused to think. 'I'm not trained in the law, not properly. But as far as I can see, judicially it makes little difference either way. He's confessed and will be executed. If Aubrey takes him to Warwick he'll sit in a cell for I don't know how long, only to confess again and die then. And all the while his family will live under that shame, that anxiety of knowing what will happen and being powerless to stop it.' He sighed and looked up at Martin. 'But all that is irrelevant, really. The main issue now is – would you do it?'

A weight landed on Martin's shoulders. He had assumed that Edwin would tell him what to do and that he'd do it, no questions asked. But now he had to *decide*. Himself. The fate of a man lay in his hands. It would be so much easier if they were facing each other on the field of battle; there, everything was simple.

'Talk to me, Martin.'

Martin ran a hand through his hair. 'On the one hand, he killed his lord; that means he should suffer shame as well as death.' A thought struck him. 'You know what you were saying a while back, about Joanna being burned because killing her husband was "petty treason" as well as murder? Wouldn't that apply to Joscelin as well?'

Edwin's eyes were wide. 'You're right! I had so much else weighing on my mind that I hadn't thought of it. But yes, a servant killing his master would be counted in the same way.'

'They'll burn him?'

'I'm not sure if they do that to men. But yes, it would be something horrible – not a quick death.'

Martin considered. 'Killing a man in cold blood is a very different thing from being in battle. But in this case it seems it would be a mercy. And …'

'Yes?'

'I have to confess, I'm not sure what I might have done in the same situation. If the only way to save Joanna, or you, or Adam, was to harm the lord earl, would I do it? I don't think I would, but it scares me to wonder how I would cope with the decision.'

'It sounds like you've made a decision now.'

'Yes.' Martin forced himself to remain calm. It wouldn't work if his hands were shaking. 'I'll do it.'

'You're sure? Think of your own soul.'

'Yes, I'm sure. As to my soul, it's no worse than being an executioner … but we'd better do it soon, before I lose my nerve.'

They went back to the steward's office, where Turold and Tom were still standing guard. 'You two get off and find something to eat. I'll stay here,' barked Martin, a little more abruptly than he had intended.

If they had any idea of what was about to happen, neither of them showed it; they followed their orders and left. How easy to be them.

Martin could feel his heart racing again, his palms becoming slick. 'You stay outside.'

'Are you sure?'

Martin wished Edwin would stop saying that – it only made things worse. Of course he wasn't sure, but something needed to be done, and he was the one to do it. This morning he'd killed a man who wanted to live, and it hadn't bothered him at all; why was he now so squeamish about killing a man who wanted to die?

He stepped inside and shut the door behind him. Joscelin looked up.

'Did you want the chance to confess to the priest first?'

'You've decided to accede to my request, then.'

Martin nodded, not trusting himself to speak further.

'No – no, I don't want to see Father Clement. That would only complicate matters.' Joscelin pointed at some parchment on the table. 'A note to my wife. She can't read, of course, but perhaps your friend might be kind enough to tell her what it says.'

'I'm sure he will. Or Joanna can read.'

'She won't want anything to do with them, I'm sure, after what I've done. But please, of your goodness, beg her to remember that my family knew nothing of it.'

'I will.'

There was silence.

Martin was aware that he was stalling, but as he did so, a thought struck him. 'It must have been you,' he said. 'You and Luke – in the stable on that first night after we arrived.'

'You were in there?'

'Yes. I'd gone to check on … well, anyway, yes, I was. I heard two people come in, and then some words that made me think you were talking of us.'

'Luke knew straight away that your party wasn't all it seemed. It took me longer to work out – your friend would actually make a very good steward.'

'But which one of you ordered the other to kill us all?'

'Pardon?'

'I didn't catch everything, but I definitely heard the words "Kill them all". But you wouldn't be ordering Luke around, and if he told you to do it then you made no attempt to do so.'

Joscelin frowned for a moment, and then his face cleared. 'You didn't hear all of it,' he said. 'Luke was all for trying to get you out of the way, and I wanted to calm him down. "What will you do?" I said. "We can't throw them out if they've claimed hospitality, and you can hardly kill them all."'

Martin made a sound of annoyance. 'And I spent all night sitting up waiting for an attack, and then when nothing happened, I thought I was going mad and imagining things.'

'You might have misunderstood the words, but you certainly didn't misjudge the sentiment. There was a great deal of violence and threat around. Luke was only stopped by the suspicion it would cause; otherwise, he might well have had you all murdered. He's – he was – a killer.' Joscelin paused and shook his head, as though a strange thought had come to him. 'As am I, of course.'

Martin looked at him in silence, aware that they had now returned to the subject that could not be avoided.

Joscelin began to tremble. 'So,' he said, between chattering teeth, 'how will you …?'

'Let me see your knife.'

The eating knife passed to him by a trembling hand was hardly a dagger, but it was long enough and sharp enough to do the job.

'I'll make it look like you did it yourself,' said Martin, trying to stay practical while feeling as though he was in a dream from which he really ought to wake up. 'Your family won't have to see you executed.'

'Thank you,' said Joscelin, simply. And then, after a deep breath, 'I'm ready.'

Martin put his left arm around his willing victim to hold him steady, then placed the point of the knife at exactly the correct point between two ribs and over the heart.

There was no sense in waiting. Really. Hesitating was only making it worse for the both of them. He had to do it.

Martin couldn't work out which one of them was shaking more.

'Please,' said Joscelin, and Martin drove in the knife as firmly as he could.

'Go with God,' he said, gently, as Joscelin's dying eyes met his own.

Death came swiftly, and Martin stood for a long moment with the body cradled in the crook of his arm. Drops splashed down on to Joscelin's face, and it took Martin some time to realise they were his own tears.

He had to get out of here. He picked up the body and set it down as though sitting at the table, letting the head fall forward and putting both hands on the knife, curling the lifeless fingers around the hilt. He moved Joscelin's letter forward, out of the way, so it wouldn't get stained, and then looked at his own hands. He'd been so efficient that there was very little blood; such as there was, he wiped on the front of Joscelin's tunic. And that was what he was – an efficient, proficient killer. He'd been killing people since the day he was born, hadn't he? Might as well embrace it.

He opened the door and took in a gulp of air. Edwin was there. He looked like he was going to say something. 'Not now,' were Martin's only words as he walked away, heading for he didn't know where.

Chapter Fifteen

Edwin awoke the following morning wondering how much of yesterday had been real and how much of it was nothing more than a nightmare.

Once Martin had disappeared, Edwin had slipped in to view the tableau and to say a quiet prayer over Joscelin's body, seeing the letter and folding it into his belt pouch. It had been a simple matter to seed the tale that Joscelin had killed himself out of shame and guilt, and that it had been a mistake to forget to deprive him of his knife while he was in captivity.

The water was beginning to recede from around the castle, and the general thought was that another day would do it; they could leave, and the three bodies could be removed for burial. Neither Luke nor Joscelin, of course, could be interred in the consecrated ground of the churchyard, but Edwin would leave their disposal up to Father Clement, with whom he had a long talk during the course of the morning. Now that the worst was over the priest was regaining some small part of his bombast, and Edwin believed that it wouldn't be long until he was back to his old self. He laid as much emphasis as possible on the need to be kind to widows and orphans and reminded Father Clement that although he himself was leaving, others now knew of his past actions. But he didn't hold out much hope for a Damascene conversion.

Edwin spent the rest of the day as quietly as possible, sitting in the solar and letting everything sink further into his mind as he prepared himself to face the long journey home. Martin, of course, wanted to spend every possible moment with Joanna, which she was happy with as long as they could be out of doors. She'd been incarcerated in the keep for so long that even the small wards of the castle seemed like freedom.

It was strange, thought Edwin as he sat, that he'd considered this all along as a female crime, based as it was – or seemed to be – on gossip and jealousy. But in the end, it had turned out to be an all-male affair, although, as ever, women had been among those who suffered most. Ada seemed the least concerned about it, but she had lost her innocence and her baby. Joanna had been on the receiving end of overwhelming hate from all sides and had nearly lost everything, including her life. Emma had lost the man she loved, as well as having her eyes opened to his real nature and lack of regard for her, and she would go on to suffer the stigma of an illegitimate birth. And poor, poor Mabel. She had sinned in carrying on her liaison with Sir Nicholas outside of marriage, of course she had. And she'd sought to capitalise on a tragic situation for her own advancement. But did any of that merit the lifelong punishment of losing her child, her first-born son? Edwin thought not.

It was late in the afternoon when Aubrey joined Edwin by the fire in the solar.

'You'll be leaving tomorrow?'

'Yes, God willing, as long as the water doesn't rise again. And so will you, I suppose?'

Aubrey nodded mournfully. 'Yes.'

'Why so sad? Surely you're keen to get away and make your report.'

'Ha.'

'Your sheriff will be delighted to hear it: Lady Joanna exonerated, two culprits identified and confessed before witnesses, and both of them now dead – no need for an expensive trial.'

'Well, yes, but none of that was down to me.'

'He doesn't know that, though, does he?'

'You mean … but I couldn't …'

'I'm not looking for credit. Only for the truth, and hopefully for a bit of peace.' Edwin turned to look Aubrey full in the face. 'If this helps to start your career by giving you confidence and a reputation, and if it helps you to realise your duty to others, feel free.'

'That's very kind of you,' began Aubrey.

Edwin waved him into silence. 'It wasn't so long ago that I was terrified and out of my depth when I was first asked to find a killer. But I had some help from a wiser, more experienced head.'

'Who was that?'

'My father.' Edwin sighed. 'He died not long afterwards, but before he went he knew he'd set me on the right path. He would have done anything for me.'

'I suppose my father was doing his best for me,' said Aubrey, tentatively, 'when he got me this position. I'm a third son, after all, so I needed to get out and do something.'

'So you'll continue with it? Working for the sheriff?'

'Yes. Yes, I think I will. And … thank you.'

———— ※ ————

Another dawn came, and it was time to leave. The castle gate was finally open: it had been swung wide at dawn. A weeping and distraught Mabel had already left, wading through the mud towards the village where her two remaining sons waited.

All was in readiness for the Conisbrough party, the baggage packed and loaded. A new mount awaited Martin: Joanna had gifted to him the horse that had belonged to her husband. It was not in the same class as Fauvel, of course, but it was the best the Brandon stable could offer, and it would get him home. The men were busy checking saddles and tightening girths, and Edwin was looking forward to being off. Not that anybody in his right mind could find pleasure in the journey itself, but the thought of being at home again was calling to him across the miles.

The only problem was that Martin was not there.

Edwin handed his reins to the loitering Matthew, who was sad to see them go but who, Edwin suspected, was going to swagger around the stables and boast of his involvement with the important visitors for years to come.

Martin, as Edwin expected, was in the solar. He looked up as Edwin approached the window seat where he was ensconced. 'I don't want to go.'

'I know you don't, but you have to.'

'Why?'

'We've been through this, Martin, and so has Joanna. Duty comes first.'

'Hmmph.'

Edwin knew what he had to do. 'Martin, get up right now and go to the stables.' He squared his shoulders. 'And that's an order.'

'An *order*?'

'Yes.'

Martin unfolded himself from the seat, and once again Edwin found himself having to look up sharply into the face of his towering, overwhelming friend. 'You're giving me an order.'

'Yes, I am. Now go.'

Martin hesitated for a moment and then stalked off without saying anything.

'Well done.' Joanna had appeared beside Edwin.

'I wasn't sure for a moment there whether I was going to survive the experience.'

'Like I said, you've changed.'

'So have we all. Perhaps it's being parents or parents-to-be. Which reminds me …' Edwin took out the parchment from his belt pouch and handed it to her.

'What's this?'

'It's Joscelin's last words to his wife and children. Please, pass it on to them, and read it if they can't. And please remember – they had nothing to do with all of this. Don't start your son's rule with revenge on innocent children.'

She unfolded the letter and gazed at it without seeing. 'I won't, I promise. There are many blameless children mixed up in all this, and I'll do my best to be fair to all of them – not just John, but Joscelin's children, Emma's, and even Mabel's.'

'You're a good woman, Joanna.'

'Yes, although one who couldn't make Martin happy, even after all that's happened. Look after him for me, won't you?'

'I don't think he needs much looking after.'

'Not physically, maybe, but he's not as tough on the inside as he looks on the outside, and you must know that as well as anybody. Just … keep an eye on him.'

'I will. But don't you want to say goodbye to him yourself?'

'Don't worry – we've already said our goodbyes, many times over.' She paused to regain her composure. 'And now,' she continued, her voice a little unsteady, 'it's you holding everyone up. I'll come with you to the gate.'

Before long they were all in their saddles. The open gate was before them, and the horses of the Conisbrough party stepped carefully through the vast patch of mud outside it until they reached the high part of the road.

Edwin turned in his saddle. Joanna was framed in the centre of the open gateway, and she raised a hand in farewell. Edwin waved and then looked to Martin, who was beside him, but Martin kept his face resolutely forward as they rode away.

Historical Note

Brandon castle had a short life but an eventful one. It was built sometime during the 1140s by Geoffrey de Clinton, the holder of the much bigger Kenilworth castle some 10 miles away, but it lasted little more than a century. In 1266 it was captured and burned by the Kenilworth garrison (then in rebellion against the king during the Second Barons' War involving Henry III and Simon de Montfort) and was never rebuilt.

In the early thirteenth century Brandon castle was in the hands of one Nicholas de Verdon, who built the stone keep sometime during the reign of King John (1199–1216). Little is known of his life, but his wife may have been called Joan de Lacy and he was succeeded by a son or grandson named John, who supported Henry III against de Montfort. Nicholas probably didn't die until the late 1220s or early 1230s; his murder in 1218 is entirely my own invention. Other than baby John, all the characters in *By the Edge of the Sword* are fictional, although – as in previous books in this series – they represent the people and professions of England in the early thirteenth century.

The castle was built on two moated platforms divided by a ditch, so that water surrounded each one separately. The moats were fed by a stream leading off the nearby River Avon, and they opened out into a larger pond on the northern side. A stone keep stood at the eastern corner of the second ward. This was small but well built, the end walls some 4 metres thick, and featured a spiral staircase in its south-west corner. The entrance seems to have been in the north wall and recesses to the south side suggest that there may have been garderobes on both levels that emptied outside the castle wall. The outer wall and the castle's other buildings were of wood, of which no trace survives today, so I have invented my own plan based on the known outline of

Brandon and on the sort of functions that would have been common in any castle this size.

All that remains now are the earthworks and some fragments of stone indicating the position of the keep. The castle is on private land and is not open to visitors; however, it is easily visible from the road and the bridge over the river. The road bridge currently in use is modern, but if you stand on the smaller footbridge to one side you can see traces of the original mediaeval one beneath it. The church, dedicated to St Margaret, is still in use and has some surviving thirteenth-century features. The River Avon runs through the area, which is very flat and prone to flooding during the winter. The surrounding fields are often under water for days or weeks at a time and the footpath that leads off the bridge is set on stilts.

The sheriff of Warwickshire in 1218–19 was Philip Kniton, who was also the sheriff of Leicestershire and thus probably quite busy. There seems to have been some political conniving going on: his appointment in Warwickshire was short and sandwiched in between those of William de Cantilupe, who held the position both before and after him. Philip would no doubt have had a number of men working for him who could be dispatched to different locations if the need arose, as represented here by Aubrey.

———◦◦◦———

We tend to think of women's lives as being very circumscribed in the Middle Ages – as they certainly were by modern standards – but on closer inspection we can find that matters were not quite as clear-cut as we might expect, and there was a huge variety of experience. To understand these women better we need to view things through the lens of the thirteenth century rather than the twenty-first. For example, a mediaeval noblewoman would simply not expect to have much control over the choice of her (first) marriage partner, but she would derive authority from that match and the course of her life would be determined by what she was able to make of her situation *after* the union was sealed. Noblewomen were routinely expected to be efficient administrators and leaders, but their activities in these areas were not highlighted by contemporary chroniclers (who tended to be male), meaning that later historians must look more carefully to find out more about them and their actions.

Similarly, women of lower rank could take advantage of the opportunities offered by marriage to run households and businesses and to influence the course of local events. Widows of any rank enjoyed a great deal more independence than their married peers, not only in financial matters but sometimes also using their position to push through a second marriage to a husband of their own choosing. Even single women could make their own way in the world if they went about it the right way. The word 'spinster', used to this day to denote unmarried status, derives from the spinning of wool, a female-dominated activity, but its meaning has changed. A spinster in the true sense of the word was not some sad old woman pining for a man but rather a canny business operator who was paid for her labour rather than donating it for free to husband or son. Women were just as active and entrepreneurial then as they are now – they just had to find a different way in which to express it.

We should not, however, go too far down the route of painting the Middle Ages as some kind of feminist utopia, because it certainly was not. The subordination of women to their male relatives was enshrined in some secular laws as well as Church ones, and even where the laws were ostensibly gender neutral, women tended to come off worst in any brush with them. For example, in the thirteenth century women committed far fewer murders than men – less than 10 per cent of accused murderers were female – but when they did, they were far more likely to be executed. The murder of a husband by his wife, or of a lord by one of his servants, was classed as petty treason (from the French *petit*, meaning 'small'), as opposed to high treason, which could only be committed against the sovereign. In the early thirteenth century petty treason came under common law, but it was later codified in the Treason Act of 1351 (and not repealed until 1828). The penalties for this crime were harsher than those for murder: women were burned at the stake and men were drawn and hanged, although they were spared the quartering that followed a conviction for high treason.

Trial by combat was still legal at this time, and indeed the practice would continue well into the fifteenth century. Anyone accused of a serious crime could opt for it, regardless of rank, as long as they had not been caught in the act by witnesses. Women and children, and men who were over 60, lame or blind, could choose to name a champion to fight on their behalf; able-bodied men were expected to take the field themselves. The combat had to be held in public, and a list (enclosed area) was marked out for it. Fighting was to the death, although either party could surrender by crying 'craven' at any point – however, as this resulted either in instant execution for the defendant or outlawry for the plaintiff, it probably didn't happen very often.

Further Reading

Given, James B., *Society and Homicide in Thirteenth-Century England* (Stanford: Stanford University Press, 1977)

Goodall, John, *The English Castle* (London: Yale University Press, 2011)

Neilson, George, *Trial by Combat* (New Jersey: The Lawbook Exchange, 2009)

Salter, Mike, *The Castles and Moated Mansions of Warwickshire* (Malvern: Folly Publications, 1992)

Schaus, Margaret (ed.), *Women and Gender in Medieval Europe: An Encyclopaedia* (London: Routledge, 2006)